"I agreed to meet to tell you I can't see you again."

"Is it because we're rivals?" Jack asked. "I thought we were getting along well."

Allie wondered what his mouth would feel like, taste like... "It has nothing to do with you. I promised myself not to get involved with anyone right now."

He pursed his lips, as if considering her explanation. "You and I hit it off at the wedding. That rarely happens to me." His sexy smile was nearly her undoing. "I'd like us to be friends."

"Just friends?"

"Just friends." He paused. "What do you say, pal?" He held out a hand for her to shake.

Slowly Allie reached out and slid her hand into his larger, warmer one and said, "Deal."

Was she disappointed that Jack hadn't pushed to have a closer personal relationship? What a ridiculous idea. She was off men and that's all there was to it...

Dear Reader,

Setting—it's an unsung hero. Many times you don't even think about it because it's such an essential part of a story. Can you imagine *Sex in the City* taking place in a small Wyoming town? Or *Downton Abbey* in the Caribbean?

Catching Her Rival is set in Rhode Island and surrounding states. I lived near Newport, Rhode Island, for several years, and if you're familiar with the area, you'll notice some elements of my story are accurate and others aren't. The wedding at the beginning takes place at a historic, entirely fictional Newport mansion. I took bits from several actual mansions and created Bellevue House. The street that Charlotte and Jack live on is based in reality. Thanks to Google Maps, I found a narrow street with houses in the Point neighborhood of Newport that fit what I pictured in my mind.

I hope you enjoy Allie and Jack's story—not just the setting!

Please visit my website, lisadyson.com, or send me an email at lisa@lisadyson.com. I'd love to hear from you!

Happy reading,

Lisa Dyson

LISA
DYSON

Catching Her Rival

⬧ **HARLEQUIN**®SUPERROMANCE®

ISBN-13: 978-0-373-60910-9

Catching Her Rival

Printed in U.S.A.

Lisa Dyson has been creating stories ever since getting an A on a fifth-grade writing assignment. She lives near Washington, DC, with her husband and their rescue dog with a blue tongue, aptly named Blue. She has three grown sons, a daughter-in-law and four adorable grandchildren. When not writing, reading or spending time with family, Lisa enjoys traveling, volunteering and rooting for her favorite sports teams.

Books by Lisa Dyson

HARLEQUIN SUPERROMANCE

A Perfect Homecoming

Visit the Author Profile page at Harlequin.com

For my sister, Jill.
For your love and support, and for all the times
people have asked us if we're twins.

CHAPTER ONE

ALLIE MILLER'S MOTHER was of the mindset that lives were meant to be lived in pairs.

"What about that nice boy you've been seeing?" her mother whispered between bites of spinach salad. "I'm sure he'd love to be your date for your brother's wedding."

How had she ended up seated next to her mother at this ridiculous bridal luncheon for Allie's soon-to-be sister-in-law? She answered through clenched teeth. "I told you, Mom, we broke up."

"This is a special occasion." Her mother brushed a crumb from the mint-green sleeve of her suit jacket. "Surely you can put your feelings aside and get along for one day?"

Tough to invite the guy to a wedding or anywhere else when he's currently in federal prison.

Her mother didn't need to know that, though. Moreover, she didn't need to know that Allie had nearly ended up in an adjoining cell.

"I don't need a date for Scott's wedding." She softened her tone. "I mean, if I don't have to worry about entertaining a date, then I can be of more help behind the scenes, right?"

Her mother's scowl was all the answer Allie needed. She turned to the sister of the bride sitting on her other side. "So what do you do?" She didn't recall her name other than it was something like Hope or Charity or Faith.

The young woman, who looked to be close to Allie's age of twenty-nine, said, "Well, I'm married to a wonderful man, and we have three little girls." Her mouth twisted as if she had to pull the information from deep within her brain. "I'm the room mother for my kindergartener, I teach an adult Sunday school class and I'm learning to coupon."

"Coupon?" *Isn't that the discount code you apply when you order shoes online? What is there to learn?*

"Yes, I'm studying several websites to learn how to save money using coupons." Her excitement grew as she spoke. "Last week our grocery bill was only twenty-two dollars and ninety-one cents."

"Please, share your secret!" The woman seated directly across the table joined the conversation, asking the bride's sister multiple questions. Allie gave a silent thanks to her for providing the opportunity to exit the conversation.

She didn't care how the woman saved so much money by couponing. Allie was too busy keeping her newly formed advertising agency afloat. Buying laundry detergent at a discount wouldn't help her pay the rents on her small office in downtown Providence, Rhode Island, and her apartment.

She ate her salad quietly. They were in the smallest of the private dining rooms at a Newport restaurant. She hadn't been to Newport in years, even though it was only about forty-five minutes from where she lived and worked.

The walls were a golden oak, and a stained-glass window on the wall at the end of the table muted the room's lighting. The white linen tablecloth touched the floor. The table was set with fine ivory china and etched crystal, accented by pink napkins and matching roses in small vases. Of course the roses were pink. What other color would a traditional June bride choose?

Despite her soon-to-be sister-in-law's penchant for everything girlie, including marriage and raising a family, Allie really did like her. Emily was personable and smart, and she made Scott very happy.

He was the youngest of her four siblings and the last to marry. Scott and her sister, Rachael, had been adopted from China, her older brothers from Russia, and Allie herself from the United States.

Allie looked around the table. She was surrounded by women like Emily. Women who were married or engaged to be married. Women who probably thought they needed their other half to complete them.

That would never be Allie. She'd thought like them at one time, but not anymore. Yes, she knew men had their uses, but even great sex wasn't worth the trade-off. In Jimmy's case, that *trade-off* had been the threat of prison.

Jimmy had promised everything would be fine. He'd told her there was no need for her to worry about getting the account. Said he had the client wrapped around his little finger. Now he was behind bars and Allie had almost ended up there, too.

"Allison, dear." Her mother never shortened her name. Allie had been named after her mother's Aunt Allison, who would never have answered to a shortened version of her name. "Would you please pass the water pitcher?"

She refilled her mother's glass.

"It really is a shame you'll be coming to the wedding alone." Her mother's disappointed tone was one Allie had heard regularly over the years, but she couldn't give in.

She was definitely off men. No other half, no soul mate, no partner for life.

No ball and chain.

JACK FLETCHER READ the details on the wedding invitation again. He'd replied six weeks ago to say he'd be there with his girlfriend.

Brenda had been his ex-girlfriend for several weeks now, but he hadn't yet let his cousin Emily know that he'd be coming alone to her wedding. It wasn't as if he thought he'd get back together with Brenda. He'd merely forgotten. Work had been his priority.

The break-up had been a mutual decision. And in truth, theirs wasn't what most people would call a real relationship. More like just having fun. But it turned out Brenda was anxious to have a domestic life in the suburbs with kids and a minivan—he wasn't. End of story, as well as of their short-lived time together.

He focused on the invitation. The wedding was tomorrow. Too late to tell his cousin there would be one fewer guest at the reception. She'd probably already given the caterer a head count. And he knew better than to upset a bride right before her big day. As kids, he and Emily had been close, but they had grown apart somewhat as adults. It would be nice to see her again.

He *could* ask someone else to go with him, but most women would take an invitation to his family wedding as a precursor to a relationship. Or at least a second date.

He refilled his coffee cup and stepped out onto the front porch of his home, located in The Point neighborhood of Newport. He enjoyed the warm June breeze and the sight of fresh potted flowers on several porches and window boxes up and down his street. Forsythia had turned almost completely from yellow blooms to green leaves, and the hydrangeas were about to bloom.

He never thought he'd be happy in anything but a high-rise apartment in downtown Providence, close to where he worked at his grandfather's advertising agency, but here he was. He'd bought the property a little over a year ago as an investment, expecting to fix it up and rent it out. Somewhere along the way, he'd begun spending nights at the house, away from work pressures. Before he could change his mind, he'd given up his Providence condo and moved to Newport.

"Hi, Jack."

He hadn't seen Charlotte Harrington sitting on her porch on the other side of the narrow street.

"Hey, Charlotte, what's up?"

"Not much." She gave him a sad smile, wiping what he assumed was a tear from her cheek. She'd lost her mother less than a year ago, not long before she moved in. She'd been raised an only child and had recently experienced her first Mother's Day since her mom's death. It had hit Charlotte hard.

Jack had met her when she bought her house. Charlotte was an artist, he'd discovered, and a somewhat successful one according to what he'd read on the internet.

"What are you working on?" Jack called out as he descended the side steps from his porch, crossed the street and ascended hers.

"A new project," she said softly, closing her laptop and setting it on the floor next to her rocking chair. "I told you I'm adopted, right?"

At his nod, she continued. "I never had the urge to track down my biological parents, but lately I've been thinking that I should at least find out my medical history."

Her adoptive mother had died of pancreatic cancer. He figured that must be an unrelenting motivator.

Jack nodded. "Any luck?"

She shrugged. "I just started this morning. 'The first day of the rest of my life' and all that." Her mouth twitched ever so slightly, and she tucked her chin-length dark hair behind one ear.

"Sounds like a step in the right direction."

"I guess so. Want to sit?" She pointed to the rocker that matched hers.

He pulled out his cell phone to check the time. "Sure, I have a few minutes before my conference call."

"You're working from home today?"

"Kind of. After the call, I'm going to visit my grandfather in Providence. He's in the hospital."

"Oh, no. Is it serious?"

"I'm not sure." He sipped his coffee, placed it on the table between their rockers and sat down. "He was admitted with heart problems. That's all I really know. I'm hoping to get more detailed information when I'm there in person."

"This is the grandfather you work for?" She drank from her plastic tumbler. Even her careful movements screamed *grief stricken*.

He nodded. His granddad had started the advertising firm forty-five years ago, and Jack was expected to take over the reins one day.

"Tell me about this search," he said. "How do people find their biological parents?"

Jack felt comfortable asking Charlotte these rather personal questions. The two of them had become friends the day she moved in. He'd come home from work exhausted and there she had been, sitting in the same rocking chair as now on an unusually warm fall day, enjoying a beer from the bottle. From across the street she'd offered him one, before asking if he knew anything about plumbing. So he'd taught her how to replace the insides of a toilet and get it to stop running constantly. She, in turn, always had a cold beer ready for him.

"I don't really know yet. I've been reading websites that explain how to start the search. They say things like, 'Ask your adoptive parents about the adoption agency or lawyer they went through.' I wish I could. Mom went so quickly that I never had a chance to bring up the subject. And until recently, I never even thought about finding my biological parents. But after losing my mom to cancer, I really need to know what might be in store for me, medically speaking. Not only for me, but for any children I might have."

"Sounds like a good idea. Did your mom have a file or anything where she might have kept that information?"

Charlotte's eyebrows rose. "Good point. I haven't been through everything yet. She saved every piece of paper that came her way. There are boxes and boxes to go through. I'll look for an adoption file next."

He'd never had a woman friend before, but he enjoyed Charlotte's company. He felt strangely brotherly toward her—a novelty since, like her, he'd been raised as an only child.

Charlotte wasn't anywhere close to the type of woman he dated. And even if there had been a slight hint of sexual attraction between them, he certainly wouldn't get involved with a neighbor. How awkward would it be when they stopped seeing each other?

Luckily Charlotte wasn't the type to make assumptions... Suddenly he had a brilliant idea. Charlotte needed cheering up and he needed a plus one. "What are you doing Saturday?"

Her eyes narrowed. "This Saturday? Like tomorrow?"

"Yeah." He grinned. "Are you free?"

"That depends."

"Depends on what?"

"It depends on why you're asking me if I'm free on Saturday." She folded her hands on her lap, waiting for him to explain.

"I need a date for my cousin's wedding." He held up a hand. "Not really a date. A plus one."

"You're asking me with one day's notice?" She cocked her head and waited for him to continue.

He let out a breath. "A few weeks ago, when I sent back the RSVP, I told Emily—my cousin—that I'd be bringing a date. You remember I was dating Brenda, right?"

Charlotte coughed to cover her laugh. "Oh, yeah, I remember Brenda."

"What's that supposed to mean?"

She shrugged. "I don't know."

"Yes, you do. Tell me."

She hesitated. "Well, she was just a little too much for me."

"Too much?"

"She wasn't real, personality-wise. She was one person with you and quite another when you weren't around."

He thought about it for a second. "Go on."

"Did she ever tell you to stay away from me?"

"Stay away from you?" He scratched his head. "No. Why would she do that?"

"That's what she said to me. She made it very clear that I was not supposed to have anything to do with you. Although I'm not surprised that she never brought it up with you."

This time *he* was the one cocking his head. "She told you to stay away from me?"

Charlotte nodded. "I don't think she understood that our relationship is friendly, neighborly. She saw me as a threat."

He chuckled. "Do me a favor. Next time you meet someone I'm dating, please let me know stuff like that. I would have dropped her sooner if I'd known she had such a jealous streak. That trait, along with the dominant domestic gene, are a deadly combination."

They laughed together, trading stories of past dating disasters. He was glad to see Charlotte smile.

"So will you go to my cousin's wedding with me?" he asked. "Anyone else I bring will expect a second date."

She winked at him. "I guess this means I'm off the hook for any other time you need a plus one."

"No, no! I didn't mean—" He glimpsed the twinkle in her eye that was rarely seen. "You're teasing."

"Of course I am." She sipped her drink. "I'd love to go. I barely leave the house since I work at home. This will be good for me."

He was glad she saw it that way. "Great! We'll have fun. I'll make sure of it." He checked the time on his cell phone and got up from the rocker. "I better go make that conference call. I'll email you the wedding details." He picked up his coffee cup.

"Sounds good." She rose, as well. "I'm going to go dig out Mom's old files that I haven't been through yet and then figure out what to wear on our nondate."

He smiled. As he turned and went down the steps, he saw her sketch pad propped against the porch railing. The ocean was churning and the sky was dark, as if a storm was brewing. He turned back and asked Charlotte, "Is this yours?" At her nod, he said, "It's so different—darker—from what you've done in the past."

She nodded, her expression thoughtful. "No matter how much I try, I just can't seem to make myself use color in any of my art these days. I'm drawn to charcoal, as if my world is black and white."

He considered her statement a moment and said in a terrible British accent, "I take that as a challenge, my lady." He swept off a pretend hat and bowed in the middle of the street, as if he were a prince and she his princess-to-be. "Until tomorrow…"

She smiled, giving him hope that someday soon she would be the happy person he knew she could be.

He gave her a little wave and a wink. "See you later," he called, and he took his porch steps two at a time.

SATURDAY MORNING DAWNED bright with sunshine, but Allie's mood didn't match the weather. Morning had come too quickly after her late night, and she craved a few more hours of sleep. But no, her mother was adamant Allie have her hair done with the other girls. She wasn't in the wedding party, thanks to some fast-talking when her sister-in-law-to-be brought it up. Allie was merely a reader at the ceremony. Regardless, her mother had insisted on her presence at several wedding-party functions.

Allie had attended the rehearsal last night like a good little girl, followed by a catered dinner at the Chinese Tea House on the Bellevue House grounds. Thanks to the bride's parents, who were members of the preservation society, Emily and Scott would have their wedding reception at Bellevue House, one of Newport's glamorous, historic mansions, recently donated and restored for members' functions. And getting married at St. Mary's Church, the same church as John and Jackie Kennedy, wasn't too shabby, Allie supposed.

If you were into weddings, that is.

After the rehearsal dinner, Allie spent hours working on her presentation for the client who could rescue her advertising agency. She had a meeting scheduled for Monday, and there was too much preparation necessary to do it all on Sunday. Now she wasn't quite done, but she'd gotten far enough along to be able to enjoy her brother's big day.

After a group breakfast with the females in the wedding party, Allie was getting her hair washed and "done" at Crystal's Salon and Spa. Allie wasn't sure what the "spa" part of the title meant. There didn't seem to be anything to the shop but a large room for washing and styling hair, a back room to mix coloring chemicals and a dryer that was presumably tumbling towels.

"I don't want anything too extreme," she told her

stylist, Shari. The young woman had a blue streak in her hair and a prominent tattoo on her bare right shoulder and down her arm.

"You have gorgeous hair," Shari told her as she combed through Allie's dark, wet tangles. "Do you want an updo like the rest of the party?"

"I'm not a bridesmaid," Allie said. "I'm not sure exactly how I want my hair done." Her hairstyle had been the least of her concerns recently.

Before Allie could decide, Shari said, "I think we keep it down and do a crimped version of your style." She scrunched Allie's chin-length hair a little to give her an idea of where Shari was headed. "What do you think?"

"That's good," Allie said. Much better than an updo, which would make her feel like she was attending her high school prom.

"So, where do you fit into all this?" Shari asked as she rubbed a squirt of mousse between her hands and applied it to Allie's hair. "If you're not a bridesmaid, then what are you?"

Allie couldn't help smiling at Shari's openness. "I'm the sister of the groom. I passed on the bridesmaid role," she said in a loud whisper over the whir of the hair dryers. "It's not really my thing, and the bride didn't need one more anyway. I'm sure she asked me only to be polite. She already had six bridesmaids, two junior bridesmaids and two flower girls."

"Wow! No wonder everyone's booked this morning."

Shari kept up a running conversation while she worked on her hair, complimenting Allie's great skin and the striking blue of her eyes next to her milky-white complexion.

This girl was definitely jonesing for a large tip. By the end of their time together, Allie was much more relaxed and decided Shari certainly deserved that tip.

Next stop, back to the downtown Newport hotel where they were all staying so she could get dressed and apply makeup. Another group event she'd taken a pass on, deciding to do these tasks on her own.

At least her mother hadn't made an issue of that, too.

ONCE CHARLOTTE FINALLY figured out what she was going to wear on this nondate with Jack, her excitement grew. She hadn't done anything for the fun of it in…well, she couldn't remember the last time.

Since her mother's cancer diagnosis a little over a year ago, Charlotte had been with her mom nearly 24/7 until her passing. Her mother had no other living relatives. After being left all alone, Charlotte's focus had been settling her mother's estate and buying the historic home she'd fallen in love with on sight. She had an art studio set up in one of the bedrooms, and she rarely left home except for necessities.

She wasn't even sure she remembered how to have fun.

She finished her makeup and spent some extra time curling her dark hair into soft waves that came just below her chin. According to the clock on her nightstand, she still had twenty minutes before Jack would come by for her. She was about to slip on her dress when she heard her cell phone.

A text message from Jack.

Running late. Visiting Granddad and he passed out. He's fine now. Will be there ASAP.

She texted back.

Glad he's OK. Do you want me to meet you at the wedding?

Jack's grandfather was in a Providence hospital, which meant Jack was about forty-five minutes away. St. Mary's church was only a short drive from her house if tourist traffic wasn't too heavy.

No. I have to change for the wedding. Didn't expect to stay this long.

When she was ready to go, Charlotte made herself comfortable on her porch. She didn't want Jack to have to wait even a second longer on her account. The wedding was scheduled to begin at two, which was almost the time Jack's black sports car came down the street. He spotted her immediately and waved as he ran from where he'd parallel parked his car on the street to his front porch steps that he took by twos. "I'll be right out."

Charlotte checked her small silver clutch to make sure she hadn't forgotten anything and then locked her front door. She walked carefully down her porch steps to the sidewalk with its cracks and bumps, and then crossed the street. She wasn't used to wearing the four-inch heels that went with the sapphire-blue dress she'd chosen, but she'd manage. Her dress was gathered on one side under the bust with a glittery silver buckle, and her strappy silver shoes completed the outfit.

"All set?" Jack appeared on his porch, straightening his gold tie and securing a gold tie bar. His dark suit jacket was folded over one arm. He locked his front door and stopped abruptly at the top of his steps. "Wow! You clean up real nice."

Charlotte's cheeks heated. She wasn't used to being complimented on anything but her artwork, even in such a flippant manner. "Thank you." She couldn't help noticing he didn't look half-bad either. "So do you."

"What, this old thing?" He grinned as he opened the passenger-side door for her and then came around the car to lay his jacket in the backseat before getting into the driver's seat. "I'm really sorry we're so late." He checked the silver watch on his wrist. "By the time we fight the Saturday tourist traffic and park, we'll probably have missed the ceremony completely. Why don't we head directly to the reception?"

"Hey, she's *your* cousin. No one will miss me," she teased. "How's your grandfather? You said he passed out?"

Jack nodded as he pulled out of his parking spot and drove up their street. "I waited until the doctor examined him. The doctor said it was probably low blood sugar because everything else checked out. Turned out Granddad didn't eat much for lunch today. I guess he's not thrilled with the food they serve."

"That's too bad. Can you bring food in for him?"

"He's on a low-sodium diet, which makes that difficult."

"No wonder he doesn't like the food, if they're leaving out the salt."

A few more minutes of small talk and they were at Bellevue House, being directed where to park.

"It's a beautiful day for a wedding," Charlotte commented as she exited the car. "They could have had an outdoor wedding. Not that planning an outdoor wedding in this area would be a smart idea."

"That could be a disaster with the wind gusts off the ocean alone, but I'm sure a lot of brides risk it when you can have the Atlantic Ocean or Narragansett Bay as a backdrop." Jack put on his suit jacket and then held out his bent arm for her. "Shall we?"

She slipped her hand into the crook of his elbow, and they headed toward the mansion with its manicured gardens and huge round fountain. "Tell me how you're related to these people. You said the bride is your cousin?" At his nod, she asked, "And the grandfather you just visited?"

"He's my mom's father. The bride is my dad's niece."

"Will your mother be here?" She hadn't thought about how much family he would have at the wedding. His grandfather had raised him, but Jack had never mentioned what had happened to his parents.

"No." He paused. "She passed away a long time ago."

"I'm so sorry. I didn't know. I should have…"

He stopped walking and looked at her. "It's okay. I haven't mentioned it because of your situation. She died when I was about ten."

He put a hand on the small of her back, and they continued walking.

Charlotte blinked away the tears that threatened. It didn't take much for her to remember her own mother.

"I always forget how impressive the mansions are," he said in an obvious attempt to change the subject.

She nodded. "Such a romantic place to have a wedding."

"If you're into those things."

She glanced sideways at him. "I take it you're not?"

"Definitely not." He grinned and then winked. "I'm not a good candidate for marriage, so a wedding is nowhere in my future plans."

Before she could ask about his plans, they reached the mansion and were directed to the terrace for drinks and hors d'oeuvres.

There must have been more than two hundred people in attendance, mostly standing in groups under the large, striped awning, while a few others sat. There were small, round tables with floor-length tablecloths and six cushioned ladder-back chairs at each. Two bars were set up, one at each end of the terrace, and both had long lines.

"What would you like to drink?" He guided her in the direction of the closest bar.

"A soda would be fine for now." She wasn't used to drinking in the middle of the afternoon. The last thing she'd want to do was drink too much and make a fool of herself.

"Oh, there's my cousin Frank and his wife." Jack scrunched his face. "I can't remember her name. Anyway, Frank's a lot of fun. I'll introduce you, and you can sit with them while I get us drinks."

Charlotte wasn't a "talk to strangers" kind of gal, but since Jack was the only one she knew in the room, she'd try her best to fake it. And it would give her an excuse to not have to stand in her high heels, which were already being troublesome.

JACK HATED LEAVING CHARLOTTE, but the whole idea of inviting her was to get her out amongst people. Ideally his cousin could engage her and keep her thoughts away from her grief better than Jack had. He should have known the subject of his parents would come up when they were attending a family wedding. At least Charlotte hadn't asked about his dad, too.

After several minutes, he was nearly at the front of the line. The couples ahead of and behind him were strangers, so he quietly looked over the crowd for people he knew. The wedding party must still be taking pictures. He didn't see the bride, groom or anyone associated with them on the terrace.

"I'd like two colas," he told the older man who was bartending. He slipped a dollar into the tip jar and stepped away with the two glasses.

He was making his way back to the table where he'd left Charlotte when he saw her in line at the other bar. She had her back to him, her arms crossed.

A moment of worry hit him. What had happened? Had she gotten tired of waiting for her drink and decided to get her own? Had she not gotten along with Frank and his wife?

Jack hurried through the crowd. He came up behind her and said, "Charlotte?" When she didn't react, he tapped her shoulder to get her attention.

"What's the matter, too impatient to wait till I got back?" he asked.

As soon as the woman he thought was Charlotte turned around, he knew it wasn't Charlotte, even though the resemblance was incredible. She wore a dress similar to Charlotte's in color, and her hair was not only the same dark brown but also styled nearly identically.

"I'm so sorry. I thought you were someone else." He couldn't help staring into her gorgeous blue eyes. Uncanny. They were exactly like Charlotte's, but somehow different.

Instead of seeing Charlotte's grief in her eyes, he saw definite annoyance.

CHAPTER TWO

ALL SHE WANTED was a drink. A glass of water would do—a shot of tequila would be better. "Did you want something?" Allie asked the man who was still staring at her.

He twisted his neck slightly and raised his chin as if his stiff white shirt collar was too tight. He held a glass of dark liquid with a cocktail straw in each hand.

"I'm sorry. I thought you were someone else." He blinked.

"You said that already."

"The resemblance is remarkable."

"I'm sure it is." Whatever that meant.

She glanced to her right and saw her very pregnant sister, Rachael, coming toward her. Uh-oh. Now what? Maybe she should have given in to her mother and found a date for this shindig instead of being everyone's errand girl. She was beginning to think her mother was looking for things for her to do to punish her for refusing to bring a date.

She turned back to the guy who'd mistaken her for another woman, but he was gone. She probably should have been nicer to him. He was pretty hot in his well-tailored, dark suit that made his dark eyes look nearly black. His almost-black hair was neatly trimmed, shorter on the sides with a little height on top, but not too much. Yeah, definitely hot.

"What do you need me to do now?" Allie asked Rachael as soon as her sister was within hearing range.

"Dad left his inhaler back at the hotel, and he's having trouble with all the blooming flowers around here."

Allie rolled her eyes. They could have stopped at the hotel on their way from the church if he'd remembered sooner. "Okay, I'll go get it."

"I could go—"

Allie shook her head. "I'll do it. You've got enough to worry about between Sophie and her little brother, who you're cooking in there." She pointed to Rachael's expanding belly and then looked around the room. "Speaking of Sophie, where is she?" Allie's three-year-old niece had developed a tendency to wander off since arriving in town, and the entire family was on constant lookout.

"Dan's got her occupied," Rachael said, referring to her husband. "If you're sure, then I'll go back to keep an eye on Dad."

"I'm sure." Maybe she could even stop for a big bottle of water while she was gone. She sure wasn't going to get a drop of it in this slow line anytime soon.

JACK SET A glass of soda in front of Charlotte, who sat alone at the table. He took the seat next to her, anxious to share what he'd seen. "Guess what? You have a doppelgänger."

Charlotte's eyes widened. "Really?"

As someone adopted as a baby, did she search crowds to find other people with similar DNA? Or was he projecting his own thoughts on the situation? As an only child, he had often found himself wondering what it would be like to have a sibling. Especially during his teenage years.

"Yeah, she's over there in line at the bar." He stood up again and surveyed the room to find Charlotte's look-alike. He squinted but didn't see her in either line. He sat back down. "She's gone. But I'll point her out next time I see her. You can't miss her. She's even wearing a dress almost the same color as yours."

He gestured to the plates and glasses left on the table across from Charlotte, where Frank and his wife had been sitting. "What happened to those two?" The last thing he wanted was for Charlotte to be by herself. She was supposed to be having some fun.

"They went to look at the collage of baby pictures of the bride and groom," Charlotte said. "I told them I'd make sure no one cleared away their food and drinks. And, just so you know, Frank's wife's name is Julia."

"That's it." He knew he'd recognize her name when he heard it. "Sorry it took me so long to get the drinks. The bartenders are in no hurry. Want some food?"

"I'm good with a soda right now, but go ahead and eat if you're hungry."

"I did skip lunch, what with Granddad's episode."

Charlotte grinned. "Then go get some food. I'm fine right here. I'll even keep watch for my doppelgänger."

"The resemblance is remarkable." He shook his head. "Anyway, I promise not to take so long this time." He spoke over his shoulder. "I'll bring enough to share in case you change your mind."

Jack kept a lookout for Charlotte's double as he made his way through the throng of people toward the food. No sign of her, though. He filled a plate with different cheeses, crackers and fruit, grabbed two napkins and hightailed it back to Charlotte. He was supposed to be showing her a good time, and instead he'd spent more time away from her than with her.

He slipped a piece of cheese into his mouth and set the plate where both he and Charlotte could reach it. "Miss me?" He winked and was pleased to see her smile. He handed her a napkin and then pointed out people he knew while they emptied the plate of food.

"We're back!" Frank and Julia appeared suddenly as the very tall glass French doors opened and everyone was invited into the ballroom.

Jack and Charlotte were seated at the cousin table. Frank and Julia were across from them, with Frank's sister, Kate, and her husband on Charlotte's side. Next to Jack was his cousin R.J. and R.J.'s girlfriend, whose name he didn't catch.

The wedding party arrived a few minutes later, and they were introduced. Charlotte whispered to Jack, "Look how many attendants there are. I've never seen so many pink dresses."

"I know. This could take all night," Jack whispered back, still watching for Charlotte's double.

After a stilted toast by the best man and a long, weepy and emotional tribute from the maid of honor, dinner was finally served. A Caesar salad and warm rolls were followed by a choice of salmon or vegetarian pasta primavera.

Without warning, Julia, who had excused herself a few minutes before, came up behind Charlotte and said loudly enough for Jack to hear, "Charlotte, I just saw someone in the ladies' room who looks exactly like you!"

"I FEEL BAD for you," Rachael told Allie at dinner. "You've missed so much of the day."

Allie shook her head and chewed the bite of salad she'd stuffed in her mouth. She was starving. She hadn't eaten since that protein shake she'd gulped down on her way to get her hair done that morning. "It's okay. Weddings aren't my thing anyway."

Rachael looked at her askance. "You know,

the day will come when you'll change your mind about that."

"I doubt it." Allie buttered a roll, not caring that she'd been trying to avoid carbs now that it was swimsuit season. She'd make up for it by running an extra mile tomorrow.

If she could squeeze it in between attending the family brunch and completing her potential client's presentation.

"You just haven't found the right guy." Rachael tilted her head at her husband, who was playing keep away with an asparagus spear he was trying to get Sophie to eat. She was giggling wildly as Dan attempted to feed it to her ear.

"You got the last good one," Allie told her sister. "The guys I meet are interested only in what's in it for them."

"Jimmy was an idiot," Rachael said, fully aware of his stupid extortion plan. "You can't compare all men to him."

Allie shrugged and took a bite of her salmon with dill sauce. It melted in her mouth, and she practically moaned aloud. "He was the last in a long line of users."

"You mean losers," her sister corrected her.

"Yeah, that, too." Allie couldn't argue with the truth. She pushed back her chair when they announced it was time to cut the cake. "I'm going to the bar. You want anything? Soda? Mineral water? Juice?"

Rachael shook her head. "Nothing for me, thanks."

She looked to Dan. He held up his hand, and it was quickly grabbed by Sophie. "I'm good, thanks," he said on a laugh.

No one else had shown up to sit at their table for her to entertain, so Allie hurried off to the bar.

"Hey," the female bartender greeted her. "You must be thirsty from all your running around. I keep seeing you everywhere I look."

"I doubt you saw *me* every time. They tell me I have a double here somewhere."

The woman's eyes widened. "Really? And you haven't seen her yet?"

Allie shook her head. The idea of someone looking that much like her was crazy. "Hard to find anyone in this crowd."

"Well, if I see her," the bartender said, "I'll tell her you're looking for her."

A lie, since Allie didn't care about this other woman, but she gratefully accepted her white wine, kept her mouth shut and headed outside, where the sun had almost set.

THE BRIDE AND GROOM'S first dance was nearly over, and Jack was still searching for Charlotte's double. Then the bride danced with her father while the groom danced with his mother.

Jack was sure he'd spy Charlotte's double once the bride threw her bouquet. Unfortunately, the woman was nowhere to be found when that time came. Maybe she was married. Not that it mattered either way. But why was she was so hard to spot?

"I wonder what happened to her." Jack craned his neck to look around the crowded room.

Charlotte laughed. "Stop worrying about some woman who looks like me. If we're meant to see each other, we will."

"How can you not be intrigued? I think it's pretty cool." Jack shrugged. He looked at her and smiled. "Want to dance?"

The "Chicken Dance" was starting, and people were forming a circle on the dance floor.

"Really? The 'Chicken Dance'?" Charlotte laughed but rose from her chair. "Sure, why not? You probably just want to get out there to see if you can spot her."

He grabbed her hand and gave her a pull. "You're absolutely right!"

They were both laughing by the time they squeezed into the circle of participants. Charlotte's laughter made him feel good. Even more so when the music got faster and faster and they messed up the motions because they were laughing hysterically.

"Do you see her anywhere?" Charlotte asked breathlessly after they finished the "Chicken Dance" and a just-as-much-fun attempt at doing the "Y.M.C.A."

He pulled her in to slow dance to a Beatles

favorite. "See, you *are* interested in finding her," he teased.

She turned her face away, but not before he saw a corner of her mouth curl up. "Maybe I am a little curious."

"I *knew* it." He squeezed her hand in his and spun them around a hundred and eighty degrees.

"Whoa!" She laughed. A wonderful sound to hear.

ALLIE SAT ON the edge of the large fountain outside the mansion. Her wine was long gone, and the empty glass sat next to her. The outside lights were the only illumination. What time was it? Almost time to go home? Could she make a break for it, or would she need to help gather and transport things back to the hotel for the bride and groom? Did she really have to stay until after they were gone? Her brother wouldn't care. He probably wouldn't even miss her.

Too many questions. Not enough answers.

All she wanted to do was go back to the hotel and get a good night's sleep. It only made matters more stressful that her incomplete Monday-morning presentation was hanging over her head. This account could make or break her agency. Where would she be if she didn't get the account?

Her parents' spare room in rural upstate New York? The same room she had growing up?

No way.

She inhaled deeply. The floral scent around her was strong. No wonder Dad had needed his inhaler. The last she saw him, though, he was enjoying a piece of wedding cake.

Her parents were wonderful people. Even when Mom was pushing her to "find the right man," Allie knew her mother's motives were pure.

That didn't preclude Allie from feeling like an outsider in her own family, though. She just didn't think or act like the rest of them.

She stood up, brushed off the back of her dress and picked up her empty wineglass. A quick stop in the restroom to touch up her lipstick and she'd get back to the party.

She adjusted her evening bag's chain strap on her shoulder and headed inside.

CHARLOTTE WAS HAVING a wonderful time. She couldn't remember when she'd laughed so much. Jack really was fun to hang out with. Since she'd moved to Newport from Burlington, Vermont, she hadn't gotten close enough to call anyone a friend. But Jack fit the bill.

The crowd had begun to thin a little, and she was slightly disappointed that she never did run into her double. She must have taken off earlier in the evening.

"We can leave whenever you've had enough," Jack told her. "Unless you want to take a short break and hit the dance floor again."

"Let me think about it while I go to the ladies' room," she said. "But if you're ready to go—"

"I'll get us fresh drinks and we can see how we feel." He pulled at his collar. "It's pretty warm in here. Why don't I meet you out in the hall? I saw a nice seating area around the corner to the left."

She nodded and headed to the restroom. Even this late, there was a line coming out the door.

"Is there another restroom to use?" she asked one of the bartenders.

"Go right around there—" she pointed down the hallway "—and you'll see a sign. You can't miss it."

"Thanks!"

Turned out the bathroom was on the lower level. It took a while for her to make her way down the old cement stairs without breaking her neck on her high heels, and then she had to navigate a maze of hallways. But once she committed, she refused to turn back.

JACK GOT THEM drinks as promised. Another white wine for Charlotte and a Scotch on the rocks for himself. He sipped his drink and waited for his "date" to return.

Very few people came by, and he wondered if Charlotte might have misunderstood where they should meet. He went back into the ballroom and there she was, on the far side of the large room. Charlotte's back was to him and she was speaking to one of the bridesmaids, which surprised him.

She was being more outgoing than he'd thought she would be. Maybe coming to the wedding had helped her remember life before grief. He had no idea what her personality had been like before her mother became ill—perhaps she'd been more outgoing, adventurous.

The DJ switched to "Shout," and the dance floor filled up quickly. Jack caught himself tapping his foot to the beat, so he set down his drinks and made his way around the crowd to where Charlotte was.

She was unaware of his presence. He came up behind her and grabbed her waist. "Let's dance." She squealed and said something, but the music was too loud for him to hear her. "Sorry, Patience," he apologized to his cousin for interrupting their conversation. Then he took Charlotte's hand and pulled her behind him onto the dance floor.

He found an open spot and then turned to face her. His jaw dropped. The woman wasn't Charlotte.

The woman he'd dragged onto the dance floor was her very angry double.

"WHAT DO YOU think you're doing?" Allie had to yell over the blaring music to be heard. She ripped her hand out of his.

The man who'd pulled her away from her conversation with the sister of her new sister-in-law stood there with his mouth hanging open.

She widened her eyes, an attempt to clue him in that she was waiting for an explanation.

"You're not Charlotte," he finally yelled back over the loud music. "But, damn, you two could be twins."

"Yeah, right. If this shtick is an example of what you think is a good pickup line, then you're in for a shock, buddy. This ain't workin' at all."

She turned to leave the dance floor. The song ended and the volume lowered as the DJ played a slow song. Instead of letting her walk away, the crazy guy spun her into his arms.

She stiffened. "What are you doing? Let me go."

He loosened his grip, though their bodies remained a few inches apart. "I'm sorry. Please, don't make a scene. My cousin—the bride—would never forgive me."

"Maybe you should have thought about that before you dragged me away from my conversation with her sister." Who must also be his cousin, if he was telling the truth.

They swayed to the music, and her anger slowly abated. She remembered the feeling of being held by a handsome man and had the urge to press against his solid form but didn't want him getting the wrong idea.

"Who are you?" His breath was warm on her cheek. "Besides being my date's doppelgänger?"

"Allie. Who are you?" She wasn't about to give him a last name, even if she did share it with the groom.

"Jack."

"Just Jack?" She looked him straight on.

"Just Allie?" he countered with a damn sexy grin.

She considered it. "Allie Miller, sister of the groom."

Jack's feet planted in place, and he stared at her. His eyes narrowed. "Really? The groom's sister?"

She got that reaction all the time. She'd spent her life explaining. "Scott was born in China. I wasn't."

Allie nearly laughed as the lightbulb figuratively came on over Jack's head.

The song was ending and Allie halfheartedly tried to free herself, but he held her hand. "Let me get you a drink as way of apologizing for my behavior." Another slow song began, and he pulled her closer.

"No need," she said a little breathlessly. "I've been hearing all night about this woman who looks exactly like me, but I haven't seen her yet."

He chuckled, his warm breath ruffling her hair against her cheek. "I know. I've been trying to find you again ever since I saw you in the line at the bar. I think Charlotte thought I was crazy until other people started telling her they'd seen you, too."

Allie nodded, inhaling deeply. She found the hint of his spicy soap or aftershave or something intoxicating. His splayed hand at the small of her back was practically burning through her dress to her skin, and it was all she could do to keep her rubbery legs from giving out. She couldn't think beyond how his thigh felt so good against hers. She was hyperaware of every cell of her body.

"Charlotte? That's her name? This woman who looks like me." A sudden thought caught her by surprise. "Is she your wife?"

He laughed from deep in his chest. "Not even close. She's a friend, my neighbor from across the street. Someone who needed to get out and have a good time."

"And yet you're dancing with me and not her." She looked directly at him and raised an eyebrow.

His smile in return was almost her undoing. His full lips revealed straight white teeth, and the gleam in his eyes had her expecting a tinkling bell to go off like it would in a television commercial.

He squeezed her hand with his much larger one and whispered in her ear, "She'll understand." His cheek rubbed lightly against hers, and her knees nearly folded.

Allie was glad this Charlotte would understand, because Allie didn't have a clue about what was happening.

One minute she was playing errand girl for her family, and the next she was in the arms of a complete stranger who didn't feel strange at all.

In fact, he felt pretty damn good.

JACK DIDN'T WANT to let her go. His attraction to Allie—who was essentially a stranger—was strong and unexpected. He could barely keep his body under control.

He needed to talk about something nonsexual. Not that anything they'd talked about had been sexual in the least. Exactly the opposite. But that hadn't stopped his body from responding otherwise. The last thing he wanted to do was scare her off.

"I should introduce you to Charlotte," he said abruptly. He cleared the hoarseness from his throat.

"Of course," she murmured close to his ear. "I'd love to meet her."

He had to stop thinking about Allie's breasts pressing against him.

"As soon as this song ends," he promised.

"Uh-huh."

He had to stop wondering what she tasted like. The nape of her neck, her earlobe, her shoulder. *Stop.*

He inhaled deeply in an effort to clear his thoughts, but instead caught a whiff of something citrus. Her shampoo? Perfume? Intoxicating, whatever it was.

The song ended.

They drew apart, but Jack held on to her hand. He opened his mouth to speak. Before he could form words, he heard another voice.

"Allie." The very pregnant Asian woman who spoke sounded out of breath as she hurried toward them. "Do you have that double-sided tape? Mom caught her heel in the hem of her skirt, and she refuses to come out of the bathroom until she can fix it."

"It's in my purse." Allie looked around the room. "I think I left it at my seat. I'll go get it and take it to Mom."

"I can do it," the woman said. "I don't want to interrupt whatever *this* is." She pointed to the two of them with a devilish grin.

"It's nothing," Allie insisted.

"Hey," Jack said automatically.

"You've had a long day," Allie reminded the woman, pointedly ignoring Jack. "Go sit for a few minutes and get off your feet."

Allie had apology written all over her face when she spoke to Jack. "This won't take long." She extricated her hand from his, and he immediately wanted to snatch it back. "By the way, this is my sister, Rachael Thompson." She said to Rachael, "This is Jack—" She turned to him with furrowed eyebrows. He'd never told her his last name.

Jack put a hand out to Rachael. "Jack Fletcher, cousin of the bride. Nice to meet you."

Allie smiled. "I'll be right back. Don't let him go anywhere, Rach. He's the one who brought my double to the wedding. I'm anxious to see her for myself."

"So you admit you're using me," he teased loudly as she hurried away.

She shook a fist in the air, and he heard her laugh as she disappeared through the crowd.

CHARLOTTE FINALLY FOUND the ladies' room on the lower level, but it was locked up tight with an out-of-order sign on the door. Deciding it would have been easier to just wait in line, she made her way back up to the main-floor bathroom.

The straps of her shoes dug into her feet and she was tempted to take them off, but of course she didn't. She needed to behave like a proper guest at Jack's cousin's wedding, not the frequently bare-foot, yoga pants—wearing, free-spirited artist she normally was.

The line was gone by the time she arrived at the restroom. She hurried past the lounge area, where two women were seated on the sofa. They were hunched over, concentrating on some task. Charlotte barely noticed them as she located an empty stall.

"Okay, Mom, I think you're all set now," one of the women said.

"Thank you, dear," the other replied. "I really appreciate your help. I'm glad you were so prepared."

"I'll see you out there in a few minutes," the original speaker said. Then Charlotte heard the opening and closing of the door leading to the hallway.

Heels clicked on the tile floor in front of her stall and someone entered the stall next to her.

Charlotte finished, exited the stall and washed her hands at the sinks. The stall door behind her opened and slammed shut as heels clicked behind her.

"It's you!"

Charlotte stopped rinsing the soap from her hands to stare at the other woman in the mirror. She couldn't form words. Everything Jack had said about her having a doppelgänger was true.

The woman stood beside her in front of the sink, her concentration clearly on Charlotte's reflection. They had the same mouth, identical noses, even a similar hair color and style.

But it was the eyes that got Charlotte. She was staring back at the same eyes that she'd seen in the mirror for the past twenty-nine years.

CHAPTER THREE

ALLIE COULDN'T STOP staring at the other woman in the mirror as she finished washing her hands. She finally swallowed and formed words. "You must be Charlotte." Allie reached for a paper towel from the pile on the counter.

The woman's eyes grew round and her lips trembled. "You know my name?"

Allie smiled, unable to comprehend their resemblance. "I was just dancing with your date. He told me your name."

"You danced with Jack?"

Allie quickly said, "Don't worry, he thought I was you at first."

"No, don't misunderstand." Charlotte's hands shook when she reached for a paper towel without breaking eye contact. "Jack and I are friends. He's been trying to find you since he first ran into you. We thought you'd left."

"I've been running around all day. I'm the sister of the groom. Do you want to sit for a minute? This is all so unbelievable." Allie gestured to the lounge area of the ladies' room. She was at a loss for words until she realized she hadn't introduced herself. "I'm Allie Miller."

Charlotte took a seat on the sofa. She hadn't

taken her eyes off Allie. "I'm very glad to meet you, Allie. This is definitely unreal."

Allie smiled. "Isn't it?" She sat in the chair that was at a ninety-degree angle to the sofa. "I can't get over how much we look alike."

"I was adopted as an infant, so I've never seen anyone who looks even slightly like me."

"Me, either," Allie said. "I was adopted, too."

"You were! Do you think we're related?" Charlotte shook her head. "What am I saying? I mean, we must be related. This is too crazy."

Allie nodded her head. "There's obviously some connection between us. People weren't lying when they said we look alike."

"I should go find Jack," Charlotte said. "If that's okay with you. He's pretty invested in finding out our connection. Besides, I've been gone quite a while." She explained her unsuccessful expedition to find another bathroom on the lower level of the building. "Man, my shoes are *killing* me." She reached down to adjust the strap over her pinkie toe.

Allie laughed. "Yeah, I gathered from our conversation that he has as many questions as we do. Not that any of us have any answers. Wait—" she bent down to unbuckle one of her shoes and then the other "—go ahead." She looked up at Charlotte. "We'll both take off these painful things."

Charlotte laughed and did the same. "Ohhh, that feels *so* good!"

"Oh, yeah!" Allie hadn't realized how much her feet hurt until she removed her shoes. "I can see how people thought we were the same person. Our clothes and even our hairstyles are nearly identical."

Charlotte touched her hair. "I don't usually curl mine, but I decided to since this was a special occasion. Even our feet look the same. Size 8?"

"Exactly." Shoes in one hand, Allie held the door for Charlotte to leave first. Charlotte toasted her with her own shoes as she passed, and Allie noticed they were the same height, too. She had to give Jack credit. Their dress color *was* very similar. At least until they were right next to each other.

Allie and Charlotte kept glancing at each other as they walked down the hall to where Jack sat with his drink. The looks from the few people they passed were hysterical. Even some open mouths and gasps.

Jack stood as soon as he saw them coming, a wide grin on his delicious mouth. At least Allie was pretty sure it was delicious. Her tongue wet her bottom lip.

She glanced at Charlotte, wondering if she'd ever kissed Jack. They both claimed to be merely friends, but were they friends with benefits?

She shoved her thought aside. She barely knew the man. Besides, she'd sworn off men for good.

Though she couldn't deny the instant connection she and Jack had made.

The seating area was comprised of two matching Louis XIV chairs across from a straight-backed sofa, and an ornate black and gold-leaf coffee table that sat in the middle. Charlotte took the chair next to Jack's, and Allie sat across from them on the sofa. Perfect spot to view this exact replica of herself. She perched on the edge of her seat, anxious to figure out this mystery.

"Tell me—"

"—about yourself."

The two women laughed when they asked the same thing at the same time.

Jack looked from one to the other. "You're speaking in stereo. This is really strange."

Allie said, "You can say that again."

Charlotte wiggled in her chair.

"What do you know about your adoption?" Allie's heart was beating furiously.

"Nothing, actually. Yet. I only started thinking about searching for my birth parents a few days ago." Charlotte told Allie about losing her adoptive mother to cancer and wanting to know her medical history. "My mom was older when she adopted me, in her early forties. She never married, so it was only the two of us."

Allie saw the sadness in her eyes. "You must miss her terribly."

"I do." Charlotte brushed at a tear that escaped from her watery eyes. "Sorry." Jack patted Charlotte's arm, and she smiled wanly as she spoke to

Allie. "Jack's doing his best to cheer me up, but I do miss her every day."

He put an arm around Charlotte's shoulders and squeezed. Allie approved of how good a friend it seemed he was being to Charlotte.

"What do you know about *your* adoption?" Charlotte brushed away another tear. "Sorry. It's still tough talking about my mom." She sniffed.

"I've never looked into my adoption," Allie said. "My mother doesn't like to talk about it. When I was younger and asked questions, she'd say, 'All you need to know is that we chose you and we love you.' By the time I was an adult, I didn't feel the need to find my biological parents. Maybe in part because I already had more family than most people."

"Then you don't know any more than I do." Charlotte dabbed at a lone tear on her cheek. "You said you had a big family? Tell me about them."

Allie smiled. "I've got the opposite situation from you. I'm one of five adopted children."

Charlotte's eyes grew round.

"My parents lost their only biological child to a rare but fatal genetic disorder that they both carry. He was only a few weeks old when he died. Instead of trying again, they opted for adoption. That's where I came in. I was their first." Allie brushed at a lock of hair tickling her cheek. "Shortly before I started kindergarten, they adopted a brother-and-sister pair from China. They were one and three when they came to live with us. Scott—the groom—is my brother." She looked at Jack. "And you met my sister, Rachael. They were both born with heart abnormalities and were sent to an orphanage so their parents could have a perfect child. Little did they know, a few surgeries later and their children were as good as new."

"So you have four younger siblings?" Charlotte asked.

"Not exactly. I was the oldest until I turned nine. That's when my parents adopted my older brothers, Grigory and Nikolay, from Russia. They were also biological brothers. Gregory and Nicholas— Greg and Nick—came here when they were twelve and ten."

"So you're the middle child of five?" Charlotte's eyes—an exact replica of Allie's—widened.

Allie forced a smile. "That's right. I'm sure there are hundreds of psychologists out there who would like to study me. 'Oldest child becomes middle child. Where does this adoptee fit?'"

"At least you can joke about it," Jack said.

Allie shrugged. "Not always."

He seemed to be considering her response before he said, "You two are obviously related. Let's get down to the pertinent stuff. When and where were you born?" He looked to Charlotte first.

"I was born on April 17—"

"1986?" As soon as Allie heard the month and day, she knew the year would be the same.

"Yes!" Charlotte said excitedly. "You, too?"

Allie nodded vigorously, but her excitement wouldn't allow her to speak for a few seconds. "I was born right here in Rhode Island, but I'm not sure where."

Jack asked Charlotte, "You were born in Rhode Island, also?"

She shook her head, her confusion evident by her pursed lips. "No. I was born in upstate New York."

"HOW CAN THAT BE?" Jack verbalized the question that had to be on all of their minds. "You look so much alike, you sound alike and you were born on the same day. But in different states?"

Jack had been sure from their birthdays that they were twins. But now he didn't know what to think.

"Coincidence?" Charlotte suggested.

"It's more than coincidence," Allie said. "We're obviously related. Now we need to figure out *how* we're related."

"Maybe we're cousins?"

"That's a possibility, but it seems unlikely. Siblings giving birth on the same day in different states... Anyway, I don't think we'd look this much alike if we were cousins unless both our birth mothers and fathers were twins."

"Wouldn't that make you genetic twins?" Jack asked.

"I think you're right," Allie said. "But what are the chances that both sets of parents would put us up for adoption? There must be more to it." She stuck out her hand, palm down, and said to Charlotte, "Put your hand out next to mine."

As soon as Charlotte did, the resemblance was remarkable. Just like their matching feet.

"You can't argue with proof like that," Allie said, "but only a DNA test will tell us for sure." The other two nodded their agreement. "There's nothing more we can do tonight."

"What about your mom?" Jack suggested. "We could ask her some questions and see if she can fill in the blanks."

Allie shook her head. "I'd rather keep her out of this, at least for tonight. She had pretty bad bronchitis six weeks ago, and between that and the wedding prep, she hasn't quite regained her strength. Besides, she should just be allowed to enjoy the rest of her son's wedding day."

"Of course," Charlotte said. "And it *is* getting late."

Allie jumped up from the sofa. "You're right. I didn't realize how late it was. I need to help pack up. Mom's probably looking for me. Let's exchange information," she said to Charlotte, "and we can get together soon."

Charlotte and Jack stood up, too. "We can help," Jack said.

"Yes," Charlotte agreed. "Tell us what needs to be done."

"Oh, wow, thanks, but I'm sure we're fine. Huge family and all."

"I understand completely," Charlotte said, and Jack nodded his agreement. Allie must really want to keep her mom from seeing Charlotte.

Charlotte retrieved her cell phone from her silver clutch. "Give me your number, and I'll text you so you have mine."

"Good idea. I left mine in the car." Allie recited the number.

Jack was trying to be cool. He could get Allie's phone number from Charlotte, he supposed. He really wanted to see her again, but she was in the middle of some big family stuff with the wedding and now meeting Charlotte.

And he didn't want to appear overeager.

"Where are you staying in town?" Jack asked Allie, trying to play it casual.

She named a popular downtown hotel. "I'll be checking out in the morning."

"Where do you live?" Charlotte asked before Jack could. "We never talked about that."

"In Providence," Allie said.

"Oh, good!" Charlotte was giddy with excitement. "I was afraid you flew in from halfway across the country. Jack and I both live here in Newport."

"My office is in Providence," Jack said, pleasantly surprised. "We should get together, maybe grab coffee or lunch this week." He made the suggestion before thinking it through. *Cool, Jack. Real cool.*

Allie smiled, and he took that as a good sign. "I'd like that."

Me, too, he mouthed.

Jack glanced at Charlotte and saw her satisfied grin—she'd obviously not missed his exchange with Allie. "You ready?" he asked Charlotte.

At her nod, he stepped back so the two women could say their goodbyes.

CHARLOTTE'S MIND WAS RACING as she sat in the passenger seat of Jack's car on the way home. Amazing! There was someone else in the world whom she must be related to. She wasn't sure yet how, but they'd soon find out. She was positive they were connected.

"You're pretty quiet," Jack said as they drove up Bellevue Avenue. "Are you okay? In shock, perhaps?"

Charlotte turned toward him and grinned. "I'm better than okay." She was definitely more excited than she'd been in a while. "I'm really glad you asked me to come to the wedding with you."

"I'm glad, too." He gave her arm a pat. "Talk about a coincidental meeting."

"I know. I'm not sure how Allie and I would ever have met otherwise."

"And she lives so close," Jack said. "It didn't hit

me until I asked where she was staying that she could have come in for the wedding from anywhere."

"I'm sure that makes *you* very happy, too," Charlotte teased.

"Of course it does. Now you two will be able to get together."

"Uh-huh."

He glanced at her quickly before returning his attention to the road. "What does that mean?"

She smirked, but it was too dark in the car for Jack to see her. "It means I'm not blind. I saw how attracted you are to her."

The muscles in his jaw tensed. "Do you have a problem with that?"

She chuckled. "I think it's great." She paused a few seconds. "We *are* just friends, right? Nothing romantic going on?"

"Of course. I don't mean that to sound harsh, but even I'm a little confused. You and I are friends, and I never considered you anything more."

"Gee, thanks."

"That wasn't meant as an insult," he said quickly. "I value friendship, probably more than any romantic stuff I've ever been involved in. So if I see you as my friend, then take that as the compliment it is."

"Got it. Are you considering Allie as another friend?" She already knew the answer.

"Maybe."

"Hah!" She was enjoying making him squirm.

"Okay, I'm attracted to her. A lot." He stopped

at a red light and looked at Charlotte. "I don't get it. She looks almost identical to you, so why am I attracted to her and not you?"

"Again, gee, thanks." Then she laughed because she really *was* teasing. "Good thing I'm not attracted to you, either, *friend*." And that was the honest truth. She sobered and asked the question she'd wanted to ask for a while now. "Why are you so afraid of getting into a relationship, Jack?"

"With you?" His tone was teasing, but his resistance to answering honestly was blatant.

"No. And I don't mean to pry. It just seems like you have a successful job, a newly renovated house. You're what, early thirties?"

"Thirty-two."

"So what's keeping you from settling down? Not necessarily married, but in a committed relationship?"

"Simple. It's an allergy."

Charlotte laughed. "Allergy?"

"I'm allergic to relationships. I inherited it from my father."

"He never settled down, either?"

"Just the opposite," Jack told her. "He settled down over and over and over again."

"And that's what caused your allergy to commitment?"

"Yep."

"Well, I think that's ridiculous. We'll have to work on that. Give me your cell phone."

He pulled it from his pants pocket and gave it to her. "What are you doing?"

She took out her own phone, too. "I'm programming Allie's phone number into your phone so you have no excuse for not calling her. In fact, I think you should call her as soon as we get home so you can make it clear that you and I are no more than friends."

It was well after midnight when Allie finally collapsed, fully clothed, on her hotel bed.

"What a day," she said aloud to the ceiling, wiggling her bare toes to bring back the circulation.

She heard a noise that sounded like her cell phone vibrating from under the pile of things she had brought in from her car. She hauled herself up off the bed, hoping it wasn't someone asking her to do something. Her energy was depleted.

She finally dug her phone from the bottom of a reusable tote bag where she'd put her shoes, makeup bag and anything else she'd thought she might need during the day while away from the hotel.

The phone number was unfamiliar. She opened the message, and a warmth went through her as she read it.

This is Jack. Got your number from Charlotte. Hope that's okay. Hope to talk to you soon.

She immediately wrote back, careful not to sound too eager. After all, she *was* off men.

Of course it's ok. Nice to meet you.

She hesitated before hitting Send. "Nice to meet you?" she said out loud. "How formal." She erased it and tried again.

Of course it's ok. Call me anytime.

Again, she hesitated. Now she sounded desperate. Or at least easy. She deleted it and considered what to say.

Maybe she should ignore his text until tomorrow morning. Pretend she was asleep when it came in.

No. She really wanted him to know she felt something with him, without actually telling him that. Even though she really was off men.

She took another approach. She texted Charlotte.

Hope this didn't wake you. It's Allie. I need advice. Jack texted me. I want to answer, but don't want him to get the wrong idea.

She only waited a minute or two before Charlotte replied.

It's obvious you like each other. Why play hard-to-get?

Charlotte had no idea about Allie's poor decisions when it came to men. She typed quickly.

I've made wrong choices before. Don't want to repeat mistakes.

Charlotte wrote back.

Give him a chance. He's been a good friend to me.

Allie considered that. She had seen firsthand how comforting Jack had been to Charlotte in the short time she'd known him.

But she barely knew Charlotte. How could she know how good the woman was at judging character? Should she take Charlotte at her word that Jack was a good guy? She looked exactly like Allie, but what if she was also as bad at judging people as Allie was?

She wrote back to Charlotte.

Thanks. Will think about it. Talk to you soon.

Charlotte replied.

Looking forward to it. Call or text me tomorrow after your family stuff. You could come over to my house so we can talk more.

Allie thought about how much work she still had

to do. She really needed to drive back to Providence, but getting to know Charlotte better had become a top priority.

Sounds good. I do have to get work done before Monday morning, so I can't stay too long.

Charlotte wrote back.

I'll search through my mom's files to see if I can find anything about my adoption before you get here. Can't wait.

Allie smiled. *Me, neither.*

She went back to Jack's message and hit Reply.

I'm glad she gave you my number. Hope to talk to you soon.

She hit Send and felt a rush of adrenaline. This could be a huge mistake.

She stripped out of her dress and underwear before heading to the bathroom, where she'd left her nightshirt hanging on the back of the door. She slipped it on, brushed her teeth, washed her face and applied moisturizer.

When she came out of the bathroom, there was a voice mail message on her phone. She must not have heard the phone ring over the water running.

She smiled as she listened to Jack's message.

"Hey, you said you hoped to talk soon, so here I am." He paused. "Guess you must be sleeping by now or maybe don't want to talk this late. I wanted to say good-night." He paused again. "So good night."

She shook her head, both amused and touched. *Damn, he's good.*

As much as she desperately wanted to call him back, she resisted.

After all, she was off men.

EARLY THE NEXT AFTERNOON, Charlotte was on a mission. She diligently went through box after box after box of her mother's papers. She'd repeatedly put off the task, but now that she'd met Allie, Charlotte had a driving force behind her.

When she'd cleaned out her mother's house to sell it after her death, Charlotte hadn't taken the time to go through everything. Instead, she'd packed the papers into plastic boxes with lids. Now she regretted not sorting through them earlier. Mom had been a saver. She had receipts and old bank statements from over three decades ago, but nothing yet that pertained to Charlotte's adoption.

She'd like to take a good look at her birth certificate, but she had it locked in her safe-deposit box at the bank, which was closed on Sunday afternoons. She hadn't used it in years.

Her phone went off, announcing a text message.

She put down the pile of papers she was sorting and grabbed it. Allie.

I'll be there in a few minutes if that's still ok.

Charlotte replied.

Can't wait. See you soon.

She'd texted her address to Allie last night. She'd been hoping that she'd have found something by now to help them make sense of the information they had about their adoptions—which was little to nothing.

Charlotte went to the kitchen to wash up, feeling gritty after handling all the dusty papers.

By the time she stepped out onto her porch, Allie was parking her car.

"Hi," Charlotte said with a wave, trying to control her excitement.

Allie grinned back and waved. "Hi, Charlotte!" As she got closer to the porch, she commented, "Great house!"

Charlotte appreciated the compliment. "Thanks! I fell in love with it the moment I saw it."

"How long have you been here?" Allie asked as she ascended the porch steps and the two women hugged.

"Since last fall, a few months after my mom died. I had given up the apartment I'd been renting and moved in with her to take care of her while she was sick. When she passed away, I sold her house because I couldn't bear to be in it without her, surrounded by so many memories." She opened the front door and stepped inside. "Come on in. I'll give you a tour if you'd like."

Allie's eyes widened. "I'd love it. These older homes have so much character."

"Character," Charlotte repeated. "Yeah, that's a nice way to put it. More like repairs when you're least expecting them."

They laughed as they went through the living room and into the dining room, then on into the kitchen. "There's a full bath in there," Charlotte said, pointing to the doorway in the dining room. "There's a shed in the small backyard, and I'm trying to grow a few vegetables in a garden, but nothing else exciting out there. Let's go upstairs."

The narrow staircase was on the side wall of the dining room, and Charlotte told Allie about the house's history as they went up to the second floor. "The house was built in 1900, and the hardwood floors are original. In the eighties, the owners made some improvements, but I've been told they didn't keep with the history of the house. In 2005, the home was sold. Thankfully, the new owners returned it to its turn-of-the-century feel by uncovering the brick wall on the far end of the house and installing more appropriate plumbing fixtures."

They reached a small hallway. "Straight ahead

is the guest room," Charlotte said, and then led the way through another doorway. "In here is where I have my studio set up."

Allie entered the room. "I love this! The light is wonderful in here."

There were large windows at eye level, as well as a gorgeous window near the ceiling that ran the length of the wall and had amazing scrollwork. "That window up there and the skylight were what sold me on the house."

"I should've asked you what you do, but you're obviously an artist," Allie said, looking around at the supplies and paraphernalia Charlotte had neatly arranged. She'd spent more time organizing in here than going through her mother's old files. "Is it for fun, or is this how you make your living?"

"I'm lucky enough to be able to support myself with my art," Charlotte said. "I've had several shows in the past few years, but not many since my mom got sick. Most of my sales right now are over the internet. My dream is to open a brick-and-mortar gallery."

"Newport is a great place for that."

"That's actually why I decided to move here from Vermont. Newport's also close enough to New York City and Boston to be able to have shows in those cities."

"This is wonderful," Allie said of a depiction of some historic Newport doorways done in pastels, hung above a shelving unit.

"Thank you. I did that about two years ago when

I came here to paint some of the historic buildings. That's when I fell in love with the town." About a year prior to her mother's diagnosis.

Allie pointed to a door on the far wall. "Is your bedroom through there?"

"Yes. Kind of an odd setup having to go through this room to get to that room. That's why I chose the other bedroom for guests." Not that she'd had any visitors except her college roommate coming through town a few weeks ago. "You said you have work to do today. What do you do?"

"I'm in advertising," Allie said. "I recently started my own agency, and I'm hoping to land a large account tomorrow. My presentation is close to being done, but it's not quite there."

"How exciting. Somehow I'm not surprised that we are both entrepreneurs."

"With a creative side, too," Allie added. "I'm not nearly as good as you, but I do a lot of freehand drawing in my line of work, as well as animation."

"Wow, that's another thing we have in common. Come on." Charlotte waved her hand. "Let's go downstairs and see what else we can learn about each other."

When they were seated in Charlotte's inviting living room, sipping cold drinks, Charlotte asked, "How was your family brunch?"

Allie rolled her eyes. "Let's just say I'm glad this weekend is almost over."

Charlotte laughed. "That bad?"

"You don't know the half of it. I'm honestly not into the whole wedding and marriage thing, but my mother lives for those occasions." *Does she ever.*

"Did you tell her about me?" Charlotte asked.

Allie shook her head. "No. Though I did make sure I was seated next to her so I could casually ask about my adoption, but she kept changing the subject. I can't help feeling she's not telling me something."

"Sounds like it," Charlotte agreed. Her mouth twisted. "I didn't have any better luck looking through my mother's things."

They talked for quite a while about everything they could think of—their childhoods, their hobbies, their likes and dislikes.

"Oh!" Allie jumped up from her seat when the mantel clock chimed. "It's five o'clock. I didn't know it was so late. I better get going."

"I didn't, either." Charlotte got up and walked Allie out to the porch. "Call me tomorrow to let me know how your presentation went."

Allie nodded. "I will. And I'll see if I can figure out how we go about getting a DNA test done."

"The sooner the better."

Allie waved and got into her car. She watched Charlotte pull a dead leaf from a hanging flowering plant on her porch before going inside her house.

Allie turned on the engine and was about to pull out of her parking spot when she saw Jack crossing the street. He was in khaki shorts and a T-shirt. His hair was damp, as if he'd just showered. She lowered her window.

"Hey," he said when he got close. He smelled delicious. Fresh and clean.

"Hey," she replied in like fashion. "You live right there?"

His smile warmed her insides.

"Yep," he said. "Did you have a good visit with Charlotte?"

"I did." She smiled back. "I'm on my way home. Work to finish for tomorrow."

He nodded. "You said you live in Providence? Do you work there, too?"

"I do." She named the office building where her firm was located.

"That's about two blocks from my office. We should meet for coffee or lunch tomorrow."

Before Allie left for home, they made plans to meet for coffee at 2:00 p.m. at a café they both frequented. Allie was surprised she'd never run into him before. Although she probably wouldn't have given him a second glance since she was off men.

Correction: she definitely would have given him more than a glance or two, but she would have reminded herself about her promise to not engage.

Yet here she was, making plans for a coffee date with Jack.

Go figure.

CHAPTER FOUR

JACK WAS UP early the next morning after a late night of prep for his ten o'clock meeting. Fighting the morning traffic from Newport to Providence made his trip a few minutes longer than expected, but it gave him more time to anticipate coffee with Allie.

What was it about her that made him feel different than he did about Charlotte? Physically, they were so much alike. Until he heard they were born in different states, he would have sworn they were identical twins. Perhaps they were sisters with the same father, different mother. Or at least cousins. The central question remained: Why was he attracted to one and not the other?

And, man, was he hot for Allie. His body reacted just at the thought of her. He shifted in his seat as much as his seat belt allowed.

His cell phone played a piano riff from the center console, announcing an incoming call. He hit the button on his hands-free device. "Jack Fletcher."

"Good morning, Jack," the female caller said. "This is Monica Everly."

He recognized the deep, gravelly voice of his potential client. "How are you, Ms. Everly?" The fiftysomething woman had started her successful organic and sustainable farm-animal food company a decade ago and was now looking to broaden her scope by introducing organic dog and cat food.

Jack was determined that *he* would be the one to make her expansion from farms into people's homes successful.

"What can I do for you?" he asked.

"I'm afraid I'm going to have to postpone our meeting this morning. I've got a family emergency."

"Emergency? I hope it's nothing too serious."

"We'll know soon enough," Ms. Everly said in her no-nonsense manner. "I'm on my way to the vet with our Daisy. She was up all night with a cough. I hope she didn't pick up that nasty kennel cough from the groomer's last weekend."

"I'm so sorry to hear that. I hope she feels better soon."

Jack had been introduced to Daisy, a sixty-pound rescue mutt with no manners, when he first met with her owner about moving the company forward into new markets. Ms. Everly claimed their current advertising agency wasn't taking her future seriously. Daisy had her own space in Ms. Everly's office, including a bed, water and food bowls and a basket of toys.

"After I know what's going on with Daisy, we can reschedule your presentation."

"That sounds like a plan," Jack said. "I hope all goes well."

Ms. Everly disconnected in silence.

Jack was beyond disappointed. The firm put all

their efforts into securing this account, and they couldn't afford a delay.

He was close to his office when the piano riff on his cell phone sounded again. He pushed the button to connect. "Jack Fletcher."

"Jack, my boy, just checking in." His grandfather sounded more robust than he had on Saturday morning. "Is your presentation up to snuff?"

Jack proceeded to tell him about the meeting being postponed because of the dog.

"The dog?" Granddad practically shouted into the phone. "Damn! We need that account now."

Nothing Jack hadn't heard before. His grandfather had been pressuring Jack constantly about luring the client to their firm. His grandfather repeatedly reminded Jack that the fate of the company rested on his shoulders, and Ms. Everly's business was their best hope.

"Did you reschedule?"

"Not yet. She wants to hear the vet's diagnosis first."

"I want you to come to the hospital," his grandfather said. "We can go over your presentation and decide how to handle this delay."

"I really need—"

"I'll see you in a few minutes." Granddad disconnected with no further discussion.

The hospital wasn't too far from the office. Jack called his assistant to update her as he entered the hospital garage and then found a parking space.

"I'm here to see Patrick Fletcher," Jack said to the woman behind a large desk in the bustling lobby of the hospital.

Her fingers clicked on the keyboard while she watched her monitor. "Room 317." She handed him a visitor badge and said, "The elevators are down that hall and around the corner to the right. Have a nice day."

"Thanks. You, too." He clipped the badge to his dress-shirt breast pocket. Then he headed to the bank of elevators.

According to the sign when he got out on the third floor, his grandfather's room was to the right. When Jack had visited him before the wedding on Saturday, Granddad had been transferred to ICU as a precaution. Yesterday he had been moved back to this floor, but to a different room than before.

"Hey, Granddad," Jack greeted him as he knocked on the doorframe of his open door.

The older man was sitting up, the head of his bed raised. He set aside the newspaper he'd been reading. "Hello, my boy. Come on in and tell me more about the animal lady."

Jack leaned in to hug him, glad to see his color improved. "Not until you tell me how you're feeling." Jack hadn't gotten a chance to ask him when they spoke on the phone. "You're looking much better than you did Saturday morning."

"Good enough to go home, but they won't let me." He went on to tell Jack about the medical tests his doctor still wanted to do. "Besides having low blood sugar the other day, he's still worried about my heart."

Jack moved the lone vinyl chair closer to the hospital bed. "Better to be sure you're okay." His grandfather lived alone in a high-rise, even though Jack had been trying to get the seventy-nine-year-old to move into a senior assisted-living facility.

"Yeah, yeah," Granddad mumbled and then changed the subject. "You feel good about the presentation? You know we must get this account."

Jack was intensely aware of the pressure he was under, even if his grandfather didn't remind him constantly. The past few years had been rough ones for Empire Advertising, and his grandfather was counting on Jack to rescue it.

Back when Granddad founded the company—thirteen years before Jack was born—he'd snagged several accounts that grew substantially. They included the company whose duck-shaped cookies became a top snack item for the under-ten set, and a juice company that saw their market share quadruple when they began mixing vegetables into their fruit juices.

Unfortunately, over the past decade, many of the CEOs of the large firms that had been the lifeblood of Empire had retired. In turn, their younger counterparts, looking for a fresher approach, sent their advertising dollars to the younger, hipper ad agencies.

From the time Jack graduated from college ten

years ago, his grandfather had pressed him to come and work for Empire. Instead, Jack had stuck to his plan to work for one of those hipper agencies based in New York City. Two years ago, Granddad had finally talked Jack into coming onboard by admitting that Empire couldn't last much longer without help. That's also when his grandfather told Jack he'd inherit the company someday. So if Jack wanted the security of his own firm, then he'd have to work for it.

After spending a few more minutes talking strategy with his grandfather, Jack checked the time. "I'd better get into the office. I'll call you later to see what your doctor says."

"Don't worry about me," Granddad said. "You get that crazy dog woman to give you her advertising money."

Jack couldn't help cracking a smile. His grandfather never minced words. He used to have a filter when necessary, but over the past few months that filter had become almost nonexistent.

He hugged his grandfather and left the hospital. He wondered if he'd be able to get any work done before meeting Allie, since he couldn't seem to get her out of his head.

ALLIE WAS HAVING a heck of a morning.

Just when she finally thought she had her act together, she found out her eleven o'clock meeting was canceled. So much for the presentation she was up until 2:00 a.m. working on.

So much for the zipper on her skirt that finally got unstuck from her blouse.

And so much for the cold shower she had to take this morning because of the broken water heater in her apartment building.

She sat at her desk in her rented office space and stared at her computer. She was eager to figure out how she and Charlotte could get a DNA test done, but that research would have to wait. Right now she needed to get down to business and find more clients so she could afford to get out of this place and into a real office. Making cold calls was one of her least favorite things. She was the idea person. Give her a product and she'd come up with a gimmick. Preferably one that she could animate.

With no funds to fall back on, Allie couldn't afford to rent more than the one office she currently occupied. It came with the use of a conference room and a receptionist, both of which were shared by seven other small offices. What was lacking was any sense of style or warmth.

It was a far cry from the office she used to work in. DP Advertising was located in one of the most prestigious buildings in Providence. When she worked for them, Allie had a plush office overlooking the city. There she led a team of talented and creative people with loads of energy. Unfortunately, the team included Jimmy, her ex-boyfriend who'd recently landed in federal prison.

Her phone rang, startling her out of her reverie. "Allie Miller." She wasn't used to having anyone call her—most of her communication was done through texts or emails. She hoped this was good news. She could use some.

"Hello, Ms. Miller. This is Joan Broadwell from the Rhode Island Animal Rescue League."

Allie had forgotten about the application she'd filled out online. "Yes, Ms. Broadwell. It's good to hear from you."

"I've been looking over your fostering application and have contacted your references. I'm happy to say that you've been approved. We should have a dog for you to foster in the next few days."

"That's wonderful." Allie tried to sound excited, but she was faking it. It wasn't that she disliked dogs. She was simply indifferent to animals of all kinds. She saw no need to have them as pets. The only reason she applied to foster a dog was to impress her potential client. As soon as she landed the account, Allie would return the dog and tell the Rescue League that being a foster parent—or whatever they called it—wasn't working out for her.

She'd hoped to get the dog before her presentation so she could bring it with her. In the end, having her appointment with the client delayed had worked in her favor.

The woman who owned Naturally Healthy Animal Food brought her own dog to her office. And it was actually because the dog—named Tulip or Rosebud or some such thing—had caught something called kennel cough that their meeting this morning had been canceled.

"Now, you do realize that since you live in an apartment, we can't give you a dog larger than about twenty-five pounds."

"Yes, I understand." She didn't need a big dog like Daisy—*that* was the dog's name. But Daisy wasn't anything close to a delicate flower, as she had proved when she jumped up on Allie, practically knocking her over.

They finished their conversation and disconnected. Not two minutes later, the phone rang again.

"Allie Miller."

"Oh, Ms. Miller, this is Joan Broadwell again. Great news! We have a dog that we think will work perfectly for you." She went on to explain that one of their other foster parents had to go out of town unexpectedly for an extended time and could no longer care for the Jack Russell terrier–beagle mix he'd been fostering for a few weeks. "When do you think you can pick up Harvey?"

Allie hit a key on her keyboard to display her calendar. Blank. The rest of the day was open except for coffee with Jack at two.

"I can come anytime after three," she said. Jack probably couldn't take more than an hour off from his job, whatever that might be. Surprisingly, that particular subject hadn't come up.

As soon as she hung up, she searched online to find out what a Jack Russell terrier looked like so she wouldn't look stupid and inexperienced when she picked up the dog. The beagle part was easy. Isn't that what Snoopy from the *Peanuts* comic strip was?

She was about to become a first-time pet owner. Wow. How weird did that sound? Almost stranger than saying she was Harvey's foster mom.

CHARLOTTE WAS DUSTY and dirty by the time she brought down the first of many boxes containing her mother's files that were still in the attic. The plastic tubs felt heavier than she remembered as she carefully made her way down the folding steps to the guest room on the second floor.

She was anxious to continue searching for clues about her adoption, deciding to go through each file meticulously, not putting the boxes back in her attic again. Of course, that would take time, but she didn't want to miss anything, and she certainly didn't want to go through them again later.

She'd covered the hardwood floor of her spare bedroom with an old sheet to protect the surface. She hadn't gotten around to furnishing the room yet, so it was a large empty space. When her college friend had visited several weeks ago, Charlotte had given Joanie her own bed, and Charlotte had slept on an inflatable air mattress in the spare room. She wasn't expecting more company anytime soon, so using the room to spread out Mom's papers should work perfectly.

"Bank statements, receipts, tax returns," she said aloud. "Even her pay stubs from when she worked at a fast-food chain in high school." Charlotte couldn't help laughing.

She had to admit that even though her mother might seem like a hoarder to some, the files were definitely meticulously organized.

A thought came to her. Would her mother have had to pay money at the time of Charlotte's adoption? If so, a receipt of such a transaction might give Charlotte a clue about who her mother had dealt with. She must have at least paid for legal or medical expenses. Charlotte searched the box for records from 1986. Nothing. Wrong box.

She carefully climbed back into the attic to find the *right* box. The two bare bulbs with pull chains didn't provide the best light, so she had to bring several boxes down before she found the right one.

With each descent, she checked the box to see if it contained the bank statements from 1986. Finally, on the fourth box, she found them.

Her heart beat wildly.

Like the others she'd found, the 1986 bank statements were in one of the small boxes inside the plastic tub that Charlotte had used in order to ensure nothing was ruined by moisture or heat in her attic.

She pulled out the small box from the plastic tub and sat cross-legged on the floor. For a moment, she simply stared at the container in front of her. What would she discover? Perhaps something life-altering? Maybe nothing at all.

Her hands shook and she laughed at her nervousness as she opened the box to find twelve identical envelopes in chronological order. She began with January, thinking there may have been a payment to someone several months prior to her birth.

She removed the pile of checks, which were in numerical order. There were canceled checks for rent, utilities, groceries, even a check made out to a local family-owned furniture store long out of business. The notation on the check said *crib*.

Charlotte's eyes teared up. Her mother had been nesting before bringing her baby home.

A single tear escaped and ran down her cheek. She brushed it away and blinked several times to clear her vision. She studied the bank statement. Nothing unusual. The only deposits were identical checks that Charlotte assumed were from the accounting firm where her mother had worked. One near the beginning of the month and one right after the middle. Direct deposit wasn't readily available in those days.

She took out the February statement. Nothing looked any different from January, except for a

check with a notation of *changing table*, made out
to the same furniture store where her mother had
bought the crib.

March was the same, but there were no extra
checks written for baby items. Mom must have
used her credit card for the other purchases. Charlotte was sure to discover those records eventually.

Finally, April. The month of her birth. She could
barely breathe. She carefully opened the envelope.
This time she pulled out the bank statement first.

She immediately saw a deposit for thirty thousand dollars. "Where the heck did that come from?"
she asked out loud. Her mother's yearly salary at
the time wasn't much more than that.

Who could have given her that much money?
Had she taken out a loan? Charlotte would have to
dig through more paperwork from 1986 to find out.

She looked at the statement again and noticed a
check for thirty thousand had been written by her
mother two days after Charlotte was born.

Who had given or loaned her the money? More
importantly, who had she written the check to?

Charlotte quickly pulled the checks from the envelope. Her fingers trembled as she went through
each one. Finally she came to the one she was looking for. Thirty thousand dollars, but it was made
out to Cash.

She quickly turned it over to see who had en-
dorsed it. Her heart sank. As hard as she studied
the signature, she couldn't decipher the scribble.

She couldn't make out the first letter in either the first or last name. Even worse, the check had been cashed at the same bank as her mother's account, not deposited, because there wasn't even an account number along with the signature.

Definitely a dead end.

ALLIE SPENT NEARLY an hour on the internet, trying to find local businesses that might need assistance with their advertising. She found three prospects to contact, meeting the daily goal she'd set for herself.

Next she went on Twitter and participated in a discussion on branding. She would check later to see if she had any new followers. Other advertising professionals would be good, but finding companies or individuals who were trying to do their own advertising would be ideal. She could assist them in improving their public presence both online and anywhere else that might be beneficial to their individual goals.

Finally, she decided her newly formed company needed a blog. She figured she could find something worthwhile to say at least twice a week, so she started on her first entry. She called it "How a Brand-New Ad Agency Handles Its Own Advertising." Her website already had a blog page ready to go, so uploading her piece would be simple.

With a draft of her blog entry set aside to review later, she turned her attention to searching for information about getting a DNA test done. Lots of ads came up with the search, but after reading some websites, she had a better understanding of the process.

She picked up the phone and called Charlotte. "Any news on your end?" she asked without preamble. "This is Allie, by the way."

Charlotte laughed. "I know. You sound like I do when I listen to myself on my voice mail message."

Allie grinned and paid attention while Charlotte told her about finding the deposit and the check to Cash in her mother's files.

"That's a good start, but it brings up a lot more questions."

"I know. Believe me, I've been making a list," Charlotte told her. "I'm guessing she got a loan for the thirty thousand dollars since it all showed up at once, and as far as I know she had no living relatives, but I haven't found any documentation. Which is surprising, since she was so organized."

"Keep looking. You're sure to find the answers. Maybe she transferred it from a savings account."

"That's true. I haven't come across her savings account records from back then yet," Charlotte said. "I don't actually know if the money in and out of her account is even related to my adoption. Just because it occurred two days after I was born, that doesn't make it conclusive. Maybe she bought a car or a really nice piece of jewelry." Charlotte paused. "Although she wasn't the expensive jewelry type."

"Back then, for that price, that would have been

a pretty nice car," Allie commented. "Do you really think she would have spent that much on a car, or anything for that matter, knowing she'd need money for the baby she was about to adopt?"

"Probably not. You're right. She never had expensive taste," Charlotte said. "She was able to pay for my education and left me more than enough money to buy my house—all on her accountant salary."

"Sweet," Allie said. "The advantage of being an only child."

"One of the few." Charlotte's voice turned somber.

Allie needed to change the subject before Charlotte's mood sank lower. "I've been checking out DNA testing online," she said. "It sounds pretty straightforward. You've probably seen it done on TV. You swab your cheek and send it off to the lab."

"How long before we'd get the results?" Good. Charlotte had snapped out of her melancholy.

"That information wasn't available on the website, so I emailed to ask and also to find out exactly what the results might tell us. If they don't contact me by tomorrow, I'll make some phone calls."

"Sounds good. Anything else going on with you? How did your presentation go?"

"Postponed. The CEO's dog might have kennel cough. Is that a real thing? I meant to look it up."

Charlotte laughed. "Yes, it's a real thing. They

give dogs vaccines for it. I would think your animal-food CEO would have had that covered."

"You'd think so, wouldn't you?" Allie checked the time on her computer and realized she had to leave in a few minutes. "Hey, can I call you later? I'm supposed to meet Jack for coffee at two."

"You *are*?" Charlotte's excitement was clear. "Why didn't you tell me? When did that happen?"

Allie told her that he had come out of his house as she was leaving Charlotte's the day before. "It's just coffee. Nothing more."

"Well, have a good time. He's really nice, and funny, too."

"And you're sure you're not interested in him?" Allie needed confirmation.

"Absolutely."

"You don't have to sound so positive about it," Allie teased. "You make it seem like there's something wrong with him. Is he a serial killer? A pervert? Please don't tell me he has a third nipple or six toes." She giggled at the thought.

Charlotte laughed, too. "I didn't mean it that way, but for all I know, he *could* have webbed feet or something equally as disturbing. I just don't have feelings for him like that, that's all."

"Okay, if you're sure. You would tell me if there's something I should know, right?"

"I swear. He's a good guy. He even seems to be the sole caretaker for his grandfather."

"That's a good reference," Allie said. "Now tell me his faults."

"I don't know him well enough to know his intimate secrets, but I should warn you about how he feels on the topics of marriage and commitment."

Please don't let him be looking for a wife. Please, please, please.

"Go on." Allie held her breath.

"He's commitment-phobic, completely against settling down. I'm not sure exactly why, but I think it has something to do with his dad."

Allie expelled the breath that was burning her lungs. "Whew! You had me worried. Have I mentioned that I'm *off* men? Sometime I'll tell you about my last boyfriend." Allie closed her laptop and put it into her rolling brief case. "I'm only having coffee with Jack so I can tell him that—that I'm off men."

"Don't be so hasty," Charlotte said quickly. "You never know how things will work out. Besides, you have other things in common, too."

"Like what?"

"Well, you're both in the same profession."

Allie's heart stopped. "The same profession?

"Yes, he's in advertising, too. I'm surprised he hasn't mentioned it." Charlotte laughed. "Wouldn't it be funny if you two were competitors?"

"Yeah, real funny." Allie wasn't laughing, though.

CHAPTER FIVE

Jack left his suit jacket and tie in his office and walked the two blocks to the coffee shop to meet Allie. He'd unbuttoned his top shirt button and rolled up his sleeves on the warm, sunny day. He hoped the weather was a favorable forecast of his time with Allie.

Meeting for coffee wasn't his usual go-to for a first date, if that's what this could be called. Drinks were more his style, followed by a nice dinner or maybe a club with a great band playing. For some reason, he didn't quite feel like himself when he was around Allie. Not that it was a bad thing. In fact, he felt pretty good when she was close by.

He reached the large front door of Café Lisbon with its thick glass panel surrounded by a wooden frame with years of worn paint. A bell tinkled as he opened the door and stepped inside.

"Hey, Jack." The barista greeted him from the cappuccino machine. "What can I get you?" She added a plastic lid to the drink she'd just created and handed it to her customer. Coffee was the main event here, but they also served a small selection of breakfast and lunch items.

"The usual," Jack answered. "Medium black coffee, dark roast if it's already made." He looked over the room of small, round tables with assorted styles of well-worn wooden chairs. There were several people sitting alone at tables either with a laptop or electronic device that they were concentrating on, or they had their noses buried in a newspaper or book. Two women sat chatting quietly at the table by the window, but he didn't see Allie anywhere.

"Here you go," the barista answered with the confident smile of a woman who knew she was attractive.

He pulled out his wallet and paid for his coffee. "This is for you." He gave her a large tip. "And this money is to pay for whatever a certain woman with chin-length, dark hair and piercing blue eyes wants." He glanced at the front door. "She should be here any minute." He didn't know Allie that well, but he had a hunch that she wouldn't allow him to pay for her coffee unless he caught her off guard.

He took his coffee and chose a seat at a table where he could watch for her. He didn't have long to wait. Even through the glass, she sucked him in completely. She wore a black blazer and matching skirt with a red blouse that buttoned down the front. Her red high heels were what made her outfit go from office attire to downright sexy.

She went straight to the counter to order without even acknowledging him. Jack couldn't hear the conversation between her and the barista, but Allie didn't have a pleased look on her face when she looked over in his direction. Her lips were pinched and her eyes narrowed.

Was she upset that he'd paid for her coffee? It wasn't *that* big a deal, was it?

She turned her back to him, dug in her purse and removed her wallet. She gave the barista money and must have told her to keep the change, because the barista dropped money from the cash register into the tip jar. Allie didn't turn around again until her drink was ready.

She was a vision as she came toward Jack, drink in hand. He stood as she came closer and was about to offer her a friendly hug when he saw the expression on her face go from ticked off to full-blown angry.

"Did you think you could make everything better by paying for my coffee?" She carefully placed her cup on the table and then yanked the chair from under the table before he could pull it out for her. She sat down across from him.

What was she talking about? *Make everything better?*

"I need more information to go on here," he said calmly while he lowered himself into his chair. "Why would I need to make things better? Did I do something to offend you?"

Her eyebrows shot up. "Did you *do* something?" She removed the lid from her coffee. "It's not what you *did*, it's what you *didn't* do."

He did a quick scan of his memory to figure out

what she was talking about. "I've got nothing," he said. "What didn't I do?"

"You're serious?" She obviously didn't believe him.

"Absolutely."

"So you thought it was okay to keep your occupation a secret?"

A secret? "I didn't do it on purpose," he said slowly. "The subject never came up." What was the big deal?

"You're right, the subject never came up. Probably because you already knew what *I* do for a living."

"Actually, I don't. What is it you do?"

She cocked her head and smirked suspiciously. "I'm in advertising."

He relaxed. "Oh, that's great. Then we *do* have a lot in common." Why would that anger her?

Allie rolled her eyes. "A lot in common? We both had presentations this morning, right? Well, after learning you're in advertising, it didn't take me long to figure out that we're both competing for the Naturally Healthy Animal Food account."

"Ah!" *Now* he understood. "I had no idea we were rivals. Honest."

"I'm supposed to believe that?" She spoke loudly and looked around to see if anyone overheard.

"Why would I keep that information from you on purpose?" he asked.

She leaned in and lowered her voice. "To sabotage me. You *knew* I was going after the account, so you thought you'd blindside me with your charm and good looks. You must think I'm a sucker for a free cup of coffee."

He blinked. "You really think I'd do that?" Although he did kind of like that she admitted he could throw her off her game. "Charm and good looks, eh?" He couldn't hide his grin.

"I've been through worse." She blatantly ignored his last comment. "But I just met you. Who knows what you're capable of?"

A thought came to him. "How do I know *you* aren't the one trying to sabotage *me*? You obviously know more about me than I do about you."

Her jaw dropped, and she gaped at him. It took her a few seconds to respond. "How could you think I knew we were both competing for the same account?"

"I could ask you the same thing." Although he was pretty sure from her surprised expression that she had no prior knowledge of their rivalry.

She held her hands up in surrender. "Okay, neither of us was aware that we're competitors. Fine."

He sighed in relief. "I'm glad you finally believe me. How did you find out what I do, anyway?"

"From Charlotte. She mentioned it when we were talking earlier today."

He nodded. "Right. Well, I'm at Empire Advertising. My grandfather's company."

"How long have you worked there?"

He explained that he'd gone first to New York City and then come back when Empire was in financial trouble. "It didn't help that the CFO had been embezzling money."

"Was he or she caught?"

"He," Jack clarified. "He was caught and brought to justice, but he died before we could get much of our money back."

"What about his estate?" Allie blew softly on her hot coffee. "Can't you collect from that?"

"We probably could if there had been anything left to collect. He used the stolen money to pay his wife's medical bills after he was able to get her into a new cancer program. He saw no other way out of his financial debt. Unfortunately, his wife died anyway.

"The thing is, if he'd come to my grandfather, Granddad would have loaned him the money—no questions asked. They'd been friends since college."

Allie shook her head. "That's so sad. For both the CFO and your grandfather."

Jack nodded. "Now that you know about me, tell me about you. Who do you work for?"

"Myself."

"Your own company? I'm impressed." That was the truth. Start-ups had little chance of surviving.

"Thanks," she said. "It's a long story, but I was kind of forced into it."

He narrowed his eyes at her. "I'd love to hear details sometime."

She cleared her throat. "That's actually why I said I'd meet you today."

"To tell me why you started your own company?"

She laughed and then sobered. "No. Not really. I agreed to meet you to tell you I can't see you again."

ALLIE WAS MET with stunned silence as she waited for Jack to say something.

"Because we're rivals?" he asked. "I'm sure we can keep that separate—"

"No, I already decided I couldn't see you again before I knew what you did for a living."

"Then what is it? I thought we were getting along well. At least once I realized you weren't Charlotte and you finally believed I wasn't using your resemblance to her as a cheap come-on."

She smiled, trying hard to stick to her mantra. "It's not you, it's me."

His mouth twisted. "Now there's a cliché if I've ever heard one."

She suddenly wondered what his mouth would feel like, taste like... She wet her lower lip with her tongue. "I meant it has nothing to do with you. I've made a decision to not get involved with anyone right now. No commitment." She swallowed. "I don't want to repeat past mistakes."

He pursed his lips, as if considering her explanation. "I get it. I don't like it, but I get it."

She sipped her coffee. "Thank you. I'm glad you understand."

"Now don't mistake my understanding as agreement," he told her. "I'm not discarded that easily."

Her eyes grew wide. What was he talking about?

"You and I hit it off at the wedding and I can't ignore that, Allie. It's something that rarely happens to me." He held up a hand. "Don't get me wrong. I'm not looking for a happily-ever-after, either."

Allie's pulse sped up and she spoke through tight lips. "Then what *are* you looking for?"

"Hey, don't get mad," he joked. "I'm not asking for a one-night stand or anything." He winked salaciously. "Unless you're into it—"

She smirked.

His sexy smile warmed her inside. "I didn't think so." His honesty made her melt. "I'd like us to be friends."

"Friends?"

His eyes lit up. "Yes, friends. People who hang out together, maybe get some dinner, go to a movie. Do you like baseball?"

She shrugged, and then nodded.

"Good. Maybe we can even go to Fenway for a game sometime."

She considered his idea. "But what about the fact that we're rivals for the same account? Who knows, we could be competing for other accounts and not even know it. And if we aren't yet, we probably will be one day."

"So we work it out as needed." He didn't seem to think it was a big deal. "Friends can compromise, right?"

"Sure, but I'm not sure how that will work with business. There's no compromise there."

"Like I said, let's take the problems as they come."

She nodded slowly. "So just friends."

"Right. Just friends." He paused. "Which means either one of us can invite the other to do something with them, because that's also what friends do." He paused again. "What do you say?" He held out a hand for her to shake.

Slowly she reached out and slid hers into his larger, warmer one. Without thinking any more deeply about it, she said, "Deal."

Was she disappointed that he didn't push her to have a closer personal relationship?

What a ridiculous idea. She was off men and that's all there was to it.

JACK SIPPED HIS COFFEE, barely cool enough to drink. "I'm thinking we need some ground rules." He liked the idea even more as he said it.

"Ground rules?" Allie asked.

"Sure. Like what we can talk about with each other and what we can't."

Allie nibbled at her bottom lip, and Jack's body reacted. He tamped down his response, reminding himself of their pact. Friends. Just friends.

"First of all, any conversation about our jobs is not allowed," he suggested.

Allie nodded. "Agreed. And no asking Charlotte questions about each other's work, either."

"Absolutely." He made another suggestion. "Maybe we should choose other occupations for ourselves."

She tilted her head as if waiting for him to explain his odd idea.

"If we pretend we have different occupations," he said, "then we're free to ask each other, 'How was your day?' without feeling like the rules are being broken."

Her lips curled slightly as her understanding became evident. "So if I say I'm a doctor and you ask, 'How was your day?' and it wasn't good, I could say, 'I lost a patient' instead of 'My client didn't like my presentation.'"

"Exactly!" Jack laughed, enjoying Allie's creativity and her ability to play along, as well as her enthusiasm for the unusual.

"Okay, then, I'm a doctor. What do you do?"

He didn't even hesitate. "I'm a garbage collector."

"Hmm." Her lips twitched. "Good thing I'm not a snob." She winked. "After all, I *am* a highly respected doctor."

"Highly respected, is it?" He grinned. "And what is your specialty?"

She hesitated, but not for long. "I'm a world-renowned brain surgeon."

He laughed. "Highly respected, as well as world-renowned. I'm very impressed."

"And you should be, since you're a lowly garbage collector."

"Ah!" He raised a finger to make a point. "Not an *ordinary* garbage collector. A well-paid and *discriminating* garbage collector."

Her eyes widened. "Discriminating? Does that mean you pick up only certain garbage?"

"Absolutely. Nothing ooey or gooey. Everything in bags. Recyclables must be separated from landfill items."

"You're pretty strict."

"You better believe it. Trash is nothing to take lightly."

They shared easy laughter until Jack realized their coffees were long gone and it was almost three-thirty. "Oh, jeez, I've got to get going. I'm expecting a call soon."

Her eyebrows rose. "A call? A garbage collector gets calls?"

She had him there.

"Of course," he answered without hesitation. "My stock broker calls every afternoon before the market closes to get my opinion on what to buy and sell."

She chuckled and shook her head. "Good one."

He merely smiled, admiring her sense of whimsy.

In fact, there was a lot about her that he admired, both intellectually and physically.

JACK AND ALLIE walked a block together before stopping at the corner to say goodbye. They were headed in opposite directions from there. Allie was sort of sad to see their time end. She enjoyed his company, especially his sense of humor.

She put a hand out to shake his, and he drew her in for a hug.

"Friends hug, don't they?" His deep whisper, close to her ear, made her shiver in delight.

She couldn't form words to answer him. She was too busy enjoying his warmth and solidness, as well as his delicious masculine scent that she couldn't stop inhaling.

He held her away from him and looked directly into her eyes. "I'm sure we'll talk soon...pal."

It took her a moment to figure out what he meant. "I'm sure we will...buddy." She grinned.

He released her, stepped back and waved. "Have a great rest of the afternoon." He turned and walked away.

"You, too." She stood on the corner and watched his body move effortlessly away from her on the sidewalk, wishing he'd suggested more than just a possible phone call in their future.

As if reading her mind, he turned around suddenly, walking backward, and yelled, "Don't forget. Friends invite friends to do things together."

Her stomach did a flip. She smiled and waved in reply. He was right. She didn't need to wait for him to suggest they get together. No silly mind games with friends.

He yelled again. "And if you ever feel the need to be more than friends, I'm available!"

She was caught by surprise at his statement and knew she was blushing. A few people passing on the sidewalk chuckled and whispered, adding to her embarrassment.

He was already close to half a block away. She couldn't reply without bringing more attention to herself, so she simply turned and walked away.

She took his interest in her as a compliment. Her step was lively as she returned to her office building, riding the elevator up to her floor. For the first time in months, she felt optimistic about life and her future. At least until she picked up her messages from the receptionist.

The dog!

As soon as she saw the message from Joan Broadwell at the Rescue League, she knew what it was about. She was late picking up the dog. Harvey. She had to be sure to remember the dog's name. It was bad enough that she'd forgotten she was even picking him up. She quickly dialed Joan and told her she'd gotten hung up, promising to come by within the hour.

Unfortunately, the rest of the messages weren't from clients. They were all from her mother. Allie refused to worry that her mother might demolish her great mood. She punched in the phone number before her mom could call a fourth time.

"Hi, Mom."

"Allison, how are you?" Her mother sounded less stressed than in recent weeks, now that Allie's brother's wedding was behind them. Maybe Allie could try again soon to get her mom to talk about her adoption details.

"I'm good. Did Scott and Emily take off okay for Aruba this morning?"

"They did." Her mother caught her up on events, even though it had been only a little over twenty-four hours since Allie had brunched with all of them.

"I should probably get back to work," Allie said a few minutes later, trying to push her mother to get to the reason why she'd called three times. "Was there anything else you wanted, Mom?"

"Actually, there is."

She knew it. Allie rolled her eyes and waited for her mother to get to the point.

"I'm wondering why you didn't tell me about what happened at the wedding."

Allie didn't know what to say. Who had told her mother about Charlotte?

"What's his name?" her mother asked.

"*His* name?" Allie was more confused. At the same time, she was relieved that Mom wasn't asking about Charlotte. "Who are you talking about?"

"I'm talking about that handsome man you were dancing with at your brother's wedding."

"Oh." How much should she tell her? "He's just a friend." Isn't that what the two of them had agreed to? At least until his last statement... "His name is Jack, and I met him at the wedding. He's Emily's cousin."

"Emily's cousin," her mother repeated as if it was a very interesting fact. "Now what? Where does he live? Are you going to see him again?"

"He lives in Newport." She purposely didn't mention how close their Providence offices were. "I told you, we're friends, Mom. I'm not interested in anything more right now." If her mother required further explanation, Allie didn't have much she wanted to share about why she didn't care to get involved with a man at the moment. She didn't want to stress her mother any more than necessary. If she found out that her middle child nearly went to federal prison because of her last boyfriend, her mom might have a nervous breakdown or worse. "Who told you about Jack?"

"Several people, actually," her mother answered. "I guess I'm the only one who missed seeing him."

"There was nothing to see." Allie tried to reassure her, wondering why people had felt the need to tell her mom about seeing her with Jack, but no one had mentioned that she'd had a doppelgänger at the wedding. "Neither of us wants a relationship right now."

"You know you can date without getting what you young people call 'serious.'" Her mother had an answer for everything.

"I know, Mom. I'm busy right now trying to keep my company afloat—I have no time for dating. Please don't go into your matchmaking mode." The words were out of her mouth before she could stop them. Now that she'd spoken up, she was actually relieved to have the subject open for debate.

"Matchmaking mode? I'm just looking out for your future. Besides, your dad and I warned you about going off on your own in business, but you were too headstrong to listen."

They'd had this conversation several times after Allie had made her decision. Her parents had no idea that she'd really had no choice—that she'd been blacklisted by every advertising agency she'd contacted after she lost her job because of her involvement with Jimmy.

"I'll manage." Allie repeated what she always said when her mother went off on the subject. At least she'd moved the conversation away from Jack. "I really do need to go, Mom."

They ended their phone call, but not before her mother reminded her that she shouldn't work so hard.

As if her company had anyone else who could keep it from going belly-up.

A LITTLE WHILE LATER, Allie's adrenaline surged as she drove the few miles from her office to the Animal Rescue League.

"I never thought you'd get a dog. You don't seem the type." Penny, the receptionist Allie shared, sat in the passenger seat. At the last minute, as Allie was running out of the office, she'd noticed that Penny was leaving for the day. Penny had experience with dogs—as evidenced by the pictures of two dogs on her desk—so Allie had invited her along for moral support.

"It'll only be for a few weeks, maybe less," Allie said to the fortyish woman she barely knew. "It all depends on how long it takes for the animal-food account to be awarded. That's why I decided to foster a dog."

"How is having a dog going to help you?"

"I figured that if I had pictures of Harvey to show the client, it would prove that I'm familiar with dogs and she should, therefore, go with my company for her advertising. I can probably even bring him in during my presentation since the owner keeps her dog in her office."

"But you've never had a dog before?"

"I've never had a pet of any kind. Not even a fish. My parents were too busy with five kids to have pets, too."

"Do you know how to take care of a dog?" Penny asked.

Allie shouldn't have been so hasty about bringing the woman along. She was supposed to support Allie, not question her wisdom.

"I've been reading up on it." That was a partial truth. Allie had skimmed an article about dog breeds and found out that she was probably getting a pretty smart one. That should save her some aggravation.

"Couldn't you have borrowed a dog and taken pictures of *it*?" Penny had a point.

"I could have, but this way I can speak from experience."

The parking lot at the Rescue League was nearly empty when Allie pulled in. She and Penny entered the building. The sound of barking dogs came from somewhere in the rear of the structure.

Penny stayed a few feet behind Allie while she introduced herself. "I'm Allie Miller, and I'm here to pick up Harvey."

The older woman behind the desk stood up and put out an enthusiastic hand. "I'm Joan Broadwell. We spoke on the phone. I'm very pleased that you'll be fostering Harvey. He's such a sweetie."

After shaking hands, Joan disappeared through a door leading to the back. Allie exchanged looks with Penny, who was less than reassuring. Should she back out, tell Joan she'd made a mistake?

Joan returned a few minutes later carrying a brown, black and white dog with floppy ears and big brown eyes. "Isn't he so cute?"

"Very," Allie answered as if on cue.

"Everything's in here," Joan said, pointing to the bag hanging at her elbow. "His last foster home sent along his favorite chew toy, and his rabies tag is on the collar he's wearing. I think there's even a leash in here."

Joan managed to produce the leash from the bag and hooked it onto Harvey's collar, all with one free hand, before setting him on the ground.

Harvey immediately barked at Allie.

"What's wrong with him? Does he not like me?"

Joan laughed. "He's saying hello. Look at his tail wagging. Ignore him until he sits quietly, and then you can pet him. If you pay attention to him before he's calmed down, then he thinks you're rewarding him for being excited, and he'll keep doing it."

Maybe having a dog wasn't going to be as simple as she'd expected.

Allie waited for the dog to sit quietly like Joan said he would, but Harvey never did. He continued to bark at her.

"Harvey, sit," Joan finally said, and Harvey did exactly that. She leaned down to pat his head. "That's a good boy."

Seemed simple enough when Joan did it.

Allie reviewed her mental list of questions for Joan. "Is he housebroken?"

"I would say partially."

"What does that mean?"

Joan smiled patiently. "That's right, you told me

this was your first dog, didn't you?" She reached over the high desk and came up with a brochure, handing it to Allie.

How to Take Care of Your New Family Member was the title of the pamphlet. "Thank you." Allie slipped it into her purse and then prompted Joan to answer the original question. "So, he's partially housebroken?"

"That means he should be easy to train once you get him home. He's old enough to learn quickly, and he is already crate-trained. Take him directly from his crate to where you want him to do his business every time."

A crate? She didn't have a crate.

Joan continued. "Take him outside right after he's eaten, first thing in the morning and last thing at night. Of course, any other time he seems to need to go, as well."

Allie nodded, wondering if he could wait long enough to make it down her apartment building elevator each time.

"What should I be feeding him?"

Joan held up another bag. "There's a few days' supply of food in here, along with instructions and the kind of food to buy. Sticking with the same food is the safest way to go as long as he has no digestive problems. He's still a puppy, so he eats twice a day, morning and evening."

Allie nodded mutely, her brain overflowing.

"Here's Harvey's shot record." Joan handed her a

red folder with the Rescue League's name and logo on the front. "He's scheduled for neutering on Friday. The vet will give you follow-up instructions."

"Neutering?" She hadn't known she'd be involved in that.

"Our policy is to spay or neuter our animals before they're put up for adoption. The address of the veterinary hospital is in the folder, as well as preop instructions. Just have him there by the time specified."

"Okay." Allie was completely overwhelmed by the magnitude of care this dog required. All to save her company by landing the animal-food account. No backing out now.

Before she knew it, Allie, Penny and Harvey were in the car, ready to drive Penny back to the office parking garage.

"I don't have a crate," Allie told Penny. "Would you mind if we stopped at the pet store on our way? I don't want to leave Harvey in the car by himself."

"That's fine," Penny said pleasantly. She was turned in her seat just enough so that she could reach into the backseat to pet Harvey. "He's a sweetie. You know, most pet stores allow you to bring in your dog."

Good to know. "Maybe next time." If there *was* a next time.

Buying the right size crate was surprisingly simple, and Allie was back in the car in a few minutes.

"Thanks for coming with me," Allie said to Penny when they got to the office.

"Anytime," Penny said. "Good luck with this sweet boy." She gave Harvey's head one last pat before exiting the car.

Unfortunately, now that Penny was gone, Harvey wasn't happy in the backseat anymore.

"Harvey, no." She spoke firmly when he jumped on the console between the front bucket seats and landed on the passenger seat. She wished she'd thought of bringing an old towel to protect the leather. Her car was several years old, but she cared for it as if it were new. Especially since her loan on it was paid in full.

She carefully maneuvered out of the parking garage and back onto the street. She began to relax, but then Harvey started barking like crazy at a man walking a dog on the sidewalk.

"It's okay, Harvey," she cooed while he continued barking and spinning in circles. "It's only another dog. No need to get excited."

Harvey wasn't paying attention to her.

Keeping her eyes on the road, she reached out her free hand to pet him, hoping that would help calm him.

Instead, he jumped onto the console and then into the backseat. He paced back and forth on the seat as he watched the other dog through the back window.

Allie did her best to drive safely the few more

blocks to her apartment building. She was about to turn in to her parking garage when Harvey went nuts again. She was startled and nearly hit a parked car as well as the cinder block wall of the garage.

She pulled out the electronic card that let her into the garage. As soon as she started opening the window, Harvey was trying to stick his head out.

"Stay back, Harvey." Of course, he didn't have a clue what that meant.

Hoping he wouldn't jump out the open window, she lowered it enough to stick her arm out to swipe her card. "Get your nose inside," she told the dog when she had her arm back in the car, trying to close the window. She decided to leave the window open until she parked, since it wasn't worth the effort to win this argument.

She pulled into her assigned space and turned off the engine. "Now you have to move your head because I can't leave my window open." She merely touched the button to raise the window, and it was enough to startle the dog into retreating. "Good boy."

Worried that Harvey would take off as soon as she opened her door, Allie unbuckled her seat belt and reached into the backseat to grab the end of the leash.

"Come here, buddy." She tugged on the leash, but he wasn't budging.

She twisted in her seat and got up on her knees

to get a better angle, but he was backed up as far as possible next to the window behind her seat.

She slumped onto the back of her seat. "Come on, Harvey. Don't you want to go see your new home, even if it's not your permanent home?" She tugged on the leash again, not wanting to pull too hard and hurt him.

Harvey barked, as if answering her question in the negative.

Allie smacked her head several times on the headrest. She was in a battle of wits with a dog. Who would have guessed?

CHAPTER SIX

CHARLOTTE SAT ON her porch, staring at her laptop. She was getting nowhere trying to figure out how her mother came to have a big chunk of money practically overnight. There was nothing more to add to the list of facts she'd compiled. She saved and closed the document.

Her cell phone rang. It was Allie.

"Hey," Charlotte said. "How are you?"

"Not great," she said, before a muffled "stop that" could be heard in the background. Who was Allie talking to?

Charlotte's heart pounded. "Are you okay?"

"Yes." Allie was breathless. "I'm not far from you—"

"Do you want to come over?"

"Yes." Again a muffled but sharp "no."

"I'll explain things when I get there." Allie disconnected before Charlotte could ask anything more.

Maybe five minutes later, Allie's car came down the street. Charlotte closed her laptop and went to the porch railing.

After parking and exiting the car, Allie waved and slowly opened the passenger door. She struggled with something in the backseat. Finally she pulled a dog from the car. It began running in circles, tangling the leash around Allie's legs.

"Do you need some help?" Charlotte asked when Allie was closer, nearly stumbling over the dog several times.

"I've got him. I hope you don't mind me barging in, but I've been having trouble with him." She pointed to the dog. "I thought a car ride might help, and before I knew it, we were headed here."

"I don't mind at all. You're welcome anytime."

"You're sure it's okay if he comes up there?" Allie stopped at the bottom of the steps.

"He'll be fine. We can put something at the top of the steps to keep him here. I'm guessing he'll probably run away if he's off the leash?"

Allie smirked. "I don't know yet, but I think that's a pretty good guess."

Charlotte bent to greet the cute puppy when he came over to smell her shoes. "He's adorable." She scratched his ears, and his tail wagged feverishly before he sat down. Charlotte scratched his chest, and she had him rolling onto his back within seconds.

Allie's eyes widened. "How'd you do that?" She turned a small table onto its side plus a few of Charlotte's potted plants to block the stairs. "That should keep him in."

"I guess he likes me," Charlotte said as she straightened. Harvey stood on all fours and shook his entire little body. "I take it he's a new addition?"

"He's temporary. I'm his foster mom."

"How nice!"

"I guess so."

Just as Charlotte was about to ask if Allie was regretting her decision, Jack pulled up in front of his house. He was whistling as he exited his car and retrieved things from his backseat.

"Hey, Jack," Charlotte called from the railing.

He turned and gave her a smile after locking his car. "Hey, Charlotte. Oh, hi, Allie."

"Want to join us?" Charlotte asked. "I have beer." Then she said to Allie, "I think he could help with Harvey." Charlotte figured this was a perfect excuse to get the two of them together.

"Let me change and I'll be right over," Jack called.

"I didn't expect to see him," Allie said quietly after he went into his house. "Though I guess I should have, since he's your neighbor."

"Are you avoiding him?"

"No. I just don't want to give him the wrong idea. I really can't get involved with anyone right now."

Charlotte decided to stop the conversation right there. "I'll get the beer. You want one?"

"I'll take a soda or water. I'll need all my wits about me with Harvey."

Charlotte grinned, picked up her laptop and went inside for the drinks. As she placed the computer on her dining room table that once had been her mother's and saw her bank statement among the day's mail, an idea came to mind.

If her mother had saved everything she thought of as valuable, that would likely have included her pay stubs. Charlotte could match her mother's pay stubs to the deposits in the bank statements. If the thirty thousand dollars didn't show up as a bonus on a pay stub, then she could rule out that possibility.

Of course, then she'd be back to having no idea where to go next.

A few minutes later, she went outside with a tray of drinks, just as Jack was walking across the street toward her house. He'd changed into jeans and a T-shirt.

"Can you make it over our barrier?" Charlotte asked as she handed him his beer.

"I think I'm good." His long legs easily cleared the table and potted plants at the top of the stairs. "What's going on? You got a dog?" He was addressing Charlotte.

"He's mine," Allie replied.

Harvey went directly to Jack, seeking attention.

"Hey, pal," Jack greeted Allie. "What's his name?"

"Harvey."

Jack reached down to pet the dog once Harvey was sitting quietly. "Like the movie?"

"Huh?"

"The old movie with Jimmy Stewart and his friend Harvey the rabbit?"

"If you say so." Allie sounded almost grumpy.

"Sorry, I grew up with those movies. My grand-father can't get enough of them."

When Allie didn't respond, Charlotte chimed in. "Allie is having trouble with Harvey. She thought a car ride might help, and she ended up here."

Jack nodded. "A car ride? What kind of trouble are you having with him?"

"For one thing, he's been running around my apartment like crazy. He jumps on all the furni-ture, and when I try to grab him, he runs to the next thing." Allie took the seat Jack had moved closer for her, and they all sat down. "Then, in the car, he paced the entire time. I thought he might relax on the ride. You know, like when people drive their babies around to get them to sleep?"

Charlotte tried to hide her grin, but Jack chuck-led aloud. "Babies and dogs aren't quite the same. Has he had enough exercise?" Jack asked.

"How much is enough?"

Jack pointed to Harvey, now asleep at Jack's feet. "Enough to make him do this."

"I guess running around my apartment and then bouncing around in my car were enough."

"Why did you decide to get a dog right now, Allie?" Charlotte asked. "Won't it be difficult to work all day and leave him alone?"

"It's only for a little while. I'm fostering him,"

Allie told her. "Anyway, what's going on with your mom's files?" She'd changed the subject away from the dog so quickly that Charlotte could have sworn she was hiding something.

Charlotte filled them both in on her search.

Jack took a long swig of his beer. "So thirty thousand dollars magically appeared one day, and then she wrote a check for the same amount a few days after you were born?"

"Yeah. I have no idea where it could have come from. It seems like a lot of money to have gotten as a bonus from her accounting job back in 1986. But that's the only explanation I could come up with."

"What about family? Might they have given or loaned it to her?"

Charlotte swallowed a mouthful of beer. "There was no other family. My mom's parents both died before I was born, and she was an only child."

"No great grandparents, great-aunts or uncles?" Allie asked. "You have no distant cousins?"

"None that Mom ever mentioned," Charlotte said. "She and I were it when it came to family." As much as Allie had complained that her large family was overwhelming, Charlotte envied her. "I do remember a great-aunt who never married, but she died a long time ago. When I was nine or ten."

"Could the money have been from her?" Jack asked.

"Not likely." Charlotte racked her brain for details about Aunt Bonnie. "I'm pretty sure she was in debt when she died. I doubt she had thirty thousand to spare. I overheard my mother talking about it with her best friend, Marie. She helped my mother sell my aunt's few possessions to pay off the medical bills."

"Is Marie still around?" Allie sipped her soda. "Would she have a clue about the money?"

Charlotte hadn't considered contacting Marie. "She moved to Maine about ten years ago. I haven't seen or spoken to her since my mother's funeral."

"Might be worth a call," Jack suggested. "What about a transfer from her savings account? Could she have saved up that much over the years?"

"I doubt it," she said. "And I haven't come across any paperwork from a savings account yet."

"You're pretty sure the money wasn't a bank loan?"

"If it was, there should be a file with the documentation. I haven't found anything yet, but I still have a lot more files to go through."

"Don't take this the wrong way," Jack said, "but she was an accountant. Could she have 'borrowed' the money?" He used air quotes for emphasis. and the twinkle in his eye cued her in that he was at least half joking. "She'd probably have a good idea of how to hide the evidence."

Charlotte couldn't even imagine such a thing. Her mother, an embezzler? Impossible. "She'd never have done anything like that. She was always the kind of person who would go back into the store to return money if a clerk gave her too much change."

"Just a thought," Jack said quickly. "I'm trying to look at all angles. Maybe jog something loose in your memory."

Charlotte wasn't offended. If she'd learned one thing about Jack since they met a few months ago, it was that he spoke his mind. "I know. I hadn't even considered it because I've never known a more honest person than my mom." Though, frankly, Charlotte knew that she *did* need to pursue all angles, so Jack's suggestion added another theory to the lengthening list. "Let's change the subject. I'm only depressing myself with all these new questions." She took a sip of beer. "How was coffee today?"

Allie and Jack looked at each other. "It was good," Allie said.

"We came to a mutual understanding," Jack added.

"A mutual understanding?" Charlotte's curiosity was aroused.

After a noticeable and slightly uncomfortable silence, Allie finally answered. "We decided that getting involved wasn't going to work for us."

Charlotte looked first at Allie and then at Jack. "Is that true?"

He nodded. "Afraid so. Seems Allie the doctor isn't interested in anything more than friendship with Jack the garbage collector."

"Huh? I'm lost."

Allie smiled. "It was Jack's idea. I'll let him explain. Anyway, I should get this guy home. Thanks for giving me a break with Harvey."

JACK SAT IN his home office and opened his laptop. He'd left Charlotte's a little while ago, passing up her offer of dinner. A cold ham sandwich wasn't everyone's idea of a gourmet meal, but he had more important things on his mind and couldn't afford to stay any longer. He took a bite of his sandwich, enjoying the spicy mustard he'd slathered on it.

He should have been working on his health services client's presentation, but instead he opened his Facebook account. Nothing interesting going on with anyone he was friends with. Then, before he could think twice about it, he searched for Allie. He told himself he wanted to find out about her advertising agency, knowing full well there was more to it than that.

She wasn't easy to find. Since he and Charlotte were friends, he checked out Charlotte's friends to see if Allie was among them. Voilà! Allie Miller, Owner of AM Advertising.

He was about to send her a friend request but decided not to.

Jack rarely became Facebook friends with women he was interested in. Made for hurt feelings when they broke up and he unfriended them. And he was definitely interested in Allie beyond friendship, even with their pact.

There was something about her that drew him in. Something in her eyes from that very first moment he had called her Charlotte when she was in line for the bar at the wedding. He'd been able to read her thoughts through her eyes. Annoyance and something more. Interest? Probably his imagination combined with wishful thinking.

To soothe his conscience, he hit the link on Allie's page that took him to her AM Advertising page. Nice graphics in the header and a professional picture of Allie as her profile picture. He hit the link for her website and found a list of a few small local accounts in Providence, which included mostly family-run businesses like restaurants and ethnic grocery stores.

Learning all he could about her business, he went back to her personal page. Allie's security settings were pretty lax, so he took a look around. There were several pictures of his cousin's wedding, ones that other people had tagged Allie in. There didn't seem to be any she'd posted herself.

He laughed out loud when, as he went through the photos, he saw one picture of Charlotte tagged as Allie.

He clicked on the Send a Message button and began writing her a private note.

Great to see you tonight and thanks for meeting for coffee today. I really enjoyed it and hope we can get together again soon. You might want to check your privacy settings as I could see private stuff on your page. Also wanted to point out that in one of the wedding pictures you were tagged in, it's really Charlotte and not you. How funny is that? Talk soon—Jack, the garbage collector

He'd barely sent the message when she posted a picture of Harvey on her page with the caption, "The newest member of my family."

He'd been really surprised to find out she'd gotten a dog. She didn't seem to know much about them, either. Taking him for a car ride like a baby? He chuckled. He actually thought that was cute.

But you really needed to be committed if you were single and owned a dog. That's why he didn't have one right now. A dog required a lot of attention, and he spent way too many hours away from home.

A sudden thought came to him.

Was it a coincidence that she got a dog just as they were both wooing the animal-food client?

She wouldn't have done this as a ploy to land the client, would she? If so, then she deserved the frustration.

Even with that in mind, he checked the time and picked up his cell phone to call her.

"Hey, pal," he said when she answered on the second ring. "It's Jack."

"Hi." She was clearly out of breath. "Get down from there!"

He couldn't help but laugh. "What's Harvey doing now?"

"The little stinker jumped on a bar stool and then on to my kitchen counter. Every time I make a move to get him down, he barks and growls at me."

"Sounds like he's trying to prove he's the dominant one in your relationship."

"Right now, he is," she said in a voice tinged with disgust. "Do you know anything about dogs? What should I do?"

"I'm not an expert, but I had a dog growing up." His dad had gotten him a dog after Jack's mother died. His dad promptly left him and the dog to be raised by his grandfather. He'd save those details for when he and Allie knew each other better. "Jack Russells are supposed to be easy to train. Do you have treats to give him?"

"Treats? Like what? A cookie or a potato chip?"

"You really aren't a dog person, are you?"

"I didn't realize you needed to have specific talents to own a dog."

He hesitated, then asked the question burning in his gut. "Did you get this dog hoping it will help you clinch the Naturally Healthy Animal Food account?"

She didn't answer at first. "You got me! But you know that's how advertising works. Sometimes you have to do things out of the ordinary. Whatever it takes. Besides, didn't we agree to not discuss our jobs?"

"Right now that doesn't matter." Why wasn't she taking this seriously? "We're talking about another life here. You have no experience with dogs. What's going to happen to Harvey after the account is awarded?"

"He's not permanent."

That wasn't the answer he'd hoped for. "You're planning to return him as if he's the wrong size pants?"

"No, no, nothing like that," she said. "No matter what you think, I'm not that cruel. I'm fostering him. This is a temporary situation for both of us until he's adopted into a good home. But, yes, I am hoping he'll give me the edge when it comes to winning this account."

"I can't believe you'd use him like that. Are you that unsure about your presentation?"

"Stop it!" There was rustling on the other end of the phone.

Jack waited for Allie to speak again. Then there was a loud crash, and she swore. Not loudly, more under her breath, but loud enough for Jack to hear.

He certainly was getting a glimpse below the surface of the put-together woman.

"Is everything okay?" he asked when there was silence on the other end.

"Not really," she answered. "Harvey knocked a vase—an expensive crystal vase full of tulips—off the counter and it broke." She sounded defeated at this point.

"Would you like help?" He made the offer without considering what he was saying. Not wanting her to think he was being forward, he added, "Friends can help each other."

She didn't answer right away. Had he screwed up? Pushed her too quickly?

She finally said, "It's a long way up here to Providence on a work night."

Was that her way of saying she didn't want him to come? "It's up to you, Allie. I'm happy to give you a hand getting Harvey settled. I can even spend the night at my grandfather's. That way I won't have to come all the way back here tonight." That should settle any questions she had about his motives.

Although the fact that he was trying so hard to make her believe he had no ulterior motives made him think that deep down maybe he did have them. Um, yeah, no maybes about it, he *definitely* had ulterior motives when it came to Allie.

Before he could back out gracefully, feeling bad about his motives, she said, "I'd really appreciate your help if you're sure it's not too much trouble."

Too late now. "I'll pack a bag and be there in about an hour. Until then, Harvey's probably better off on the counter. Be careful cleaning up the glass for both your sakes. Neither of you need the stress of stitches on top of everything else."

"Good point," she said. "Except that he knocked over the vase when he was getting down from the counter, and now he's made himself comfortable in the middle of my bed."

Jack's mouth went dry as he imagined what her bed might look like.

Only he wasn't imagining Harvey in the middle of it, but himself and Allie.

No question about it. He had ulterior motives.

ALLIE HUNG UP with Jack. Had she made a huge mistake by letting him come over tonight? He *did* sound like he knew something about dogs.

At least more than she did, which apparently was not much at all.

She was surprised he'd offered to help after his obvious disapproval of her business methods. He couldn't possibly say he'd *never* done anything like this before. Everyone in advertising did it. Maybe he'd even copy her idea and foster a dog of his own.

The sound of light snoring came from her bed. Harvey was sawing wood as he slept peacefully.

Remembering the mess in the kitchen, she took advantage of the moment. Thankfully, the broken vase wasn't anything meaningful to her. Before starting the cleanup, her stomach growled a reminder that she hadn't eaten since noon. She decided to make herself a salad for dinner. She poured a glass of white wine and ate standing up, far away from the broken vase.

No longer famished after finishing her salad, she dropped the torn and wilted tulips into the trash can, followed by the large pieces of glass. Then she sopped up the water and bits of glass with paper towels.

"Ouch!" Blood dripped from her left index finger. She inspected it carefully and pulled out a tiny shard of glass.

There was a knock on her door, startling Harvey awake. He went running to see who was there, bouncing and barking furiously. Allie grabbed a fresh paper towel to wrap around her cut finger and, after checking the peephole to make sure it was Jack, she opened the door.

"What happened?" The expression of horror on Jack's face made Allie look down and realize she had bled onto her white shirt.

"It's nothing." She held out her wrapped finger. "A little cut from cleaning up the broken glass."

He entered her apartment, and she quickly closed the door before Harvey escaped. Not that he seemed particularly interested in escaping. He was more fascinated with the new person in the room. He crazily jumped at Jack's leg, but Jack simply ignored Harvey the entire time.

"Harvey, no!" She tried to act like the boss, but the dog wasn't buying it.

Jack shook his head. "Ignore him like I'm doing. Don't give him the attention he wants until he calms down."

That was what Joan Broadwell had told her. Allie should have taken notes.

Several minutes dragged on before Harvey finally gave up. As soon as he was tired of failing to get Jack's attention, he sat down at Jack's feet.

Jack immediately leaned down to pet him, scratching him behind the ears and rubbing his chest. "That's a good boy," he cooed. "You remember me, don't you?"

When Jack straightened, Harvey stood up, and after a few seconds of indecision, the dog headed back to Allie's bedroom. She supposed he was taking up his former spot in the middle of her bed. She'd tackle that misunderstanding later.

"That was amazing!" she told Jack. "You're a dog whisperer!"

He laughed. "Not quite. I just retained a lot from when I had a dog as a boy. At first my grandfather had threatened to give away Sheba, my German shepherd, because she wasn't behaving—though I don't think he would have gone through with it. But I made him a deal, anyway. If I couldn't get her trained in a month, Granddad could give her away. But if I could get her to stop jumping on people and sit on command, I could keep her."

Allie invited him to sit down by pointing to the white contemporary sofa and black-and-white print chairs in her living room. "Seeing you with Harvey, I'm guessing you were able to train Sheba."

He followed her to the seating area and chose the chair across from where she sat on the sofa. "You better believe it! I'd already lost my mom, and then my dad left me with Granddad. There was no way I was gonna lose my dog, too."

His words obviously had a lot of pain behind them, but she didn't want to pressure him into explaining. She didn't know him well enough to pry into his life. There was plenty of time to learn more about him. They were friends now, after all.

"So how'd you learn to train your dog?"

"I went to the library and read every book I could find about dogs. Once I went through those, I got my au pair to drive me to the bookstore, and I used my entire savings from my allowance to buy several more books."

An au pair? The thought of how well-off his family must be crossed her mind, but instead she asked, "How old were you when you did this?"

He considered it a minute. "Ten or eleven."

She stared at him. "Ten or eleven? What were you, a child prodigy or something?"

He grinned and his eyes sparkled. "Not even close. More like determined. I'm very goal-oriented."

Not unlike herself. Although she didn't always go about getting there by the standard or even easiest route.

"What do you suggest for Harvey?" She looked toward her bedroom and listened for movement. No sound. She hoped that meant he'd gone back to sleep. Even if it was probably on her bed.

"First, do you have a crate? Dogs need their own space, much like humans do."

"Yes, I have one." She was pleased that she could say she was prepared. "I had to leave Harvey alone in my apartment while I got it from my car, but I had no choice. Unfortunately, that's when he decided to chew one of my shoes. Oh, no." Her hands flew to her mouth as her thoughts suddenly ran to whether or not she'd shut her closet door. "The crate's over there." She pointed to the wall in the dining area as she hurried out of the room. "I'll be right back."

She ran into her bedroom. There was no sign of the dog. "Harvey?" She listened but heard nothing. He wasn't in her bathroom. That left her closet.

Afraid to look, she slowly went around her bed to the open door. Harvey was asleep on top of one of her shoes. Not the match to the shoe he chewed before, but one of her more expensive shoes.

At that point, she slumped down to the floor on her knees, wondering why on earth she'd decided that getting a dog would help her win the account.

CHAPTER SEVEN

JACK WASN'T SURE what was going on when Allie disappeared into another room. He heard what sounded like a sniff. Was that a sob?

He slowly walked in the direction she'd taken and hesitated at her bedroom door. "Allie?"

There was a mumble from the far corner of the room, but nothing distinct.

"Is there something I can do?" He took a few more steps into her bedroom. On the wall facing the doorway, there was a door on each side of her bed. The one on the right appeared to be her dark bathroom. The opened one on the left was obviously her closet. He continued walking toward it.

Harvey wasn't on the bed, which didn't look anything like what Jack had pictured, with its jewel-toned comforter in a bold geometric design. Most of the women's bedrooms he'd been in were frilly with flowers and ruffles. Many were decorated with muted pastels and definitely girly. Not that he paid a whole lot of attention to women's interior design choices. By the time he made it to a woman's bedroom, he had other things on his mind.

This was probably a first for him. Stepping into a woman's bedroom for the single purpose of—

"Oh, no," he said quietly when he saw the damage Harvey had done to Allie's shoe. Jack crouched down and helped her to her feet. She was in his arms before he realized what he'd done.

"I should've remembered to shut the closet door." She groaned into his chest.

She suddenly pulled away and turned her back to him, wiping her cheeks with her hands.

"It's okay to be upset," he said and reached for her arm to turn her around.

"I'm not crying. I never cry."

"I didn't say you were." He gathered her into his arms, and she didn't pull away. He stroked her head, his fingers tangling softly in her silky hair. A citrus scent tickled his nose.

She sniffed and drew the back of her hand under her nose. "After he chewed the first one, I should have been more vigilant. I forgot to close the door after I changed my clothes."

She looked up at him, and that was his undoing. Those darn eyes of hers. He wiped a stray tear from her cheek with his thumb.

His breathing came faster, and he touched his lips to her forehead. She leaned into him, her breasts pressed against his chest. His hand curled around the back of her neck, his fingers tangled in her hair and he angled her head back. Their eyes met in mutual understanding.

As his mouth was being drawn to hers, a background noise grew louder until Jack gave it his full attention.

He turned his head toward the sound. Harvey was not only growling but also baring his teeth.

Not at Jack, but at Allie.

ALLIE HAD BEEN sure Jack was about to kiss her, but he suddenly set her away from him.

"What's wrong?" she asked before belatedly hearing the growling coming from Harvey.

"I'm pretty sure he thinks you're trying to hurt me," Jack told her.

"Why would he think that?"

"In his dog brain, he's protecting his master. And since I'm the one who came in here like an alpha dog and took charge, he thinks I'm the leader of the pack. I hate to say it, but I'm pretty sure he's trying to dominate you."

"There's really such a thing as a pack order?" She was trying to make sense of what he was saying.

He nodded. "If you think of dogs in the wild, they naturally have a pack leader. One who keeps things in order. Much like the way our laws—and those who enforce the laws—affect the way we live and keep us safer with than without them."

Harvey had stopped growling the moment Jack released her, leaving her wanting for his touch. Even if she knew kissing him was a terrible idea. Friends. That's what they were. Nothing more.

She was *off* men.

Without thinking, she grabbed his hand to lead

him out of her bedroom. Harvey barked, startling
her. She stopped walking and released his hand as
if she'd been burned.

Obviously, Harvey knew about her feelings on
relationships and was helping her diffuse the situation. Yeah, that's what he was doing.

"Now what?" she asked Jack.

"Let's walk out to set up the crate," Jack said.
"Just ignore Harvey."

"But what about the rest of my shoes? I can't
afford to have him chew any more of them." As it
was, he'd chewed her nicest and most expensive
pair. The shoes she wore for client meetings because they made her feel successful—the way she
used to feel before DP Advertising fired her.

Jack nodded. "You go into the living room. I'll
stay back and close the closet door and then your
bedroom door. Better to keep this guy in as small
an area as possible. Then, as he settles down and
you can trust him, you can gradually give him more
freedom in the apartment."

She did as Jack suggested and pulled the crate
out so they could put it together. Jack talked calmly
to Harvey as he closed doors. She was relieved
to see the dog had responded, following right on
Jack's heels.

"He really likes you," Allie told him as he
began unfolding the crate to snap it together. She
couldn't help but notice his broad shoulders and
narrow waist as he crouched on the floor. Her fin-

gers itched to touch him, massage his neck, whisper in his ear.

"He likes you, too."

"What?" Allie pulled herself out of her daydream. "Oh, right."

"It's that dominance thing right now," he said over his shoulder as if he hadn't noticed she was practically drooling over him. "He sees me above him and you below him." He stood up and turned to her. His wink made her stomach do a flip.

"Great," she muttered, trying to ignore the mental image she had of being *under* Jack in the most literal sense.

"It's not a permanent situation," he said quickly. "It'll just take some training to correct."

"Like obedience class?" How much would that set her back? "I can't afford to spend more money on him."

He shook his head, and he smiled. "No, not for Harvey. *You're* the one who needs the training."

"Me?" She cleared her throat and brought her tone down an octave. "Me? But he's the one who's misbehaving."

"Correct. And to make him behave the way you want him to, *you* need to learn how to act around him."

"Oh. I guess that makes sense."

He picked up the completed crate. "Where do you want this?"

She pointed to a corner of the living room. "Over there, I think."

Harvey had remained by Jack's side the entire time he put together the crate, sniffing at the metal contraption and even the pile of packaging.

"Has he had dinner yet?"

"Not yet."

After the dog was fed, Jack said, "Let's take him for a walk, and then we can settle him into his crate for the night." He gathered the packing material. "You have a recycle bin downstairs?"

"Yes." Allie hurried to where she'd left the leash and held it out to Jack.

He shook his head. "This is your first lesson. Time to learn how to take a walk."

She was unsure of this outing but she followed Jack's directions anyway. She got Harvey to sit so she could clip on his leash. She went out the door first and *then* invited Harvey into the hallway. She kept him on her left and didn't let him lead. Jack even had to remind her to get a small bag in case she had to clean up after Harvey on their walk.

"There's a lot to remember," she said as they rode down in the elevator.

"You're catching on quickly," he assured her. "Before you know it, you'll do it all without thinking."

"Easy for you to say," Allie mumbled.

Jack chuckled. He tipped his head toward Harvey, and she looked down to see the dog was sitting nicely on her left side.

She looked from Harvey to Jack and couldn't help but grin, proud of her accomplishment. She whispered, "Look! And he's not even growling at me."

Jack's eyes danced and before Allie could look away, the elevator doors opened. Luckily she had a tight hold on Harvey's leash, because he was out of the elevator before the doors were completely open.

So much for successful training.

TAKING HARVEY FOR a walk with Allie turned out to be a pleasant experience. The dog behaved himself, for the most part, and Jack was able to learn more about this multifaceted woman.

Almost like a second date...*if* she were willing to be anything more than friends.

"You're doing a great job." Jack was impressed at what a quick study she was. By the time they walked around the city block and stood in front of her building's elevator, it was as if she'd been walking dogs her whole life.

Allie smiled at his praise and then stumbled into the elevator when the doors opened. He caught her by the arm.

"Thanks." Her face reddened, and she looked away. She gestured to Harvey sitting patiently at her side. "He's a good dog, isn't he?"

"You're becoming a good master," he told her.

She shrugged. The elevator doors opened on her floor.

A few minutes later, they had Harvey settled in his crate with the chew toy his previous foster parents had sent along.

"I should be going." Jack didn't want to overstay his welcome.

He avoided looking at her mouth, hoping to keep his mind off their near kiss. But looking at any other part of her had the same result.

"You could stay for a drink if you want." She sounded almost shy. "Unless you really need to leave."

He was torn but answered before thinking too much. "I can stay a few more minutes. Granddad's place is only about ten minutes away, on the other side of Johnson & Wales University."

She visibly relaxed at his reply and then listed the choices for drinks.

"Ice water, please." As good as a beer sounded, he didn't need alcohol to stir his libido, and caffeine this late was a bad idea with work early tomorrow morning. He took a seat on the sofa, resting his foot on the opposite knee.

She returned quickly with two glasses of ice water and handed him one. With her legs curled under her on the chair across from him, she took a sip of water and said, "You mentioned your grandfather made you train your dog when you were a kid. Did he raise you?"

He took a long swallow of water. "He did. I should probably start at the beginning."

Allie straightened. "You don't have to talk about it if you don't want. I didn't mean to pry."

"You weren't. I don't talk about my family much." He set his glass on the end table. "My mother died when I was ten. She was in a car accident. It happened right after she and my dad had a huge argument—which they often had. She'd caught him cheating, and she stormed out of the house. They didn't know I was listening at the top of the stairs."

"Did you even understand what was going on?"

"Not then," he said. "But I later figured out that when she said 'cheating,' it didn't mean cheating at a board game or on a math test. That's when what happened after she left finally made sense." He took another drink of water to soothe his suddenly dry throat. "She hadn't even pulled out of the driveway before my dad was calling someone. He told me Shelley was a coworker when she arrived within a few minutes, but I found out years later that she was the woman he was seeing at that time."

"At *that* time?" Allie prompted.

"Yeah. Seems he was a serial cheater who kept getting married. His marriage to my mom was his longest relationship. That's probably because he never stayed faithful to her, or anyone else as far as I know."

"Where is he now?"

"After my mother died, my grandfather was devastated at losing his only child. He blamed my dad and threatened to ruin his reputation as a college professor. Shelley was a grad student at the university where my dad taught, so Granddad had plenty of ammunition. He arranged a new teaching position for my dad at a small college on the other side of the country. Then he made my dad promise not to have any contact with me until after I turned twenty-one."

"Did he live up to his side of the deal?"

"Oh, he more than lived up to it." Jack's bitterness was difficult to suppress. "My twenty-first birthday came and went with not a single word."

"I'm sorry."

"Don't be. My dad's a loser. I finally contacted him out of curiosity and discovered he'd been married five times since my mother died." Unable to sit still, Jack rose from the couch. "Five times. I've had five stepmothers and never met a single one. Who knows how many more wives he's had in the ten years since I last talked to him." He paced across the room and turned to Allie. "I mean, other than Elizabeth Taylor or Mickey Rooney, who gets married that many times?"

Allie uncurled her legs, stood up and walked to him. She stopped two feet away and laid a hand on his forearm. "I didn't mean to bring up bad memories. It must be difficult to have lost both of your parents. At least in my case, I never knew my biological parents."

He shook his head. "It's fine. I just don't understand my dad. Not that he's ever tried to explain."

Allie was looking at him again with those expressive eyes of hers. Her vulnerability was obvious. He had to do something to tone down his overactive libido, because Allie didn't look like she'd object if he suddenly picked her up and carried her to her bedroom.

"Now I really should go." He quickly turned to his glass on the end table, intending to take it to the kitchen. He reached for it.

"I'll take that," she said. Their hands collided when she reached for the glass at the same time. "Oh."

Their eyes met, and Jack's baser instincts kicked in. How she came to be in his arms, he hadn't a clue. Their mouths met in a hot vortex. Trying to catch his breath, he kissed her nose, her cheek, the sensitive place on her neck. He shoved the collar of her white shirt aside and nipped the skin above her collarbone.

The back of his hand grazed the roundness of her breast when he undid her top button. He exposed her shoulder and tasted her, moving his mouth slowly from her shoulder and up her neck. Finally, he returned to her lips. He couldn't get enough of her.

ALLIE COULDN'T STOP HERSELF. She wanted Jack, no matter how bad an idea it was. She needed to find the strength to tell him to stop.

But he felt so damn good.

His hands were large and strong and touching her in all the right places. Well, *most* of the right places.

She really should end this before he got that far. Maybe when he stopped kissing her...in a few hours or so. Although it would be difficult for him to stop since both of her hands firmly held his head in place.

He tasted wonderful. Hot, sexy. She wanted to devour him. Mmm. Delicious.

Oh, that was it. Right there. His hands moved down her back. Lower. Lower, until he cupped her backside, lifting her so her legs were wrapped around his waist.

She moaned, and he took it as encouragement. He was carrying her in the direction of her bedroom.

She reluctantly pulled her mouth from his and leaned her forehead against his. "Wait."

He stopped midstride.

Why couldn't she have kept her mouth shut?

He groaned, and she silently agreed with his sentiment. But continuing into her bedroom would be the wrong move.

"Second thoughts?" he asked.

She silently nodded. He released her to slide slowly down his body until her feet touched the floor. She stayed there a moment, her cheek resting on his chest.

She finally raised her head and looked at him. "I've made some stupid mistakes when it comes to men, and I really don't want to add you to that list."

He smiled and set her away from him. "Then you better stop looking at me like that, or I won't be responsible for my actions."

"How am I looking at you?" She cocked her head.

"Like you're starving and I'm about to be your next meal."

Her face heated, and she couldn't look at him. "I—"

"Don't be embarrassed, *Dr.* Miller." He leaned forward and kissed her forehead. "I'll talk to you soon, pal."

She relaxed at his playfulness and patted his upper arm. "I hope tomorrow's a light garbage day for you, buddy."

He winked and gave her a little wave before heading out the door.

She stood where she was, wondering if she'd dreamed the past few minutes. The open button on her shirt and the tingling of her lips told her it hadn't been her imagination.

She looked over at Harvey, thankfully fast asleep in his crate. They'd both had an exhausting day.

By late Wednesday afternoon, Allie had gotten into a routine with Harvey. She found using his crate in her backseat kept everyone on the streets of Providence safer.

Right now he was sleeping in his crate in the corner of her office. She actually had more energy after walking him several times a day. Her creativity was at an all-time high. And if she made sure Harvey always had a chew toy available, he stayed away from her things.

Her only regret was that she hadn't heard from Jack. Not a call, a text. Nothing.

She'd replayed their time together over and over in her mind. Had she been too aggressive? A bad kisser? Not aggressive enough? Was he the kind of man who got upset because she'd stopped them from moving to her bedroom?

He didn't seem like a guy who took "no" poorly. But then, what did she know? Her last boyfriend was in federal prison.

Besides, it was good that Jack hadn't contacted her. She was off men. Even if that fact was nearly impossible to remember whenever he was around.

Her phone rang. She was tempted not to pick up because caller ID showed it was her mother instead of a client. But the call would transfer to Penny's desk, and she'd transfer it back to Allie's phone anyway because Penny knew Allie was in her office.

"Hi, Mom."

"Hello, Allison. How are you?"

The same as I was on Monday when you called.
But instead she said, "I'm fine. What's up?"

"I'm planning a family get-together."

Oh, no. She'd need an excuse to get out of it.
"When were you thinking you'd have it?"

"This weekend at our house," Mom said. "Scott
and Emily will be back from their honeymoon. I'd
like to get everyone together before they move to
Texas at the end of next week."

Scott's job as an engineer for an oil company
was moving to their company headquarters outside
Houston. He and Emily had planned a fall wedding until the company's move was announced.
Moving the wedding date up had worked Allie's
mother into an all-out frenzy to find a new venue
for the rehearsal dinner, because the one she'd already booked wasn't available for the new date.

Allie *would* like to see Emily and Scott before
they moved. Who knew when she'd see them next?
She certainly didn't have the money to travel right
now. She didn't have extra money to do anything,
including buying gas for the weekend.

"I'm not sure I can make it," she said. "I got a
dog this week, and I can't leave him home alone—"

"A dog? *You* got a *dog*?" Her mother didn't need
to sound quite so shocked.

"Yes, I'm fostering a dog."

"Oh."

She'd gone and disappointed her mother again.

Might as well take the opportunity to bring up another subject that her mother didn't like. "But maybe if I can make it, we can find time to talk about my adoption."

Silence.

What was her mother hiding? Why would she never speak about it? "What is it you don't want to tell me, Mom?"

There was a long pause before her mother spoke. "You need to understand, Allison. I buried my only biological child." Another pause. "When you came into our lives, I was overjoyed." Her voice cracked when she said, "Please forgive me for wanting to block out the idea that you were adopted and cling to the fantasy that you and your siblings are my biological children."

Allie had never before heard her mother speak like that about her children. "I get it, Mom. I'm sorry to bring it up." That didn't mean Allie would let the matter drop permanently.

Her mother cleared her throat. "So, this weekend." Mom's demeanor was suddenly back to normal. "Why don't you plan to get here by noon? And if you can pick up Emily and Scott at the Albany airport—they have a three-something flight—that would be a great help."

"I really don't know if I can make it. Unless I can bring my dog with me." That might be the answer. Her mother would never allow a dog in her house.

"Isn't there anyone who can take care of it?"

"I don't think so." Allie's friends were mostly singles with apartments that didn't allow pets. "Besides, he's getting neutered on Friday, and he'll probably need extra care." She really had to find out beforehand what she needed to do for him.

"What about that man you danced with at the wedding? Emily's cousin."

"Jack? I couldn't ask him to watch Harvey." Actually, she could, but only if he happened to contact her. Somehow after sharing those passionate kisses with him, they'd canceled out the idea that they were just friends.

"That's not what I meant," her mom said. "He's Emily's cousin. What about including him this weekend? I could have Emily invite him. She's also inviting their cousin Frank and his wife, as well as her sister, Patience. I'm sure she'd like to spend time with Jack before she moves. Then you can get to know him better, too."

"No, Mom, please don't play matchmaker." Allie had already screwed up any friendship they might have had, if his silence was any indication.

"I'll get back to you with details," her mother said as if Allie hadn't spoken. "Meanwhile, you figure out something to do with that dog."

That dog. Allie looked at Harvey, his brown eyes watching her as if he knew what was happening on Friday—he wasn't even appreciated by her mother. Poor doggie.

Was she actually beginning to bond with the cute little guy?

They disconnected, and Allie stared at the phone. Then she recalled how every year on her siblings' birthdays, Allie's mother would recount their adoption stories. Every one of her brothers and sisters got long, drawn-out stories. All Allie ever got was, "We chose you and brought you home to make us all one happy family."

She'd never cared about any of it until now. She hadn't *wanted* to know about her birth parents, what their situation was that led to giving her up.

But it wasn't like she ever had to stop her mother from reciting the tale, either.

What was it about Allie's story that her mother didn't want to talk about? And did it have anything to do with Charlotte?

CHAPTER EIGHT

THURSDAY MORNING DAWNED sunny and bright with a slight chill in the air. Jack drank his coffee at his kitchen table and opened his personal email on his tablet.

Nothing from Allie. He hadn't heard from her since Monday night at her apartment.

How were she and Harvey getting along? Jack wanted to contact her, but he also didn't want her getting the wrong idea. He really did want a friendship, preferably with benefits, but definitely not a relationship.

He chuckled when he saw an email from his cousin Emily. Even on her honeymoon, she couldn't stay away from her devices. She wanted to know if he could join them in upstate New York for a going-away party this weekend at her new in-laws' home. As young children, he and Emily had been pretty close. At least until his mother died and his dad left him with his grandfather. This sounded like a great way for them to reconnect.

Of course, little did Emily know that he'd met and befriended her new sister-in-law. Would Allie be there, or would she find an excuse not to attend? The party was at her parents' home. Maybe she wouldn't even want him to attend.

Regardless, he'd wait to reply to Emily until after he visited Granddad at the hospital. Depending on the state of his health, Jack would decide whether or not going out of town was a good idea.

He worked for a while from home, putting finishing touches on a new idea he had for a current client. After showering, he headed to see his grandfather.

"Jack!" Granddad greeted him with a huge smile as Jack entered the hospital room. He folded the newspaper he'd been reading and set it aside. "So good to see you. Tell me about the pet-food account."

Jack smiled at Granddad's automatic shift into business. "Hello to you, too." They hugged, and Jack pulled a chair closer to the bed. "There's nothing to tell. The owner hasn't rescheduled."

"Maybe you should call her," Granddad suggested. "Give her a push in the right direction. Show her you're a go-getter and that you'll hustle to do a good job for her."

Jack didn't think pushing Monica Everly was a good idea, but he nodded to please his grandfather. "How are *you* doing?" He'd already spoken to Granddad's nurse and found out he was scheduled to be transferred to a rehab facility.

"I want to go home."

Not what Jack was hoping to hear.

"They don't think you're ready to go home just

yet," Jack said gently. "But they do have a bed waiting for you at Saint Agnes."

Granddad crossed his arms and pouted like a five-year-old. "I'm not going to any nursing home. I'm going back to my apartment, even if I have to walk there myself."

Great. There was little chance of changing Granddad's mind whenever he got like this. Stubborn could have been his middle name.

Jack kept his tone calm. "You can't live alone until you can take care of yourself."

"I've always taken care of myself." Granddad's eyes narrowed as if challenging Jack to disagree.

"I'll speak to your doctor." At least he would warn the doctor that Granddad wasn't about to go to the rehab center quietly.

Granddad visibly relaxed, thinking he'd gotten his way. "Good idea."

Not that anything would change, except that someone else could argue with Granddad about whether he could live alone or not.

CHARLOTTE'S ART SHOW was barely three weeks away, and she still didn't have enough inventory to make the trip to New York City worthwhile.

She went through the charcoal sketches she'd done since her mother's death. They weren't necessarily depressing views of Newport's historic sites, but they were far from uplifting like the pastels of the Boston area she'd done before Mom's diagnosis. The majority of the pastels had sold at her last show. That had been good at the time, but now she wished she had more.

Her cell phone rang, and she pulled it from her back jeans pocket. Caller ID showed Jack's name. "Hey, Jack. What's up?"

"You got a minute?" There was noise in the background.

"Sure. Where are you? It's kind of loud."

"At the hospital," he said, then quickly added, "visiting my grandfather."

Charlotte's heart settled into a more normal pace—she'd thought for a minute Jack had been hurt. "Oh. How is he?"

"As cantankerous as ever. I'm waiting to talk to his doctor." Jack explained that his grandfather was scheduled for transfer to a rehab facility. "The reason I called was to ask if you've talked to Allie recently."

"Sure, we talk every night." She and Allie had gotten close in a very short time.

"Has she mentioned the party at her parents' this weekend?"

"That must be the one she was trying to get out of," Charlotte said. "How'd you know about it? Did she talk to you about it, too?" Jack's name had been brought into their conversations more times than Charlotte could count.

"No. I haven't spoken to her. I wanted her to

know that I can pass on my invitation if she wants me to."

"*You* were invited to Allie's parents'?" *How odd.*

"Don't sound so surprised. My cousin married Allie's brother, and the party's for the newlyweds. They're moving out of state and I guess this is sort of a goodbye party."

"Oh, that's right. I forgot your connection. Well, why don't you just tell Allie yourself?"

"I'm not sure she wants to hear from me," he said.

"Really? I didn't get that impression from her." What was going on with these two? "Did something happen between you guys?"

There was a long pause. "Not really."

His answer made her even more curious.

The background noise on his end grew louder. "Listen, Charlotte, I've gotta go. The doctor is free to talk to me now."

Before she could ask any of the burning questions that came to mind, he disconnected.

JACK WAS ABOUT to leave the small waiting room where he had discussed his grandfather's medical status with the doctor when he got a call from his potential client.

"Hello, Ms. Everly," he greeted her. News that Jack had heard from her might placate Granddad, soften the blow of the rehab facility. "How are you and Daisy doing?"

"That's what I'm calling about." Her tone was brusque. "Daisy is much better, and I'd like to schedule a meeting for this afternoon."

"This afternoon?" He mentally reviewed his schedule for the rest of the day.

"Yes, I'd like to do a combination meeting with you and the other two advertising firms competing for the account. I need to get this settled quickly. Does three o'clock work for you?"

He hesitated a few seconds as he contemplated the ramifications of all three companies being brought in together and said, "I'll be there." They needed the account, and if this was how he had to win it, fine—he would do whatever was necessary.

The next few hours had him scrambling to make sure his presentation was perfect. He was ten minutes early and was surprised to see that Allie was already there. She and Harvey sat in the reception area of the corporate offices of Naturally Healthy Animal Food. She'd actually done it—brought Harvey to pretend she was a dog owner.

She looked up from her phone and smiled confidently when he walked in. His body temperature rose dramatically, thanks to a number of issues that included her proximity to him as well as his building irritation over her business methods.

As soon as Harvey saw Jack, he sprinted over to say hello, his tail wagging furiously and his leash dragging behind. Thankfully, the distraction gave Jack the opportunity to pull himself together.

Waiting for Harvey to settle down before petting him, Jack asked Allie, "How are you doing with him?"

"Pretty good." She got up and grabbed the leash. "Harvey, come back here." She guided the dog back to where she'd been sitting.

Jack was about to bring up the party at her parents' when Monica Everly came into the reception area from the back offices. He stood to greet her.

"Thanks to both of you for making time in your schedules to come here this afternoon." She looked to Allie and smiled. "Is this your dog?"

Allie had also risen. "Yes, it is. This is Harvey. I hope you don't mind him joining us."

Monica patted Harvey on the head and said, "Glad to meet you, buddy." She straightened and spoke to both Allie and Jack. "The third company wasn't able to join us today, so let's get started. Why don't all of you follow me back into the conference room?" She said to Allie, "I'm sure Harvey and Daisy will get along splendidly."

Once they were seated on opposite sides of the long conference table with Monica at the head, she said, "Ladies first, if that's okay with you, Jack?"

"Fine by me." He glanced at Allie. She was trying to get Harvey to stop barking at Daisy, who couldn't have cared less.

As much as he wanted a friendship or more with Allie, he wasn't about to hand her this client without a fight. He *could* have taken control of Harvey and allowed Allie to begin her presentation, but the fate of his grandfather's company was at stake.

He was ready to open his mouth and suggest he go first if Allie preferred, but Monica spoke up. "Don't worry about a little barking, dear. Just start your presentation." Monica sat back in her rolling armchair. "Is this your first dog?"

Allie immediately said, "Oh, no. I've had dogs my entire life. Harvey's just a little excited, is all." She avoided looking at Jack.

Now she was telling an out-and-out lie to get the account.

After Allie completed her presentation, with Harvey at her side, and answered Monica's questions, it was Jack's turn. He was impressed by Allie's animated presentation and thought her concept, which focused on humanizing pets as if they were eating at a dinner table, was great, but that didn't diminish the fact that she'd lied.

His presentation focused more on branding with a new logo, as well as a bigger web presence and a television spot that included all the animals—from those on farms to pets—that would benefit from eating the animal food.

"Thank you very much to both of you. I'd like the weekend to consider your presentations," Monica said when Jack finished. "I'll let you know my decision on Monday."

Allie and Jack shook hands with Monica and left in silence until they got outside. "You lied in there," Jack whispered loudly. "You've never had a dog before this week."

Allie shrugged, seemingly nonplussed. "You know how this business is, Jack. Sometimes you need to stretch the truth."

"Are you kidding me?" He was appalled. "You haven't even had Harvey a week. That's a little more than *stretching* the truth."

"You're really that upset about a little white lie?" She looked both ways in the parking lot on the way to her car.

Instead of going to his own car, he followed her. His pulse sped up, and this time it wasn't because of his attraction to her. "You have obvious talent, Allie. Why do you feel the need to lie to get what you want?"

"I told you, that's how you survive in this business. Are you saying you always tell the truth, no matter what?"

"I try to."

"And how do I know *that* isn't a lie?"

Her question caught him by surprise. "Because I'm telling you the truth. I've never lied to you, Allie." They were getting nowhere. They obviously had different views on how to do business.

"If you say so." They reached her car, and she loaded Harvey into his crate in the backseat. She turned to Jack and abruptly changed the subject. "Did you get invited to my parents' this weekend? My mother was pushing for you to come."

"Yes." His answer came out harsher than he intended. "I was going to talk to you before I replied." He tried to read her expression but couldn't. "If you don't want me to go, I don't have to."

She looked at the pavement instead of at him. "Do what you want. I don't care either way."

"Hey." His anger dissipated, and he brought her chin up with his index finger until their eyes met. "What's wrong? Don't be mad at me because I don't agree with your business tactics. I'm just being honest."

"It's not that."

"Then what is it?"

"It's the party. My mother really wants me to go, but I can't leave Harvey. He's getting neutered tomorrow, and I don't want to leave him with just anybody."

Was she beginning to have feelings for Harvey? Good to know. "Can't you take him with you?"

"I suggested that, but my mom isn't a pet person. She didn't exactly say no, but she asked if someone could take him for the weekend."

"I could keep him while you're gone."

"But then you won't be able to see your cousin, and they're moving to Texas next week. I couldn't do that."

Jack considered the options. "Then let's take Harvey with us."

"Us?"

"Sure. I *would* like to see my cousin before she

leaves. There wasn't much chance to catch up at the wedding. And if I'm going, we might as well drive together. Do you really think your mom will make a big deal out of Harvey coming along if *I'm* there?"

"You're willing to go, even though you hate the way I do business?"

He hesitated before answering. She had a good point. "I think we decided to stay away from discussions about business. I broke the rules by calling you out on your dog ownership, but I'll try to do better. Now, what time do you want to leave on Saturday?"

She stared at him as if trying to decide whether to believe him. "My mother wants me there by lunch, and it's about a two-and-a-half-hour drive from Providence. That means leaving by nine or nine-thirty—I have to pick up Scott and Emily around three o'clock. Will that work for you?"

"Sounds perfect. I'll text you when I'm on my way."

"You don't have to pick me up, you know. I can drive to Newport, and we can go from there. In fact, we should take my car to New York. You're already going out of your way to help me with Harvey."

"I don't mind. I'll check the map," he said, "but I have to go north to get to I-90 anyway, so I might as well pick you up."

Allie fiddled with the bracelet on her slender wrist, looking down at the asphalt. Her pale gray

pants were a perfect match for the bits of dog hair
that clung to them below her knees. The darker
gray heels she wore showed no visible bite marks.
As his gaze roamed her body, taking in the frilly
bright blue blouse that gathered at her narrow waist,
his temperature rose.

What was it about her that never failed to turn
him on? Even when he was irritated by her actions,
he wanted her.

And then their gazes collided. Damn those eyes
of hers. Dark blue like her blouse, with a distinctive
ring around the outer edge of her iris. Could he see
into her soul if he looked hard enough?

She was talking, but he didn't catch what she
said. Something about him not feeling obligated,
with his grandfather in the hospital.

"They're moving my grandfather into a rehab
facility today. His doctor told me that he's done re-
markably well, but he wants to make sure Granddad doesn't have any more dizzy spells before
letting him go home."

"That's good news," Allie said.

"If only Granddad thought so." He told her about
his visit to the hospital that morning. "I haven't
heard anything since. I'm hoping his doctor convinced him the rehab center is the best place for
him right now." He shifted his weight from one
foot to the other. "I'll visit him tomorrow at the
new place to make sure he's settled in. I can be

reached by cell if they need to contact me while we're away."

"I guess everything's settled, then." But she didn't sound convinced.

"I'm still sensing something's wrong."

"I'm dreading this trip," she confessed. "My mother is an unapologetic matchmaker. She thinks everyone should be paired up and make families."

"And you disagree?"

"Wholeheartedly. I've been in my share of relationships, but I'm not interested in one right now. But that doesn't mean my wishes have any bearing on my mother's actions." She twisted her bracelet. "I need you to remember that my mother's views on marriage and mine are total opposites. And if it looks like she's trying to get us together, she is."

He grinned. "Works for me." He chucked her under the chin. "Don't even worry about it. I'm a big boy. I can handle myself."

Her shoulders relaxed, and before he could consider his actions, he pulled her in for a friendly hug.

Wow. What a mistake—a mistake that felt *way* too good.

Her arms immediately wrapped around his waist and, with heels on, her face came to his neck, where her warm breath just above his collarbone sent his pulse into overtime.

There was that citrus scent of her hair again, tickling his nose. His hands slid from her lower back up to her head, sliding through the silky strands of her hair. His body screamed out for him to do something about this pull she had on him, but his mind remained in control.

The parking lot was deserted, but they weren't alone. People walked by on the sidewalk, but there were several rows of parked cars between the sidewalk and where he and Allie stood.

Allie pulled away, taking a step back.

"I'm sorry." They both spoke at the same time.

"Don't look at me like that," Jack pleaded.

"How am I looking at you?"

"I don't know. But there's something in your eyes that makes my brain go blank."

She smiled, and that made him want her more.

He groaned inwardly and checked his watch. Almost five. He could ask her to go for a drink, since trying to get any work done at this point would be fruitless.

Harvey barked from inside his crate as if he knew they needed a referee.

"I should get Harvey home," Allie said. "He probably needs some exercise after spending the afternoon in that conference room."

Jack nodded. Going their separate ways was the smart decision. "I really liked your presentation, Allie. You know you didn't need Harvey. Your talent stands on its own." He couldn't help himself. The words came out automatically.

She cocked her head. "Thank you, I think. I liked yours, too. Those branding ideas were genius."

"Thanks. But I mean it, Allie. You can rely on your talent. You don't have to deceive people to win them over."

Allie narrowed her eyes. "That's easy for you to say. You have no idea what I've been through or how hard it is for me to get new business. You have your grandfather's company and reputation behind you."

"That doesn't mean I don't have to work extremely hard to win accounts." Did she really think he had it that much easier than she did just because his firm was established? "Nothing is handed to me because of my grandfather."

Allie stared at him a minute as if she didn't believe him. He decided to change the subject, unwilling to leave things between them on such a sour note. "Who did your animation? I loved the different personalities of the dog family with puppies that were picky eaters."

"I did it all," she said stiffly. "I can't afford to hire anyone right now. Anyway, animation has been a hobby of mine since I was a kid."

"Really? That's very cool."

Her face colored. "Yeah, I used to make those little books of pictures that you fan and the characters move. Now there are websites you can use to do it all."

"But you do the actual drawings of the characters?"

She nodded. "Even though we haven't figured

out how Charlotte and I are related, we did discover that both of us have an artistic streak."

"That's amazing. I've seen Charlotte's work, and she's very talented."

"Isn't she? I'm a hack compared to her."

"Like I said before, don't doubt your talent," he chided her. "You have different points of view."

She seemed to consider that. "I like that. Different points of view. Maybe I'll use that the next time my mother tells me animation is a hobby, not a career."

Right there, Jack decided that this weekend he would need to stick up for Allie if her mother belittled her obvious talent, or otherwise.

Was that why she didn't feel she could rely on her talent and had to be dishonest to succeed?

EARLY FRIDAY MORNING, Allie was leaving the vet hospital without Harvey. She hadn't realized how attached she'd become to him until now. Poor guy didn't have a clue about what was about to happen to him.

According to the vet, Harvey should have no trouble traveling tomorrow. She only hoped her mom would accept having him in her house. Allie had already figured that Harvey would need plenty of exercise this weekend since he'd probably be relegated to his crate indoors. And if her mom gave her a hard time, she would just get a room at a local hotel.

She got into her car, and before starting the engine, she called Charlotte. "Tell me Harvey is going to be all right," she moaned in greeting.

Charlotte laughed. "He'll be fine. Vets do this operation all the time. It's no big deal."

"Maybe not to the vet, but it's a big deal to Harvey. Do you think he'll hate me after this? I was just getting him to like me better than—or at least as much as—Jack. I'd hate to go backward in our relationship."

Charlotte laughed again. "Stop giving him human reasoning and reactions. He won't even know what happened. He's certainly not going to blame you."

"I hope not." She changed the subject to the real topic she was calling about. "I was wondering what you're doing this weekend? Would you like to come to my parents' house with Jack and Harvey and me?"

"You want me to come with you? Why?"

"Yeah. I thought maybe you could help me pressure my mom into telling me about my adoption. She's got to realize there's something screwy when she sees how much you and I look alike."

"I'd love to come, but maybe another time," Charlotte said. "I've got *so* much to do for my showing in a few weeks. I don't have nearly enough inventory."

"I understand, but I just thought I'd ask. I probably shouldn't drop you on her like that anyway. I should at least give her some warning, I suppose."

"I think you're right. Are you going to push her for answers?"

"I'm gonna try," Allie said. "My mom's a champ when it comes to changing the subject if she doesn't want to talk about something." She'd done it several times in the past week alone.

"At least she's still around to answer questions." Charlotte spoke softly. "I wish you and I had met before I lost my mother. Then I would have been able to ask her questions. Like why she had an extra thirty thou lying around when I was born."

"Still no answers?"

"Nada."

"Well, keep at it. I'm sure some clue will appear when we're least expecting it." They were still waiting for the DNA kits they'd requested to arrive. They couldn't come soon enough where either of them were concerned. They needed answers.

"Speaking of not expecting it," Charlotte said slowly, "what's the story with you and Jack? Are you two seeing each other now? I mean, going away for the weekend. Meeting your parents. Sounds pretty serious."

Allie's face heated, and she was glad Charlotte couldn't see her. "I told you, we're just friends."

"Uh-huh. Sure."

"We *are*!" Allie laughed.

"So you're taking him to your parents' this weekend because you're friends?"

"He's going to see his cousin," Allie reminded her. "That's the only reason he agreed to go. Didn't I tell you all this last night when we talked?"

"Yes, but I didn't believe you any more then than I do now."

"You're as bad as my mother with your matchmaking," Allie said. "She's trying to find someone perfect for me just like my father is for her."

"Tell me again why you're so against being in a relationship? I know your last boyfriend is in prison, but not all guys are like *him*."

"That's what you think," Allie said. "I've met, and been involved with, more of them than you'd believe. Somehow I attract the kind of guy who is nothing but trouble. I'm not even sure if I'd recognize Mr. Right if he stood in front of me. I've made so many mistakes, I don't trust my own judgment anymore."

"Give me another example of a bad boyfriend."

Allie thought a minute. She had so many losers to choose from and hadn't thought about many of them in years. "How about the guy I worked with at a seminar in Charleston, South Carolina, who was using me as a cover to pass off copycat cosmetics?"

"How did you figure that one out?"

"I didn't. I was so enamored with the guy that I didn't see what was right in front of me. It was the assistant manager at the hotel where the seminar

was held who figured it out." And he'd probably
live up to his promise to have her arrested if she
ever showed her face in Charleston again.

"But Jack's a nice guy," Charlotte said. "He's not
like these other jerks you've been involved with."

"And he's no more interested in a relationship
than I am."

"I think you both protest too much," Charlotte
teased.

"This weekend is going to be pure torture."

"Because you'll be surrounded by chaperones?"
Charlotte asked.

"Stop it!" Allie laughed. "Go paint some pictures."

"Charcoal."

"What?"

"I'm working in charcoal," Charlotte explained.
"Not paint."

"Oh. I thought you worked in pastels."

"I used to."

"Before your mother's diagnosis?" Allie finally
began to understand. Charlotte must still be grieving the loss of her mother. Allie had never experienced grief to the same extent, but she would
definitely do some research to help her newfound
look-alike through hers.

CHAPTER NINE

THE WEATHER SATURDAY morning was drizzly and downright dreary. Exactly like Allie's mood.

Yesterday, Harvey had made it through his neutering procedure like a champ and slept most of the night. Unfortunately, Allie wasn't so lucky. She woke about every two hours to check on the dog and then couldn't get back to sleep because her mind was racing with thoughts of how the weekend at her parents' would go.

Jack had texted fifteen minutes before that he was on his way, so Allie double-checked her overnight bag and purse to make sure she had everything. She was taking a separate bag for Harvey's bowls and toys, plus she needed to fold up his crate and the blanket she used to line it.

There was no way she could take everything down in the elevator all at once, so she chose Harvey and his crate for her first trip—she still didn't trust him to behave when he could run free in her apartment. She didn't have long to wait before Jack pulled up.

"Good morning!" He looked fresh and appealing as he got out of his car at the curb. He wore an untucked blue plaid shirt with rolled-up sleeves over a navy T-shirt and jeans that fit him extremely well.

He was sexy enough to make her knees buckle.

Why couldn't she just forget her previous disastrous relationships and her vow to *not* get involved?

What would it hurt to have a fling with this man who'd made it clear that he was more than a little attracted to her, too?

Jack sprinted around the front of his sports car and lowered the seatback for the crate that Allie had reassembled while waiting for him to arrive. She'd found an overhang next to the apartment building to stand under.

"You're bright and cheery today." Allie held an umbrella over the two of them while they loaded Harvey into the crate inside the car.

"I'm looking forward to this weekend," he said.

Allie mumbled, "That makes one of us."

"Two whole days off and no talk of business or rivalries." He patted her shoulder and shut the door, and they stepped back under the cover of the building. "Come on, let's make the best of it." He lowered his voice. "How's Harvey doing after his big operation?"

"Amazingly well. He hasn't eaten much and has slept a lot, which is what they said would happen. It was a lot easier than I expected, but I'm glad he's coming with us." She handed him the umbrella. "I have the rest of my things upstairs. I'll be right back."

The road trip went quite smoothly. Their agreement not to discuss business seemed to work for them.

About halfway there, Harvey got antsy, and they stopped at a rest area so he could relieve himself. Other than that, the trip was actually pleasant.

So enjoyable that Allie didn't want it to end—probably because she wasn't looking forward to facing her mother and her matchmaking tactics.

"It's the house up there on the right with the wagon wheel in the front yard," she told Jack. The street where Allie grew up reminded her of a typical neighborhood from sitcoms in the fifties and sixties. Which was likely why her old-fashioned parents had chosen it in the late seventies shortly after getting married and had remained here ever since.

"Is there meaning behind the wagon wheel? It looks pretty old."

Allie shrugged. They passed several children playing. "No clue. It's been there as long I can remember."

Jack glanced at Allie. "Maybe I'll have to find out from your mom if there's a story." He pulled into the driveway. "I'll park on the street after we unload."

The engine was still making noise as it turned off when Allie's mother came out the front door, her ever-present dish towel flung over her shoulder. She wore navy pants with loafers and a short-sleeve, floral-print V-neck shirt. Her elfin short gray hair framed her smiling face.

"You must be Jack." Her mother ignored Allie and went straight to him. Mom put her arms out, and he dutifully hugged her. "I'm very glad you were able to join us. We love your cousin Emily, and we're so happy she's part of our family now." She slipped her arm through his and continued talking as she led him toward the front door. "That makes you part of the family, too."

Jack looked back over his shoulder at Allie. "I need to give Allie a hand unloading the car, Mrs. Miller."

"Oh, please, don't be so formal. Call me Eleanor."

He smiled pleasantly. "Eleanor, do you have a place where you'd like me to set up the dog crate?"

Her mother stopped midstride and glared at her daughter.

Would Mom make a scene in front of Jack? Allie had warned him, so he shouldn't be surprised.

"I thought we decided you'd find someone to take care of your dog this weekend, Allison."

Standing behind her mother now, Jack mouthed over her head, *Allison?* He winked, and Allie had a difficult time maintaining her composure.

"I could get a hotel room—"

"If you'd prefer, Eleanor," Jack interjected before Allie could finish, "I could get a hotel room and keep him there with me. Allison didn't feel right leaving the poor guy with someone else after his operation."

Allie's lips twitched at his use of her full first name. She'd pay him back when the time was right.

"No need for you to stay in a hotel," her mother said quickly.

Jack's expression said he knew Allie's mother wouldn't want him to stay anywhere else. Though, they both knew that she might have allowed Allie to stay at a hotel if Jack hadn't cut her off.

"We have plenty of room." Her mother narrowed her eyes at Allie and said, "I'm sure we can find a place for the dog's crate."

JACK TOOK A BITE of homemade potato salad. "Does your mom always make a big lunch like this?" Growing up with only his granddad, he'd been on his own for most meals after he'd outgrown his au pair.

"She lives to cook for others." Allie sat across from him at the long farm table in the kitchen eating area. No one else had arrived yet, and Allie's parents had already eaten lunch. Her mom had disappeared as soon as she'd served them, and her dad was out running errands for the party. "Don't overeat, because there will definitely be an afternoon *snack*."

"I take it that you're saying it'll be more like a meal?" The remoulade on his crab cake sandwich dripped onto his plate, and he sopped it up with the roll before taking a bite.

"Unless you consider heavy hors d'oeuvres like pigs in a blanket and chicken wings a light snack."

He swallowed the delicious mouthful of crab cake. "I'd gain a ton of weight if I lived here."

"No, you wouldn't," Allie said. "Mom puts everyone to work, and you burn off the calories as fast as you consume them."

"I have no problem helping out while I'm here."

"Don't worry, she already has us lined up to pick up Emily and Scott at the airport this afternoon. Part of her plan to make sure *we* spend more time together. I'm also sure there will be more to do for tonight's party when we get back."

"Do you really think she has matchmaking on her mind when she's expecting all this company?"

Allie pursed her lips. "She doesn't know how to turn it off."

He chuckled. "Should we take Harvey with us to the airport?"

"I don't know," she said. "He was resting in his crate in my bedroom when I left him a few minutes ago."

"We can take him for a long walk before we leave," Jack suggested. "You can show me the neighborhood, tell me stories of your childhood."

"Sounds good, except for the childhood stories part."

"Oh, come on. There must be something you'll share." He grinned and took a long drink of his milk.

"I had a typical childhood, I guess. My parents worked hard to make sure we had an idyllic upbringing."

"But?" There was obviously more to her story.

"But what?"

"But it sounds like in your case they didn't succeed."

Allie turned her head in both directions. They were alone in the kitchen, but she still spoke in a low tone. "It's not that they didn't succeed. I just felt like an outsider."

"An outsider?"

She shrugged. "My younger siblings are biologically related, and so are my older siblings. I love them all, but I'm the only one without a biological brother or sister." She sucked in a breath. "I'm different from them, and I'm certainly nothing like my parents, who do everything by the book."

"Sounds like a lot of pressure to assimilate, to be who your parents expect you to be." Jack doubted Allie shared these intimate details often.

"I always felt like something was missing." She covered her face with both hands and shook her head. "I sound crazy, don't I?"

He chuckled softly and reached across the table to take her wrist and move her hand from her face. "Not at all." He released her, wiped his mouth on his napkin and pushed his chair back. "Come on! Let's go get Harvey, and we can compare childhoods."

After they cleaned up after themselves, Jack

followed Allie through the house. "Was this always your bedroom?" He took in the room's feminine touches—floral comforter on the queen-size bed, matching floral window treatments over lacy sheers. After having seen her apartment bedroom, it was obvious she and her mother had different taste.

"I shared it with my sister, Rachael. We used to have twin beds in an L-shape. My mother redecorated after we moved out." Allie pointed to the center of the bed. "We would set up our Barbie dolls right here. Between the two of us, we had all the important stuff: house, car, even an RV and tent. My mother made clothes for them, and we would spend hours arguing about whose Barbie would marry Ken." She shook her head and wore a look of disgust. "I should have let her Barbie marry him so mine could have a career and be independent."

He laughed. "Sounds like a typical childhood to me." He sobered. "Career is that important to you?"

She nodded. "What else can prove I'm a useful human being if I don't have a successful career?"

"What if you fail?"

"Then I'd have to depend on someone else to provide for me, and I could never be happy. That's why I can't fail."

CHARLOTTE DROVE AROUND NEWPORT, trying to decide where to go for inspiration. She desperately needed to add to her inventory, but she'd been so caught up in this mystery involving her adoption, as well as Allie's, that she'd barely thought about work all week.

She stopped at a red light near downtown and fully took in her surroundings. *The doorways.* Newport was famous for its doorways. Each one was unique. Although many artists had reproduced them in different media, she was sure they would be well-received at her show since she'd done them in the past and they'd been very popular.

Recognizing a lucky break, she found a parking spot on the street. She grabbed her camera from the case in the backseat and began walking, taking pictures from different angles of the many doorways she came across.

She'd walked several blocks away from her car when she saw them. Two little girls, maybe nine or ten, sitting on a stoop. As she got closer, she realized the girls must be sisters or at least related. They had fair skin and dark-brown hair that they brushed back from their faces in an identical manner. Their noses turned up slightly, and they shared the same Cupid's bow mouth.

"Good afternoon," Charlotte greeted them as she got close.

They looked up from the magazine they were giggling over, and Charlotte saw a picture of the latest preteen heartthrob on the cover.

"Can you take our picture?" one of them asked while the other nodded.

Charlotte never took pictures of strangers, especially children. She didn't draw people either, only places.

"I'm not sure—"

The front door of the house opened, and a woman who was the adult version of the two girls stepped out. "Who's this?"

Before Charlotte could say a word, the girls piped up. "We want this lady to take our picture."

Charlotte hastened to explain. "I'm an artist. I'm taking pictures of the doorways. I was about to tell the girls that I don't take people pictures."

The mother cocked her head. "How unusual. Most people these days only take pictures of people, especially themselves."

She had a point. "I don't like to invade people's privacy."

"Are you an artist I should know? Do you have anything in any of the shops downtown?"

"I'm Charlotte Harrington." She put a hand out to the mother, then dug in her little purse that she wore across her body for a business card.

"I'm Joanna, and these are my daughters, Kayla and Maura." The woman took the card from Charlotte and read it. The list of Charlotte's upcoming shows were on the back. "Very impressive to have shows in big cities." She pocketed the card. "I've been wanting to get something besides a photograph of these two, a painting or some kind of drawing. I know this is sort of out of the blue, but is that something you might consider?"

Charlotte hadn't in the past, but her world seemed to be changing by the second. "It's not what I usually do, but let me think about it." She took down Joanna's email and promised to get back to her soon.

The girls smiled, and Charlotte couldn't resist asking, "So how old are you two?"

"Almost ten." They answered in unison.

"You're twins?"

They bobbed their heads.

They didn't dress alike, not even close, but their body language was identical. One wore a frilly pink top with pink jeans, and the other wore regular blue denim jeans with a T-shirt that sported the Boston Red Sox logo.

Charlotte looked at Joanna, who shrugged. "What can I say? They haven't allowed me to dress them alike or even similarly from the time they learned the word 'no.'"

Charlotte laughed. "I guess they learned at an early age to be independent."

"You're telling me."

At the girls' urging and their mother's okay, Charlotte took several pictures of them in different poses. "Let's do a serious one now," she suggested, posing them back-to-back on the stoop with both looking at the camera. "Perfect!"

After promising to email the pictures to the girls' mother, Charlotte continued on her walk.

As an only child, she often wondered what it would have been like to have had a sibling or two. Would they be close, or would they have drifted apart as they became adults?

She would hope that after losing their mother, they'd have been close, even if they hadn't been before.

It didn't matter. Family was a dream—she had no one left. She would never know what growing up with siblings felt like. A single tear ran down her cheek, and she brushed it away. She could count herself lucky to have several close friends, including new friends Jack and Allie, with whom she could form her own "family."

But how great would it be if she and Allie were truly related?

JACK AND ALLIE stood in the small entryway of her parents' home. "I can drive my mom's car to the airport." She held up the keys. "There's no need for you to drive since you drove all the way here this morning. In fact, you can stay behind and relax if you want."

Not that her mother would let him relax, but he was a big boy who could take care of himself.

"I really don't mind driving."

She cocked her head at him. "Are you one of those control freaks?"

"Control freak? Me?"

"Yeah, you don't seem to like giving control over to others. Do you *ever* let anyone else drive?"

He grinned. "Yes, I let other people drive. I figured you didn't need the added stress. That's all."

"Oh." She'd been duly chastised. "Thank you."

"You're welcome. Now, let's go. Didn't you say their flight was coming in early the last you checked?"

She nodded. Instead of three-forty, it was now expected at three-twenty. "If you're sure?"

"I'm positive. Now get in the car."

They had a companionable ride to the airport, and before she knew it, they were following the signs for parking.

"There's no cell phone waiting area," she told Jack. "The short-term lot is free for thirty minutes. We can keep an eye on the time, but Scott should be texting me that they've landed before that."

They'd no sooner parked when Allie got a text from Scott, and they promptly found the newly-weds waiting with their luggage.

"Thanks for picking us up," Scott said when they were finally back on the road. Allie had done the reintroductions while Jack and Scott quickly stowed the luggage in the trunk.

"You're welcome," Jack said. "How was your trip?"

"We had a great time," Emily said. She and Scott

were both tanned and relaxed. "I didn't want to come home."

Emily hit the highlights of the trip and then asked, "So you two met at our wedding?"

Allie and Jack looked at each other. "News travels fast," he quipped. Allie turned partway toward the backseat.

Emily smiled. "I vaguely remember seeing the two of you together, but then the entire wedding is pretty much a blur. I can't wait to see all the pictures."

"I have some I meant to email," Jack told her. "And you actually may have seen me with Allie's double. I brought Charlotte as my date."

"You're dating Charlotte?" Emily leaned forward as far as her seat belt allowed.

"No, she's my neighbor. Just a friend." He glanced at Allie, but she pretended she didn't notice.

"Then are you two dating?"

"No." Allie's answer was instantaneous. "We're just friends." Then she mumbled, "But Mom might answer that differently."

Scott laughed. "Is she up to her old matchmaking tricks again?" He squeezed his wife's hand. "You know she set Emily and me up, don't you?"

Allie's eyebrows rose. "No, I didn't know that. I thought you met through friends."

"That's partially true. Mom's regular hair salon was booked, so she made an appointment to have her hair done by Emily." Scott's wife managed her own hair salon.

"She was so nice, and we hit it off immediately," Emily gushed. "She invited me to the family's Fourth of July picnic, and there was Scott. The rest is history."

"Mom strikes again," Allie grumbled.

Thankfully, Jack moved the subject away from Allie's mom. "So you work around here, Emily, but you went back to Rhode Island to get married? How'd that happen?"

"I've always loved the mansions in Newport and the stories surrounding them. I go back every chance I get, and I've toured the homes that are open to the public so many times that I could probably give the tours myself." She laughed. "So that's where I've always wanted to get married."

"Great choice. I love Newport."

They were quiet for a few minutes until Allie blurted out, "I hate to revisit the subject, but I think Mom's at it again. She pushed pretty hard for Jack to come this weekend. She was adamant that I give him a chance and that 'not all men are like your previous boyfriends.'" Allie felt the need to voice her concern—plus, she knew she couldn't battle her mother on her own. "Will you guys please, please, please help us out and not let her get too out of control? I cannot deal with her games right now."

Scott grinned. "This could be fun. Maybe I'll let you flounder for a while."

"Hey!" Allie pouted.

"I'm kidding." He looked at Emily. "Although, you have to admit that Mom knew what she was doing when she got us together."

Allie was practically indignant. "Well, she's wrong in our case, right Jack?"

He looked in the rearview mirror at Emily and Scott. "Absolutely. We're just friends." He glanced at Allie. "Right, buddy?"

"You bet, pal. Neither of us wants a relationship."

Scott shook his head. "Won't work. She will look at it as a challenge. I told Mom that I wasn't the settling-down type either, but she proved me wrong. I'm sure you can come up with a plan to outmaneuver her or avoid her. You always do."

"We could take off for Providence as soon as we drop you two off," Allie quipped.

"Not up to your standards," Scott told her. "You can do better, Al."

Allie wasn't sure why she hadn't thought of it sooner. The best way to get her mother off her back was to go along with her. "Jack, we should pretend we're a couple."

He flinched. "What? Are you sure?"

"That's perfect, actually," Scott said from the backseat. "Mom won't know how to react."

"But how is that the answer?" Jack asked. "She'll think she got what she wanted."

"Exactly." Allie was really liking the idea. "Mom will think her work is done, and she'll leave us alone." Allie looked at Jack as he kept his eyes on the road. "What do you think?"

He shrugged. "You guys know her better than I do, but it could be fun. I guess."

"Yeah, fun." So much fun that her mother wouldn't know what hit her.

A few minutes later, they were pulling into her parents' driveway and unloading the car.

"Here she comes," Jack whispered close to Allie's ear when her mom came out the front door to greet them. "Let's give her what she wants." He slid his arm around Allie's waist and settled his large hand on her hip. He pulled her tightly against his side, all the while pretending to whisper in her ear.

That's all it took for Allie to get lightheaded.

If they were going to fool her mother, then Allie definitely needed to steel herself against the instant arousal Jack could invoke every time he was near.

A LITTLE WHILE LATER, Jack was on the covered cement patio with a glass of iced tea in one hand and Allie's hand in the other.

Until Allie pulled out of his grip. "She's not around right now."

He kind of liked holding her hand, their fingers laced intimately, but he didn't dare tell her that. "Your dad's right over there." He pointed to where her father was checking his gas grill. "Don't we have to fool him, too?" Her dad scratched his head, his thinning gray hair neatly trimmed.

Allie shook her head. "He doesn't care one way or the other. He only cares that Mom's happy."

Jack enclosed her hand in his again and gave her a penetrating look. "All the more reason for us to pretend in front of him, as well." For good measure, he leaned close and kissed her cheek.

Truly the wrong thing to do. The mere touch of his lips to her soft cheek, the light scent of her shampoo, were enough to make his blood heat. He should have remembered that from a few minutes ago when he was whispering sweet nothings in her ear and the same thing happened.

"Well, look at you two! This is pretty cozy." Allie's mom came up behind them. She looked directly at her daughter. "And you swore to me that you and Jack weren't dating, Allison. All that 'bad boyfriends' business you're always telling me about. This is more like it."

At Allie's slight tug to pull her hand from his instinctively, he tightened his grip and didn't let go. "I guess you knew better than we did," Jack told her.

Eleanor had such a pleased expression on her face that Jack nearly felt guilty about deceiving her.

"What can we do to help you out with the party, Mom?" Allie obviously wanted to change the topic.

"Well, let's see. I think we're in pretty good shape, but you could set up some chairs out here." She pointed to the garage door off the patio. "You'll find them right through there. Oh, and they might need some cleaning off. Dad can give you a rag to use."

Then she went on her way. Allie turned to Jack, snatching her hand back as she sputtered, "I changed my mind. I don't like this at all. Now my mother thinks she's won, and when she finds out we've been lying to her, I'll be the one to pay the price."

"This was your idea. Let's just keep her happy," he suggested. "Did you see the look on her face?"

"Yes, I did." Allie pursed her lips and glared at him.

He had a sudden thought. "What's wrong with keeping her in a good mood for when you talk to her about your adoption?"

CHAPTER TEN

ALLIE STEPPED AROUND her three-year-old niece to get the veggies from the fridge and put them out for the party. Rachael and her husband, Dan, had arrived about thirty minutes ago. Sophie had chosen the kitchen floor—right in the middle of all the action—to play tea party with a doll and two stuffed animals.

While Allie arranged baby carrots and cauliflower florets on a platter, she caught a glimpse of Jack through the window. He had set up folding chairs on the patio and now was on a ladder, changing a lightbulb in the party lights shaped like hamburgers and hot dogs strung around the perimeter of the metal roof that sheltered the cement patio.

It was his own fault that he got put to work. She'd warned him.

He suddenly turned and looked at her through the glass as if he knew she'd been watching. He grinned and waved, making her insides all gooey.

She shook off the effects he stirred up and continued getting out veggies for the platter. "Where do you want this?" she asked her mom when she had added grape tomatoes, celery and broccoli.

"Let's put the appetizers on the dining room table," Mom said. "That way we don't have to worry about bugs, and the boys won't have to set up another table outside." She'd already gotten Dan to bring up a card table from the basement for cups, napkins and bottle openers, and set it up next to the large buckets of ice that contained drinks.

Allie glanced outside again, careful not to let Jack see her checking on him. Both he and Dan were opening beers, and Jack turned to her before she could look away. He held up the beer and pointed to it.

Allie shook her head. She needed a clear head to deal with this ruse she'd concocted. Pretending to be attracted to him was as easy as it came. Too easy—which was the problem. Adding alcohol to the mix would be like throwing a propane tank onto a campfire. Instant explosion.

Rachael sidled up next to her and whispered in a singsong manner, "I hear you have a boyfriend."

"Shush," Allie said, and then added from the side of her mouth, "Did you really fall for our act?"

Rachael turned ninety degrees toward Allie, her very pregnant belly coming between the two women. "It's an act?"

"Quiet!" Allie looked to her mother, who was searching for something in the dining room hutch. Thankfully she hadn't overheard. "I'm trying to keep Mom from matchmaking, so we're pretending her work is already done."

Rachael's eyes widened. "Brilliant!"

Allie was glad that her sister thought so.

"You two had me fooled," Rachael said. "Although I can see that it wouldn't be difficult to pretend to be attracted to Jack. He's pretty hot."

Allie put a hand up. "Settle your pregnancy hormones down, missy." They both laughed and ended the conversation when their dad walked through the kitchen. Rachael sliced the rolled-up ham, cream cheese and pickle appetizers their mom had made earlier while Allie got a plate for them.

When they were alone in the kitchen again, Allie said to Rachael, "I need to talk to you about something."

Rachael didn't look at her when she said, "Sure. What is it?"

Allie didn't know how to word her question, so she just blurted, "Why do you think Mom won't tell me more details about my adoption?"

Rachael spun around, her expanding waistline making her nearly tip over in her rush. "You make it sound like a conspiracy. Why would you think she's not telling you everything? I never paid that much attention, but I naturally assumed she'd given you more details privately than what she told in front of us."

Allie shook her head. "She either avoids the subject completely or comes up with a lame excuse like she doesn't want to talk about *any* of our adoptions because she considers us all her biological children."

"Well, that makes no sense. She's always been very open about when she and Dad flew to China for Scott and me."

"I know. You guys have great stories that she tells all the time. That's why I'm coming to you. To see if you have any idea what she might be hiding."

"You really think she could be hiding something?" Rachael asked. "Like what?"

Allie shrugged. "I have no idea. I was thinking I should go talk to Dad about it. Do you think he might know why Mom is so secretive?"

"It's worth a try. But you know Dad. His job is to keep Mom happy. He takes that 'happy wife, happy life' thing seriously, and Mom eats it up. If he thinks telling you something will make her unhappy, then—" She pursed her lips and raised her eyebrows. "So you and this Charlotte really think you might be related?"

"We've got to be," Allie said. "The more we get to know each other, the more we realize how much alike we are. Not only looks, but we sound alike and we're both artists, too. Well, *she* is. That's how she makes her living."

"So are you, Allie. I'd give anything to have as much talent and creativity as you have in your little finger." Rachael popped ham and a pickle slice into her mouth. "Anyway, how great would it be for you to find a blood relative? There's nothing like having that connection to someone. Seeing yourself in someone else." Rachael and Scott were only two years apart, but people had always thought they were twins until Scott grew much taller in high school.

Their mother suddenly appeared in the kitchen doorway. "Greg and Nick are here." Allie's older brothers both lived and worked on the other side of Albany. Neither of their wives had been able to come this weekend because of job commitments.

She and Rachael exchanged glances. Had their mother heard them talking? Allie straightened her spine. She had to face her mother and get her to spit out the truth.

But now wasn't the time.

Now *was* the time to go talk to her dad. She headed out the door to the backyard.

"Hey, Dad." Allie sauntered over to the gas grill, where her dad was fiddling with the ribs he'd been slow-cooking for several hours now. The grill was far enough away from the patio that Allie was confident they couldn't be overheard, even if her mom came outside.

He looked over the grill at her and smiled. "Hi, sweetheart. What's up?" The apron he wore said "Don't distract the cook, unless it's with beer."

"Can I talk to you about something?"

"Of course. Shoot."

Her hands grew moist, and the butterflies in her stomach fluttered. "I'd like to know about my adoption."

Her dad immediately dropped the tongs he was holding.

Not the reaction she'd expected.

He bent to pick them up. "Sorry, Allie, I need to go wash these off." He took a step toward the house, and Allie grabbed his arm.

"Wait."

He looked at her then, and she was shocked by the panic in his eyes. His normally ruddy complexion was even more pronounced. "I really need to—"

"What are you and Mom not telling me?" There. The question was out. Waiting for him to answer it.

"Not telling?" He laughed, a choked sound that contained no humor.

"Exactly. Neither you nor Mom will tell me any details about my adoption. My sister and brothers have heard their stories over and over, but when I ask about mine, I get stonewalled."

"We're not hiding anything, Allie. Your adoption was typical, nothing unusual. We brought you home and here we are. End of story. There's really not much to tell. Besides, you know how forgetful I am. If there was anything else to tell, I've probably forgotten it." He held up the tongs and started toward the house. "I really do need to clean these off."

Allie stood there in shock, watching him abandon her. Forgetful? He played bridge as often as possible and did *The New York Times* crossword puzzle religiously. He was about as forgetful as a computer.

A little while later, her back was to the door as she arranged crackers in a wicker basket. She knew Jack had entered the kitchen before he said a word. Especially before he came up behind her, caught her by her hips with both hands and kissed the back of her neck.

Without turning around, she picked up a cracker and fed it to him to keep his mouth occupied. She turned her head as far as it would go. "No need to go overboard."

His breath tickled her ear when he murmured, "Not overboard. Look who's watching us."

She glanced over her other shoulder to see her mom in the doorway. She quickly turned away in case her sudden guilt over deceiving her mom showed on her face.

Jack kissed her cheek and released her, leaving her to wonder how she would ever make it through the weekend without throwing herself at him.

PRETENDING TO BE attracted to Allie was no hardship for Jack. He had more trouble keeping his hands off her. She didn't want a physical relationship. She'd made that very clear. He needed to remember that, because her actions and reactions said otherwise.

Her acting skills were definitely first-rate.

He took a swig of his beer and decided to switch

to soda after this one. Alcohol would muddy the situation, and he needed a clear head if he hoped to continue this ruse and not succumb to his baser instincts.

When Emily's parents arrived, Jack spent time on the patio with his aunt and uncle, filling them in on his grandfather's condition.

"Have you heard anything from your dad?" Aunt Monica was his dad's half sister, but she had about as much contact with him as Jack had.

He shook his head and changed the subject. "Have you tried the jalapeño cheese? It's got quite a kick."

Allie came outside then. Perfect timing.

"You probably already know Scott's sister, Allie," Jack said to his aunt and uncle, motioning for Allie to join them.

"Of course," Aunt Monica gushed. "How nice to see you again, Allie."

His aunt hugged Allie, and then Uncle Aaron hugged her, too. "Great to see you again," he said.

Out of the corner of his eye, Jack saw Allie's mom come outside. He slipped an arm around Allie's waist.

Aunt Monica's mouth formed an O and she asked, "You two met at the wedding?"

Allie and Jack nodded.

"How romantic!"

Were all women matchmakers, ecstatic when men and women were paired? Growing up without his mother and then not having a woman to look up to beyond his au pair, his education was lacking in that area. In truth, his knowledge of women was mostly sexual.

Allie leaned into his hip as they stood talking. He enjoyed the contact so much that he missed what she said to him. "What?"

"I said, can you give me a hand with something in the house?"

"Of course." Then he turned to his aunt and uncle and said, "Duty calls."

They were no sooner alone in the living room when Allie turned on him. "You don't have to be so handsy, you know."

He was taken aback. "I wasn't trying to be. It's just an act."

"Don't you think I know that?"

He wasn't sure why she was so angry.

What he did know was that, even angry, she was the sexiest woman he'd been around in quite a while.

From her orange-painted toenails in white flip-flops, to her exposed ankles and shins below her white capris that sculpted her thighs and backside, to the top that showed a mere peek of skin because it tied right above her waist, to the white-and-dark-blue check of said top that matched her eyes perfectly.

Those eyes.

Damn those eyes.

He heard the front door open and close and used it as an excuse to pull Allie into his arms and kiss her. He had no idea if someone came in or went out the door. No idea if it was one of Allie's parents or merely someone who already knew about this fake relationship—specifically Rachael.

He didn't care. He cared only about tasting Allie's mouth while her body was plastered against his. His body reacted instantaneously when Allie deliberately moved her pelvis against him.

Her mouth was hot. He could have kissed her for hours. Not since high school had a kiss been this intoxicating.

They were alone, so his hands roamed her body freely. She didn't stop him. She didn't complain again that he was being too handsy. She was obviously enjoying it as much as he was.

Her hips again grazed his erection, and he pulled his mouth from hers to whisper, "Stop. You're killing me."

She froze.

"This isn't fake," he whispered close to her ear. "I want you. I've wanted you from the moment I first saw you." He swallowed before continuing. "I know you're afraid to take this beyond friendship. You're afraid to make a mistake with me." He sucked in a breath. "You have to know I won't hurt you."

She didn't say anything, still pressed against

him. Finally she took a step back. Without meeting his gaze, she turned and fled upstairs. Presumably to her bedroom.

ALLIE THREW HERSELF on her bed, facedown. She pounded her fists on the mattress and kicked her feet, screaming out her frustration, muffled by the comforter.

Once she'd released her emotions, she rolled over onto her back and stared at the ceiling.

Harvey began pacing in his crate, whimpering. He probably had to go out. At least get some exercise. "Just a minute, Harvey." As if he understood her words, he curled up on his blanket.

What had she been thinking when she came up with this crazy plan with Jack?

That was the problem. She hadn't thought at all. She'd only felt. And, damn, but Jack felt really, really good.

She covered her face with both hands. How could she face him again? She'd claimed to want just friendship, and then she'd been the one to suggest this pretense. Taking it a step further by practically throwing herself at him was plain stupid.

Stupid, stupid, stupid.

Concentrate on the important things—keeping her business afloat, so she could grow it into a successful company.

She removed her hands, lifted her head and sat

up. As she breathed in and out slowly for a few minutes, her equilibrium returned.

Knock, knock, knock.

Her heart rate accelerated. She didn't want to talk to Jack.

Knock, knock, knock.

The rap on the door was louder now.

"Allie?" Not Jack, but Rachael.

Allie swallowed and said, "Come in."

Rachael peeked around the doorjamb. "Are you okay?"

"Sure." She tried to sound upbeat.

"You're positive?" Rachael came into the room and shut the door behind her.

"Yes, I'm fine. Why would you think something was wrong?"

Rachael's color heightened, and Allie knew immediately why her sister had come looking for her. "Did Jack send you?"

Rachael's scrunched expression said it all.

Allie shot up from the bed, hands on her hips. "I'm fine. You can tell Jack I just needed to get away from everyone for a few minutes."

Rachael remained silent, merely listening as Allie blathered on. "Just because we kissed a few times, he's under the impression that I'm attracted to him. I guess my acting skills are better than he expected."

"Are you sure you're acting?" Rachael finally

asked. "I've seen the way you two look at each other."

Allie turned her back on Rachael and straightened the bed. "I told you, Rach, my acting skills are spot-on."

"Uh-huh."

Allie spun around to face Rachael. "What does that mean?"

"Nothing." Her tone couldn't sound more innocent.

"It's true. I don't want more than friendship with Jack, no matter what *he* wants."

"I'm glad."

Allie thought she'd heard wrong. "What did you say?"

"I said I'm glad you're not getting involved with Jack. I think you need a break from men to figure out what you want."

"You do?" Allie wasn't used to having someone agree with her reasoning. Should she be suspicious of Rachael's motives? "Are you only agreeing with me so I change my mind?"

Rachael laughed. "No, I mean it. Jack seems like a really nice guy, but I don't think you're ready to get tied down to one person right now. You barely know him."

Allie considered her sister's words carefully.

"What does Jack want?" Rachael asked.

"He's very open about wanting a physical relationship with me."

"And you don't?"

Allie shook her head. "It's not that I don't, but I can't take the chance of getting hurt again." She lowered herself onto the edge of the bed and looked at her sister. "I don't trust my instincts anymore when it comes to men."

"Are you saying you'll never have more than a friendship with a man? That's not you, Allie, and I didn't mean to imply that you should never get into a relationship again. Just take your time. Besides, you're always happiest when you're in a committed relationship." She paused. "Until it ends."

"Usually disastrously." Being single did feel unnatural to her, now that Rachael brought it up. Maybe that was why she was so conflicted. "I don't know. Maybe I should sleep with him and not expect anything more. That's what he wants, so why not?"

"Because that won't make you happy, either. I think you should take your time, get to know Jack as a friend, but don't rule out the idea of a relationship in the future."

"You're right. I'll only get hurt again if he turns out to be less than what he seems." She was a champ when it came to attracting losers and users.

There was a knock on the door.

"Who is it?" Allie called.

"It's Jack."

Allie's stomach did a flip, and she looked at Rachael.

"No quick decisions," Rachael said before opening the door to let Jack in. Then her sister slipped into the hall and shut the bedroom door, leaving Jack and Allie alone once again.

And this time they were alone in a room with a bed.

ALLIE AND JACK stared at each other. He was right inside her bedroom door, and she hadn't moved from where she sat on the edge of the bed.

He took a step toward her. There was a whimper from the corner of the room.

"Harvey needs to go for a walk," Allie said, hoping Jack would get the hint and not talk about what had happened between them in the living room.

"Would you like me to take him?" he asked.

Did he have to be so nice? It was difficult to remember she was off men when he stood right in front of her being his sexy self and acting all sweet to her on top of it.

"I can do it." She reached for Harvey's leash, and the dog began pacing in his crate in anticipation. She opened the crate door and attached the leash to Harvey.

Without looking at Jack, she left her bedroom—and he followed. Not just into the hall, but down the stairs and out the front door.

"I said I can do it." She quickened her pace, and Harvey quickened his even more.

"I heard you." Jack walked on her right side, while Harvey was on her left.

After another two blocks, they reached a park with athletic fields and a playground. Harvey stopped to do his business, which made it difficult for Allie to walk away when Jack started questioning her.

"This was your plan, Allie. We were supposed to act like a couple. Why are you so mad at me?"

She looked at the ground, unable to come up with an answer. Telling him the truth was out of the question. He didn't need to know that she couldn't control herself around him. That she wanted him so badly she didn't care if he broke her heart or not.

"I'm stressed about my mother. I really want to talk to her about my adoption, and I don't know how to get her to open up." That was a partial truth. Her mother was more interested in matchmaking than answering Allie's questions. "I'm sorry I'm taking it out on you."

"We could talk to her together."

Allie glanced up to see if he was serious. "You'd do that?"

"Of course." He winked. "Your new boyfriend is as interested in your history as you are."

She slapped at his arm. "Don't be wise." She pulled out the plastic bag she'd stuffed into her pants pocket and cleaned up after Harvey. "Good boy," she told him and then tossed the bag into the public garbage can. "I think it would be better if

I talk to my mom alone. I don't want her to think we're ganging up on her."

"Good reasoning. If you change your mind, I'm here."

"Thanks. I really appreciate it. Ready to head back?" She started walking before he answered.

"Wait."

She stopped and turned to him. He walked the few steps to her. "What is it?" she asked.

"I think we need a code word."

What the heck was he talking about? "A code word? For what?"

He tilted his head. "I'm pretty sure I'm not the only one who feels this intensity between us."

She didn't respond verbally, but her internal temperature rose significantly at the memory of their last physical interaction.

"I'm having a hard time distinguishing between real and pretend with you," he admitted. "You're good at stretching the truth in business, but I don't understand you well enough yet to know if the sexual signals you're giving off are the real thing." He paused. "They certainly feel genuine."

She swallowed, still unable to respond. He was right. She wasn't faking her attraction to him, and apparently he knew it, too. "What can I say? I'm a good actress."

"If you say so." He scratched his head. "Anyway, I'm thinking if we had a code word that we could use when we thought things were getting out of control between us, maybe it would cool us down."

That made sense. A code word could work like a bucket of cold water.

She cleared her throat and said thickly, "Okay, so what word should we use? Since *you* seem to need one to stay in control."

He answered almost immediately. "How about 'monkey lips'?"

CHAPTER ELEVEN

THE EVENING WAS ENJOYABLE, and although Allie considered her mother kind of a pain, Jack thought she was very pleasant, as well as an excellent hostess.

Dinner was ribs that fell off the bone and sides of potato salad, coleslaw and cornbread. All homemade by Allie's mom, except for the ribs her dad had slaved over all afternoon.

He wondered if Allie could cook that well. Not that it mattered. She had other attributes that kept him interested.

"You play pool?" Allie's dad asked him when it was nearly dusk. They'd just finished eating cake that Allie's mom had baked and decorated with wedding bells for his cousin and her new husband.

"Sure." His granddad had had a game room outfitted when Jack was a teenager so he would bring his friends over. Besides a pool table, there were arcade games and a game table, where he and his friends would play Texas Hold'em whenever they were home from college on breaks.

"Grab a beer and follow me."

Jack did as he was told. The basement held both a pool table and an old-school pinball machine.

"Wow! I haven't seen one of these in years. Does it work?"

Allie's dad grinned. "You bet! Go ahead and play it if you want."

"That's okay. I'll check it out later, after I cream you at pool." They both laughed and chose pool cues from the rack on the wall.

Allie's dad set up the balls. "House rules say visitor breaks." He removed the rack from around the balls and hung it on the wall while Jack chalked the tip of his cue.

They had each taken a turn or two, and things were going well, when Allie's dad asked, "You're in advertising like Allie?"

"That's right, Mr. Miller. We're competitors."

"Bart. That 'Mr.' stuff won't fly around here."

Jack nodded, feeling pretty good about Bart's show of friendship toward him.

They talked a little while about advertising, the economy and the state of the world, followed by Bart's rant about the latest exploits of a professional basketball player off the court.

Bart changed subjects so abruptly that Jack wasn't prepared when he asked, "What are your intentions when it comes to my little girl?"

Jack's hand bumped his pool cue where it was leaning against his side. He caught it before it fell.

"I'm not sure what you mean. Allie and I met only a week ago." He chalked the tip of his cue and realized he had gone from relaxed to nervous, all with one question. It had been a long time since he'd met a woman's father. Even longer since a father had warned him against hurting his daughter—which was obviously Bart's intention.

"I want you to understand that she means a lot to her mother and me." Allie's dad pocketed three solid balls in a row. "She thinks we don't have a clue about what's going on, but we know things aren't as good as she'd like us to believe. She didn't start this new company of hers on a whim." He took another shot, and it went wide. "We're also aware that she didn't choose to leave her last job. She got fired. All because of that jackass she was involved with who's now sitting in federal prison."

This was all news to Jack. That guy must have been one of those bad choices in men she'd told him about.

He lined up his shot and tried to sound nonchalant. "How did you find all that out?" Jack didn't want to let on that Allie hadn't confided in him.

"We have our sources."

Jack dropped the subject and took his turn. He'd decide later whether he would tell Allie her parents weren't as clueless as she thought. He wouldn't be surprised if they also knew he and Allie weren't actually a couple. "I really like your daughter. I don't know what the future holds, but I promise I'll do my best not to hurt her." Better not to mention that he wasn't a settling-down kind of guy.

He tamped down his guilt over deceiving both

of Allie's parents about their relationship, or lack thereof. Maybe he'd talk to Allie about coming clean on a multitude of subjects.

Their discussion ended when Allie's brothers Nick and Greg joined them. Bart changed the topic to a more neutral one, baseball. He and his sons were long-time Yankees fans and Jack was a die-hard Red Sox fan, but that was still a less contentious topic than the previous one.

"I wondered where you boys got to," Allie's mother said when she reached the bottom of the stairs a little while later. "Emily's parents are leaving."

"We'll be right up, Ellie," Bart told her, and then proceeded to clear the table.

When they went upstairs, Jack didn't see Allie anywhere.

"She took Harvey out," Rachael said as if reading his mind. "You seemed to be searching for her."

He smiled. "Thanks. You heading out, too?"

She nodded and patted her expanding abdomen. "We get tired pretty early these days." She tipped her head in her husband's direction. "And it's way past her bedtime." Dan was carrying a sleeping Sophie, already comfy in her PJs, her head nestled on her daddy's shoulder.

"I'll walk out with you. See if I can find Allie."

Rachael tugged on his arm. "Jack?"

He faced her.

"Please be careful with my sister. She's a good

person, and she's been through some tough times. Don't lead her on if you don't mean it."

Jack spoke from his heart. "I swear I have been completely honest with Allie about everything. I don't foresee changing that approach." In that moment he also promised himself to stop pushing her for a physical relationship. After hearing about her last boyfriend, he'd feel like he was taking advantage of her.

Rachael nodded. "That's good." She walked past him to the front door and added over her shoulder, "Because you never want to piss off a pregnant lady."

ALLIE HAD ALREADY said her goodbyes to those who were leaving before taking Harvey for a walk down the street a few blocks. She was on her way back when she saw Jack striding toward her. She immediately recognized his body shape and powerful gait.

"Rachael told me you were headed in this direction." He caught up to her and turned a hundred eighty degrees to walk with her back to the house. "She and her family are leaving."

"I know. I already said my goodbyes. How was pool with my dad?"

"Fun. He's good."

"You let him win?" She peered at him as they walked at a slow pace. As if neither of them was anxious to return.

Jack shrugged. "Figured I'd make a better impression that way."

Allie smiled. She needed to find this guy's faults. Immediately.

"We talked about you." Jack spoke matter-of-factly. "He gently warned me about hurting his little girl."

Allie stopped walking, mortified. "He *what*?"

"Don't get bent out of shape. He's concerned. Both of your parents are. You know, after what you've been through."

She cocked her head, eyes narrowed. "What are you talking about?"

"Maybe you should talk to him yourself."

She grabbed Jack's forearm and spoke through gritted teeth. "Tell me what he said." Allie had to know what her parents thought they knew.

"He didn't give specifics." Jack removed her hand from his arm, and she realized her nails had been digging into him. "He mentioned how you lost your last job because of your ex-boyfriend."

"Did he say anything else about him?"

"Like how he's in federal prison?"

"Damn." Her legs turned to rubber, and she lowered herself onto the curb. Harvey sat quietly next to her, as if recognizing she was upset. "How did they find out?"

"Your dad wouldn't say." Jack joined her on the curb and put a comforting hand on the center of her back, rubbing it gently. "They're concerned about you."

Allie straightened her spine and pulled herself together. "Well, they don't need to be. I'm fine. I survived and I've moved forward. They taught me well."

Jack didn't say anything. She wondered how much her dad actually knew and how much he'd shared with Jack.

"Did my dad say why my ex went to prison?"

"No. He seemed to think I already knew about it, so there was no need to talk details. I went along with it. I figured you'd tell me if you wanted me to know."

She debated whether to tell him what had happened and in the end figured he might as well know the whole truth. It couldn't be any worse than what he was probably imagining.

"I met Jimmy when he came to work for DP Advertising. I'd been there only a few months myself, but he sought me out to help him get familiar with how things were done there."

Jack moved his hand up and down her back as she spoke, a comforting touch rather than sexual.

She inhaled and continued. "A few months later, we were put on the same team for a family-owned grocery store–chain account. Jimmy and I had been dating for about six weeks or so by then, and I figured the more time we spent with each other, the better." The wind kicked up, and she tucked a lock of hair behind her ear. "Somehow, even all that time together wasn't enough for me to realize what Jimmy was up to." She turned to Jack, looking him in the eye. "He was threatening the chain's owner, saying he was watching his wife. If the owner didn't use DP for their advertising, he couldn't guarantee his wife's safety."

Jack's eyes grew round. "You're kidding!"

Allie shook her head. "I wish I was."

"The owner believed your ex?"

"He had pictures of her at different places around town." Allie had been horrified when she'd learned the details.

"And you lost your job because of what he did?"

"I almost ended up in jail right next to him."

"But you didn't know what he was doing." He didn't ask a question, merely stated it as fact.

"Try making the police believe that. *I* couldn't even believe I didn't know anything about it. We were spending almost all our time together." She covered her face with her hands. "I was so stupid. I didn't suspect a thing. You can see now why I'm so afraid to get involved with anyone. I don't trust my own judgment anymore."

"You're certainly not stupid," Jack told her. "He was obviously very good at deceit."

"That's true. Looking back, I should have suspected something. He'd always go for coffee around the corner at the same time every day. He'd bring back my favorite and usually complain about how long the line had been. In reality, he'd been driving around town, taking pictures of the guy's wife."

"What a scumbag."

"I should have noticed when the grocery chain owner was way too agreeable about whatever we suggested for marketing. I thought he was a nervous type, but it turned out he was only nervous around Jimmy."

"It's easy to look back and second-guess yourself, but you couldn't have known what he was up to just from these things."

"But we were practically living together. I never once questioned anything he did."

"You shouldn't have had to. He's the criminal, not you." Jack turned his body slightly toward her, and their knees touched. "How did you convince the police you weren't involved?"

"I didn't. They wouldn't believe me, no matter what I said." The memory of those hours and hours of questioning made her stomach rebel. "It wasn't until they offered Jimmy a deal, and he swore I had no knowledge of what he was doing, that they finally stopped harassing me. By then, I'd been fired from DP and subsequently blacklisted by every agency in town. That's when I started my own firm."

"You're pretty gutsy."

She grunted. "I had no choice."

"Of course you did. You could have come back here to your parents and hidden out until your ego was soothed and everyone had forgotten what happened. Instead, you took your life into your own hands and moved forward."

He was only being kind, but his words were comforting. As was the heat coming off his body.

They locked gazes, and before she could consider her actions, her eyelids fluttered shut and she leaned into him.

The moment his lips touched hers, she was suddenly hyperaware of every cell in her body. Each one reacted to him, and she couldn't think beyond the physical pleasure he invoked.

The voice in her head finally screamed that this was crazy, but her body wanted him so badly.

He cupped her face in his large, warm hand. His touch was as stimulating as anything she'd felt in a long time. Maybe ever. She covered his hand with hers, not wanting him to stop touching her.

She placed her other hand on his muscular thigh, and she felt and heard his moan. She withdrew her hand, but he retrieved it, placing it where it had been.

His mouth trailed from her lips to her cheek to her ear and down the sensitive column of her neck to her collarbone. He cupped her breast through her shirt, his hand warm and stimulating. He rubbed her tightened nipple with his thumb. His mouth replaced his thumb as he took her sensitive nipple between his teeth.

This time she was the one who moaned. She

felt his chuckle rumble through her body, and her insides heated to a boil.

"I need to say something," Jack gasped before his mouth captured hers again.

Between kisses, she managed, "Say whatever you want." She struggled for breath. "Just please don't let it be 'monkey lips.'"

JACK GRINNED AND RECOVERED his senses. "You said it first." He kissed her again, more as a punctuation mark to his sentence than a continuation of their scalding make-out session. "I was going to say maybe we should move this somewhere more private."

Allie pulled back. "Oh."

Jack immediately backpedaled after her reaction to his suggestion. "Or not." He stood, reached for her hand and helped her up, too. Then he took Harvey's leash from her and put his other arm around her waist. "You know how much I want you, but you're the boss." As much as he ached for her, he knew in the end he'd only hurt her. He couldn't give her the future she deserved.

They began walking back to her parents' house, not saying anything more about what had just happened. By the time they returned, everyone who wasn't spending the night had left. Allie took Harvey upstairs, and Jack headed to the kitchen, where he heard Allie's parents talking.

"Can I do anything to help?" he asked when he saw they were cleaning up.

Bart answered, "I think we're about done. But thanks for all your help setting up this afternoon."

Eleanor chimed in over her shoulder while drying a platter in front of the sink. "Yes, thank you. It's nice to have so many young, strong men around to help with the heavy lifting."

"I enjoyed it," Jack said. "It's nice to see all of your family together like this. I don't have much family nearby."

Eleanor inquired about his family while she wiped down the counters and then asked, "Can I get you anything? Something to drink? There are leftovers in the fridge." Bart headed out to the garage with a trash bag.

"No, thanks." Jack patted his stomach. "I'm stuffed. Everything was delicious. Thanks for including me."

"I'm glad you could come," Eleanor said. "You're welcome here anytime." When Bart came back inside, Allie's parents excused themselves to go to bed. Jack hadn't realized how late it had gotten.

Emily and Scott had disappeared before Jack and Allie came in from their walk, probably getting settled in the room across the hall from Allie's. Jack had been relegated to the smallest bedroom, the one Allie's mom used for sewing.

The room was furnished with a daybed, and upon seeing it earlier that day, he'd assumed it wouldn't be a very comfortable night's sleep. A twin bed was definitely better than nothing, but he preferred to sleep without his feet hanging off the end. Or, in this case, off the side, since the daybed had a high wicker railing around three sides.

Jack turned off the kitchen light as he left and went up the stairs to his room. The light was on in Allie's room, and he hesitated at her door. He wanted to say good-night, but would he be able to keep his hands and mouth off her?

Better not chance it. He walked down the hall to his room. He grabbed his shaving kit and took it into the bathroom with him so he could brush his teeth.

By the time he was finished, the light in Allie's room was off. Was she asleep yet? He pictured her in bed, a slight smile on her face, her hair dark and silky against the cool sheets. What did she wear to bed? He decided she wore nothing at all.

"Keep walking," he mumbled to himself and headed toward his assigned bedroom.

He'd been right about the bed. He was too tall, or the bed was too short. Maybe both. Eleanor had told him that was where little Sophie slept when she spent the night with them.

Perfect size for a three-year-old princess, not so much for him.

He tossed and turned until he found a comfortable position on his side, in a modified fetal position.

As he was close to drifting off to sleep with

thoughts of Allie running through his head, quiet footsteps in the hallway brought him back to consciousness.

The footsteps stopped, and for a time he didn't hear anything else. Then there was a soft rap on his door.

He got out of bed. Was Allie here to continue what they'd started outside?

He pulled his khaki shorts on and opened the bedroom door.

Allie.

She was sexier in her oversized T-shirt than most women were in provocative lingerie. Even in the dark he could see that her face was scrubbed clean, but her cheeks were pink. She wet her lips with her tongue, and his body jumped to life.

"Hi," he whispered, trying hard not to look at her long, bare legs showing from beneath the shirt.

She shook her head and put her finger to her lips. Then she took his hand in her smaller, warmer one and pulled him behind her.

"Wait," he whispered.

She stopped suddenly, and by the light of the nightlight in the hallway, he saw that alarm shone in her face.

He took a step back to the door and closed it quietly so no one would suspect he wasn't sleeping in his own bed. Understanding dawned, and Allie smiled. An angelic smile—hopefully an anticipatory one, too. He smiled back and held out his hand, all the while knowing he should stop and turn around immediately. She took his hand, leading him down the hall to her bedroom. They entered and she shut the door.

ALLIE FLIPPED THE switch to turn on the overhead light in her bedroom.

"Jeez!" Jack squinted and covered his eyes.

"Sorry. I should've warned you first."

"I don't mind the light on. In fact, I prefer it to see what I'm doing. But, yeah, warn a guy first." He was still squinting, his hands shielding his eyes.

He was also shirtless.

When she'd realized she needed him, she hadn't thought about what he might or might not have on. His physique was exactly as she'd pictured it after running her hands over his chest and biceps earlier. His shorts weren't buttoned at the waist, and they hung low enough for her imagination to run amok.

"I'm sorry if I woke you." Her voice sounded unsteady to her own ears. "This couldn't wait until morning."

He grinned and took a step forward, reaching out to her. She suddenly realized he'd misunderstood why she'd brought him in here. "No, no! That's not—"

But he was still coming toward her.

She spun around and pointed to Harvey's crate. "It's Harvey. I'm worried about him."

Jack stopped and looked at the dog. "Why? What is it?"

"There's something wrong around his stitches." She opened the crate door and got Harvey to roll onto his back. She pointed to his incision. "It wasn't this red earlier today. Do you think it's infected?"

Jack got down on his knees and looked closely. "I think it's red because he's probably been licking it. I don't see any other sign of infection, although I'm not a vet." He stood up. "Did the doctor give you a collar for him in case he did this?"

Allie had completely forgotten that the clinic had given her a bag of items for Harvey. "He's done so well, I haven't needed to go through all the stuff they gave me. Let me check." She had the bag in the corner of the room. She dumped brochures, gauze pads and various other things like coupons and free treat samples onto the bed. "Here it is." She picked it up and turned it over. "Do you know how to put it on?"

"I'm sure it's fairly simple." He removed the outer crinkly plastic. The collar wasn't very big, obviously made for a dog Harvey's size.

"Here you go, boy." He spoke gently to Harvey, and Allie was amazed the dog allowed him to put on the collar without a fuss.

Jack stood up again when Harvey's crate was shut. The dog went in circles for a couple of minutes, knocking the collar against the metal sides a few times. He finally gave in and curled up as best he could, but didn't look happy.

"That should stop him for tonight, and we can check his incision again in the morning."

Allie nodded. "Thank you. I'm so glad you were here." She reached out to give him a hug, but he caught her by the upper arms.

"Don't start anything you can't finish...buddy." His words were gentle, but his eyes meant business.

She blinked. "I'm not trying to be a tease."

"I'm not saying you are." He released her arms. "But if you have as little on underneath that T-shirt as I'm imagining you do, then you need to keep your distance. Or I can't guarantee what'll happen."

"Oh." She looked down at herself. Her nipples strained against the worn material of her favorite sleeping shirt. She crossed her arms over her chest. "I never meant—"

He kissed his finger and put it to her lips. "I know. Good night."

Before she could find her voice, he was gone.

EARLY THE NEXT MORNING, the light streaming through the window woke Jack. He pulled the sheet over his head, but there was no chance he'd be able to get back to sleep. He'd barely slept after he came back from Allie's room anyway. Between the too-small bed and thoughts of what *could have been* with her, he'd gotten twisted in the sheets more times than he could count.

He got cleaned up before anyone else was awake. Once he was freshly shaved and showered, he packed up his things and straightened his bed. He and Allie had decided to leave after breakfast.

He made his way down the hall with his duffel bag, noticing Allie's bedroom door was open and Harvey wasn't in his crate. He smelled fresh coffee as he went downstairs. What a great idea. Caffeine.

Allie and Harvey were coming in the front door when Jack reached the bottom of the staircase.

"Good morning," he greeted her.

"Hey." She didn't look at him. Something wasn't right.

"Everything okay? How's our boy's incision?" He wasn't wearing the collar, although the dog didn't need it when he went for a walk.

Allie focused on Harvey, petting his head as she answered. "He's fine. I think you were right. It looks a little better this morning since he couldn't lick it through the night with the collar on."

There was more she wasn't saying. "And?" he prodded.

"And what?"

"What's up?"

"Nothing. I'm fine."

"I doubt it."

She began to walk past him, Harvey on his leash, and he stopped her. "Did I do something?" he asked.

"What? No." Her shoulders sagged. "If you must know, come with me and I'll tell you what's wrong."

He followed her upstairs to her room, and she shut the door. Instead of putting Harvey into his crate, she gave him the freedom to roam the bedroom. Her suitcase was packed and standing next to a bag of Harvey's things. She'd already stripped the bed, and the comforter was neatly folded. She was apparently ready to make her escape.

He sat in one of the two hard-backed chairs in the room and waited for her to speak.

She perched on the bed facing him, taking a couple of deep breaths before speaking. "Like I told you before, I'm a little stressed over talking to my mom about my adoption. I'm more convinced than ever that she's hiding something." She went on to explain that her mother had always avoided the subject and that her dad even did it when she talked to him yesterday.

"Maybe if you're honest with her, she'll be honest with you."

"What do you mean?"

"If you confess that we were pretending to be a couple, maybe she'll reward you with the truth. I don't know. Might be worth a shot."

"What if she gets mad and shuts down? She might never tell me what I need to know."

He considered it, remembering his talks with both her dad and Rachael about not hurting Allie. "I guess that's a chance you'll have to take."

CHAPTER TWELVE

IT WAS NOW or never.

Nothing like having clichés running through your head when you were trying to figure out how to get your mother to finally tell you the truth about where you came from.

Allie was sure the butterflies in her stomach were reproducing at an alarming rate. She hadn't even been able to eat breakfast.

"Hey, Mom," Allie said when she walked into the kitchen to find her mother brewing a fresh pot of coffee.

"Good morning, dear," she said over her shoulder. "Did you sleep well?"

"I did," she lied. She'd been awake off and on all night, dreading this moment. "It was a nice party yesterday."

"Everyone seemed to enjoy it." Her mom put bread in the toaster oven and turned it on. "Can I get you something to eat? Or have you already eaten? I heard you up early."

"I'm fine, Mom. Thanks. I didn't mean to wake you."

"Oh, I was already up. You know me."

Yes, Allie knew her mother very well.

She took a deep breath to help herself focus.

This was it. "There's something I need to talk to you about."

"Sure, what is it?" Her mother got a plate from the cupboard, not looking at Allie.

"It's important, Mom. I need you to sit down and talk to me." Allie's heart beat loudly in her chest. She couldn't back down now.

Her mother appeared curious as she took a seat at the kitchen table. Allie sat down across from her. "Okay, dear, what is it? Is this about Jack? It is, isn't it? Are you finally going to settle down?"

"Mom, I've only known him a week."

"I fell in love with your father in less time than that," Mom said. "I've seen the way you two look at each other. In fact, I can't remember the last time you went this long without being in a relationship. I'm glad Jack came along."

Allie squirmed in her seat. "I'm happy you like him," she said slowly, "but I have a confession to make."

Her mother leaned in and whispered, "Are you pregnant?"

"Mom!"

"It's okay, dear. These things happen. I'm sure Jack will marry you. Does he know?"

Allie rolled her eyes. She'd gone from a fake relationship to a shotgun wedding. *Great.* "I'm not pregnant, Mom. I'm trying to tell you that Jack and I aren't a couple. We never have been." Why did that confession make her feel a slight bit sad?

"Never?" Mom crossed her arms over her chest and sat back. "Then why would you tell me you were? You put on quite a show." Her mother's tone had turned judgmental.

"I'm sorry, Mom. I didn't know what else to do."

Mom's eyebrows furrowed behind her glasses.

Allie filled her lungs and continued. "You're always matchmaking. You think I need a man to be complete. I figured if I told you Jack and I were already together, then you'd give me a break."

Mom frowned. "I'm sorry you feel that way, Allison. I only want you to be happy. That's all I've ever wanted for you."

Allie swallowed with difficulty. "I know and I love you for that." She reached out a hand, and her mother slowly put hers into it. Allie squeezed and Mom squeezed back.

"You know I want the best for you," her mother said. "And when you're in a relationship, you seem to make better choices."

That stopped Allie cold. She pulled her hand back. "What do you mean?"

"You know, like when you were in college and you came home after your sophomore year to say you and what's-his-name—Todd something— broke up and you were quitting college. Everything was fine while you were together."

Allie resisted the urge to roll her eyes again. "I didn't say I was quitting. I said I was going to take a year off because I was offered an internship in the marketing department of a cosmetics firm. After that, I finished my degree."

Mom nodded, ignoring her toast when the toaster oven dinged. "True. But that coincided with you getting back together with Todd."

"And that was a stupid decision on my part. We broke up originally because he cheated on me. I never should have taken him back when he came begging. Once a cheater, always a cheater."

"Oh. I'm sorry you got hurt, dear. But—"

"I know, Mom. I know you want the best for me. It's just that I've made some big mistakes when it comes to men, and right now I need a break from them. So maybe you could give *me* a break and not try to pair me up with anyone. At least for a little while?" She smiled at her mother, trying to soften her plea.

Mom nodded. "I can do that." She started to get up from the table.

"Mom? I have something else I need to talk to you about."

She turned toward Allie. "Of course. What is it? Money? I know starting a new business can be financially draining."

"No, Mom, I don't need money." That was a definite lie, but not what she wanted to discuss right now. "I need to know about my adoption." There. She'd begun the conversation and wouldn't let up until she got all the answers she needed.

"What would you like me to tell you?"

Allie cleared her throat "What do you know about my biological parents?"

The color drained from her mother's face. "I don't know anything. I never met them."

"Can you tell me their names?"

Mom hesitated. "Does it really matter?"

"Yes, it matters. I need answers."

Mom had her arms crossed on the table, and she lowered her head to rest her forehead on them. Her words were muffled. "I knew this day would come. Even though most of your life you seemed uninterested in this information, I knew someday you'd want to find your biological parents."

Allie's heart nearly broke. She reached across the table and put a hand on her mother's shoulder. "Please don't be upset, Mom. I love you and Dad very much. You'll always be my parents. I just need to understand where I came from."

Her mother's eyes were filled with tears when she raised her head. "Can't your father and I be enough?" Her voice cracked.

"You don't understand. You are *more* than enough. I don't want to get to know the strangers who gave me life. Until last week at Scott's wedding, I didn't even care who they were."

"Then why?" Mom brushed at the tears on her cheeks.

"Last week at the wedding, I met someone who looks exactly like me."

"Really?" Mom's eyes widened.

"Yes, her name is Charlotte Harrington and she lives in Newport. In fact, she lives across the street from Jack. He brought her to the wedding."

"So he's dating this Charlotte?"

"No, no. They're just friends. She lost her adoptive mother to cancer not too long ago, and Jack was trying to get her out of the house and out of her funk."

"I see. So you've talked to this Charlotte? Compared notes? You said she was adopted, too?"

"Yes. We have the same birth date, but we were born in different states. She was born in New York." Allie stopped to breathe and continued. "She recently began searching for her birth parents, and now I am, too. We've even ordered a DNA test to see if we're related. We're thinking cousins because of the different state thing." She took her mother's hand again, cupping it in both of hers. "Charlotte's mother never married, so she has no one left to answer her questions about her adoption. And like me, she has no information. But we have *you*. Please, Mom. Please help us."

Mom's tears flowed freely then and Allie, who never cried, felt her own eyes fill to overflowing. Mom brushed her tears away with both hands, and Allie retrieved the box of tissues in the powder room for herself.

"I'm sorry, Allison. I should have been honest with you. I was so ashamed of what we did, and I never wanted you to think poorly of us, especially me. Your father only went along with it to make me happy."

What could her mother be ashamed about? Was this the answer she and Charlotte were looking for?

"Start at the beginning, Mom." She took her mother's hand again. "No judgment here. I promise."

Mom swallowed and began talking, her focus on her hands and not Allie. "You know about our first child, your brother Grant, and how he died."

Allie nodded, but her mother wasn't looking at her, still concentrating on her hands.

"After that, we were so afraid to have another child with the same medical problem. I even had my tubes tied so I wouldn't be tempted to gamble on the chance that we'd conceive a healthy child." She paused. "When your dad and I were far enough along in the grieving process to consider adoption, we found it very difficult. I was determined to adopt a newborn. I didn't care about race. I only wanted a baby in my arms again. But they were few and far between. Waiting lists took years and we couldn't—*I* couldn't—wait that long."

Though her mother had fed her lies about her adoption the other day, Allie was certain she was about to hear the truth.

"And then one day, a miracle happened." Mom looked at Allie, her face blotchy from crying. "There was an ad in the newspaper. A lawyer who brokered private, legal adoptions of newborns. We didn't have the internet back then, so there was no way to search for adoption lawyers outside of our local area phone book. Your dad was suspicious, but I saw this as our road to happiness."

Allie rose to get two glasses of water. Her mouth was parched. She placed one in front of her mother.

"Thank you." Mom drank half the glass at once. She took a few breaths and continued. "We met with this lawyer, and he assured us he could get us a baby. A newborn." She looked at her hands clasped tightly. "There was only one thing we had to do."

Allie held her breath. "What was that?"

"This is the reason I never told you the whole story."

"It can't be that bad, Mom. What is it?"

"He wanted money." Her mother could barely speak. "On top of the medical expenses, he charged a lot more money."

"He was basically extorting money from you in exchange for an infant?"

Mom nodded. "I was so ashamed. I never wanted you to know we paid for you like that." She spoke faster, as if trying to get all her thoughts out at once. "It's why we adopted your brothers and sisters. We wanted to make up for what we'd done by adopting older children and medically challenged children who might never have a chance for a family."

"You had nothing to make up for, Mom. You've

been wonderful parents, and that's worth all the money in the world."

"But we did something illegal to get you." She whispered, "We *paid* for you as if you were a new car."

"And if you hadn't, then someone else would have." Allie was well aware that these transactions happened all the time. A thought came to her. "How much money did you pay him?"

"That's not important," Mom said quickly.

"Actually, it is. Was it thirty thousand dollars?"

Mom's eyes widened. "How did you know?"

"An educated guess," Allie said. "Charlotte has been trying to figure out where thirty thousand dollars came from in her mom's checking account. She wrote a check to Cash for the same amount right after Charlotte was born."

"That's a huge coincidence," her mom conceded. "Our check was written to Cash also."

"I think it's more than a coincidence." Allie moved on to a different question. "Do you have my original birth certificate? The one I have has you and dad as my parents. There's no information about my birth parents."

Mom shook her head. "That's the only one we ever received once your adoption was finalized."

"Is the lawyer still around?" He might be able to help locate her birth parents. He might even have her original birth certificate in his files.

"I haven't seen or heard from the lawyer since he

sent us the legal paperwork. I didn't want to have anything more to do with him. He was a reminder of what we'd done." Mom wiped her nose with her balled-up tissue. "I wanted to focus on you. My sweet baby girl."

"You told me I was born in Rhode Island. Is that true?"

"Rhode Island is right as far as I know," Mom said. "We traveled there to pick you up because that's where the lawyer was located."

She had to push just a little bit more. "Do you know *anything* about my birth parents? Even their names would help."

Mom looked defeated. "I'm so sorry. I should have gotten that information, but to be honest, I didn't care. And I guess I always hoped you wouldn't care, either."

"I told you, Mom, I *don't* care about those people. At least not for me. Charlotte is the one without family. Wouldn't it be great if she and I were somehow related? Then she could share this huge family you and Dad gave me."

Mom perked up at Allie's words. "That would be nice, wouldn't it? Although we could include her either way. Tell me more about her."

While Allie listed the things they had in common, her dad came into the kitchen. "Someone forget about this toast?"

Mom ignored his question. "Bart, you've got to hear about this woman Allie met at the wedding last week. She says they look so much alike they could be twins."

Her dad finished pouring a cup of coffee and turned to them, his expression serious. "That's amazing, but certainly impossible. We'd know if you had a twin."

"Dad, do you remember the name of the lawyer who handled my adoption?"

Before he could answer, her mom said, "I'll go find the file. I'm sure it must have his name, but I don't know how much more information you'll find in it."

While her mom did that, Allie filled her dad in on everything she knew about Charlotte. "She lives across the street from Jack. He's the one who brought her to the wedding." When her dad's eyebrows shot up, she added, "As a friend, Dad. He was trying to cheer her up. She's had a difficult time since her mother died."

"Ah." He nodded and drank his coffee. "I'm surprised your mother told you about your adoption."

"Why's that?"

"Because she's always felt guilty about it."

"I think we've gone past that. Mom and I had a good talk."

"I'm glad to hear it. It's good to have it out in the open."

Jack came into the kitchen then. "Am I interrupting?"

"No." Allie had been about to confess to her dad

that she and Jack weren't a couple, but she didn't want to put Jack in an uncomfortable position. She or her mom could fill Dad in later. "Mom went to get my adoption file. We're hoping at least to find out the name of the lawyer who handled the adoption."

"That's great news." Jack poured a cup of coffee, then set it and his phone on the counter. "I'll go pack the car while my coffee cools."

Allie got up to pour her own cup of coffee and heard Jack's phone vibrate. They'd been careful not to discuss business all weekend, but now that she'd gotten some answers about her adoption, her thoughts turned to the animal-food account. Could the text be about that?

Her dad was reading the newspaper at the kitchen table, so she casually picked up Jack's phone. She only wanted to know if an advertising firm had been chosen, one way or the other. The beginning of a text message could be seen on his screen.

Confidential: City of Fairleigh, CT, wants ad campaign.

She put the phone back next to Jack's coffee exactly as he'd left it.

A campaign for Fairleigh. Her excitement grew until she was ready to burst. The beach town had been devastated by a hurricane two years ago. It must still be having trouble attracting the normal influx of tourists.

Now that she had this inside information, she could do her own research and presentation. Getting the animal-food account, as well as the town's account, would ensure that she could stay in business.

And Jack would have no idea that she'd discovered the information from his phone. It was just a lucky break. No harm done.

ON THE DRIVE back to Providence, Allie filled Jack in on all she'd learned from her parents. He wasn't surprised to hear her parents had been keeping the secret about paying the lawyer an exorbitant amount of money to broker the adoption.

"I wonder if he's still practicing law," Jack said aloud. "You'd think a guy like that would have screwed up along the way and at least lost his license."

"That's what I was thinking, too." Allie had the folder her mother had given her on her lap. "This letterhead says his office is in Cranston."

"That's about fifteen minutes from your apartment. Want to drive by the address before I drop you off?"

"I'd love to, but it's out of your way." Allie shut the folder and set it on the floor by her feet. "I can do it later."

"It's only a few minutes longer. Besides, I have

a stake in this now. If I hadn't brought Charlotte to the wedding last week, you two never would have met."

"You're right about that," Allie conceded. "And I never would have bothered with this adoption stuff." She looked at him. "If you're sure you don't mind, I'd love to go by this guy's office. I'm sure there's no one there on a Sunday, but if there's a shingle with his name on it, then I can contact him this week."

Jack had a thought. "Did your parents mention how much they paid him?"

"That's the exciting part—thirty thousand. The same amount Charlotte found in her mom's checking account." She turned her body in his direction.

He glanced at her. "That's great!"

"Could it really be possible that she and I might be that connected? Isn't it more like an impossible coincidence?"

"No, it isn't. This lawyer *could* have brokered both adoptions. That is, *if* Charlotte's mom's thirty thousand was used for that purpose."

Jack's phone vibrated in the console.

"Want me to check that for you?" she asked.

"Nah. Just a text, probably nothing. I'll check it later." If it was about his grandfather, they would have called rather than texting. The message was probably from his colleague, Stan. Ideally he had more information about the campaign the town of

Fairleigh had in mind. Stan had found out about it accidentally through his niece, who worked at Fairleigh's town hall. Getting the early heads-up that they were looking for a new ad campaign was extremely valuable.

Allie's cell phone rang, and she answered. "Hello."

Jack looked over at her. She was listening closely, her expression tense. She was obviously not pleased with what she was hearing.

"Thank you for the opportunity," she said stiffly. "I hope you'll think of me for your future needs." She disconnected and stared out the side window for a few minutes.

He didn't want to interrupt her. She'd obviously gotten bad news.

His phone rang.

She didn't even turn toward him as she spoke. "That's probably about the Naturally Healthy Animal Food account. I didn't get it, so she's probably calling to say you did."

Normally he would have used Bluetooth to answer hands-free, but he didn't want to subject Allie to his conversation. They'd been in Massachusetts for about fifteen minutes, where texting while driving was banned, but cell phone use wasn't.

"Jack Fletcher."

"Hello, Jack. This is Monica Everly from Naturally Healthy Animal Food."

"How are you?" He held his breath. This could

be the break Empire Advertising needed to make a comeback.

"I'm pleased to tell you that we've chosen you to do our advertising."

Internally he was jumping up and down like a ten-year-old, but outwardly he maintained his cool. His company desperately needed the client, but he knew Allie's did, too.

"That's wonderful, Ms. Everly. Thank you so much for letting me know. You won't be disappointed. I'll be in touch first thing in the morning to go over details." He disconnected. Between this account and the one Stan had just found out about, Empire should be okay. At least for this quarter.

What a pleasant shock it had been, getting the text from Stan earlier today saying the town of Fairleigh, Connecticut, wanted Empire to put together some advertising for them. After being devastated by the hurricane two years ago, the town's tourism hadn't yet recovered, and they didn't have time to put a bid out for the work. Empire seemed to have the account free and clear.

Jack glanced at Allie, who was watching him.

"Congratulations," she said without much enthusiasm.

"Thanks. I'm really sorry it worked out this way. Not that Empire doesn't deserve it, but you did a great job, too."

"You needed the client as much as I did." Her tone was matter-of-fact.

"I meant hearing it this way."

"Oh." She went back to staring out her window. "It's fine."

"Are you mad at me?"

"Why should I be mad?" She sounded mad.

"Because you needed the account, too." He racked his brain, trying to come up with something to soothe her ego. "Listen, there will be other accounts. This just wasn't the one." He paused. "You know, there *is* a good side to this."

"What?" Her interest wasn't overwhelming.

"We're no longer competitors. We don't have to be so concerned about talking business."

"I guess."

Well, he definitely saw that aspect as a positive. Plus, he wasn't up to competing against someone who used the somewhat underhanded tactics Allie preferred.

"Maybe you should take me straight home," she said.

He turned in her direction and then back to the road. "Why? Because I got the account and you didn't?"

She shrugged. "I just don't feel like going to Cranston right now."

He assumed she meant she didn't want to go with him.

At least he wouldn't be up against Allie for the

Fairleigh account. Having this competition for
business between them was a barrier he could
live without.

ALLIE WAS IN a bad mood. She couldn't help it. How
could she be excited about Jack getting the account
when she needed it so desperately?

Thankfully they were almost at her apartment
building. She and Jack hadn't spoken for the past
half hour.

Her cell phone rang. She went digging in her
purse, not recognizing the number once she retrieved it.

"Hello?"

"Allie Miller?"

"Yes." She spoke quietly.

"This is Joan Broadwell from the Rescue League.
We have someone interested in Harvey. They'd like
to take him home to see if he and their other dog
get along." Joan gave her specific details.

"Tomorrow evening at six is fine, Joan. I'll see
you then." She ended the call and stared at her
phone.

"Is everything okay?"

She looked at Jack. "That was Joan Broadwell
from the Rescue League." She paused. "They have
someone interested in adopting Harvey. She's picking him up from me tomorrow night to see if he'll
work out with their other dog, and then they'll
adopt him."

"Just like that?"

"Uh-huh." She'd had Harvey for only a week. She hadn't expected to feel anything at the thought of giving him back. That had been the plan all along. He hadn't even helped her get the animal-food account.

But she *did* feel something…

She didn't say anything until they reached her apartment building a few minutes later. "Thanks for everything." She reached for the door handle without looking at him. What a miserable ride home. First she'd lost the account, and now she was about to lose Harvey.

Jack touched her left arm. She looked in his direction. "What?"

"Have dinner with me tomorrow night." The invitation came out of nowhere.

"Dinner?" As if the word didn't make sense to her.

"After Harvey gets picked up."

Recognition dawned. "I don't know."

"I *do*. You can't sit home and mope about Harvey. I'll come by after work. You said he's getting picked up at six?

She nodded.

"Text me when he's gone, or I'll come earlier if you want me to."

She hesitated and then figured, why not? "Okay."

He kissed her before she had a chance to react.

It took only a few seconds before she slanted her head and participated fully.

He cupped her cheek and deepened the kiss. She wanted to be mad at him, at the Rescue League, at the world. But right now, she didn't care.

"I'll walk you to your apartment," he suggested in between kisses to her neck. He struggled to catch his breath.

She stiffened. She wasn't mentally ready to let him get any closer.

"Or maybe you should go by yourself?"

Her hand traveled from the side of his head, across his shoulder and down his arm to his hand before entwining her fingers with his.

"I think the second option is best," she whispered, squeezing his hand for emphasis. "I'm really not up for company tonight." She paused. "I'll text you tomorrow about dinner."

With that, she withdrew from him and was out of his car before he could say another word.

A LITTLE WHILE LATER, Allie sat on the floor in her living room with her laptop open on her glass coffee table. Harvey was curled up next to her, his head on her lap.

Since she had a mere twenty-four hours left with Harvey, she'd give him as much attention as she could.

She used one hand to stroke his back and the other to do an internet search for the adoption lawyer, Gerard Stone. She didn't have much luck locating him, although she finally found an obituary for someone by that name, also a lawyer, who'd died almost five years before.

She printed out the obit and added the page to the file her mom had given her, then went back to her computer. Maybe she could find one of the lawyer's relatives. They would know if this was the right person and, if so, where his files might be.

She first searched for the wife and discovered she'd died late last year. Next, the first daughter listed. Caroline Stone Walden. The only thing Allie found on her without paying for a background check was that she was on Facebook. Allie clicked on the link and sent her a private message.

I'm trying to locate information about Gerard Stone, who was a lawyer in Cranston, Rhode Island. He handled my adoption almost thirty years ago, and I'm very interested in finding any available information about it. If you are the daughter of this Gerard Stone, please contact me as soon as possible.

She added her email address and cell phone number. Without hesitation, she sent the message, hoping for the best.

There was another daughter as well as a son listed in the obituary. Allie repeated the process and found them all on Facebook. She left similar messages for them.

Unable to do much more, she was about to call Charlotte to update her when she called first.

"Jack told me about Harvey," Charlotte said in greeting. "How are you holding up?"

"I'm okay." She patted the dog's head and couldn't help but flash back to Jack's way of making her feel better. Heat built in her core. She wanted him as much as he wanted her, but she needed to keep her vow to herself about men. "I'll survive." She'd survived a lot worse.

Allie told Charlotte about the file from her parents and how far she'd gotten in locating the lawyer. "The best news is that my parents paid a big chunk of money to the adoption lawyer. Want to take a guess at how much?"

"Thirty thousand?" Charlotte's excitement came through the phone.

"Yep."

"That's wonderful," Charlotte enthused. "Wouldn't that mean we were both adopted through the same lawyer?"

"Not necessarily, but I hope that's the case. Being born in two different states is what's confusing. Especially since this lawyer was in Rhode Island. Could he have a law license in both Rhode Island and New York, where you were born?"

"You'd have to take the bar in both states. Darn. There must be a logical explanation. At least you got more information than I did."

"Nothing new?" Allie asked.

"I left a message for my mom's best friend, Marie, but I haven't heard back from her yet. I've spent most of my time over the weekend working. I could use a little magic to make my artwork create itself."

Allie understood. She ought to be working, too. "Speaking of work, I didn't get the animal-food account. Jack got it."

"I'm so sorry," Charlotte said. "Will you be okay without it?"

"I honestly don't know. I'll have to run the numbers and see if I can make rents this month."

"Rents?"

"My apartment and my office."

"Could you consolidate? Just have one?"

Allie had already considered that. "I could, but then I wouldn't have a conference room. Some of my clients have small businesses and nowhere for us to meet at their work spaces."

"If there's anything I can do, let me know."

"Thanks. I appreciate it." Allie meant it. They hadn't known each other very long, but it didn't feel that way. "I guess I should go. I'll let you know if I hear from anyone related to the lawyer."

"Sounds good." Charlotte paused. "Allie?"

"What?"

"I'm worried about you."

Allie smiled. Even if it turned out they weren't related by blood, she had a friend for life in Charlotte. "I'll be fine. In fact, I've got some inside information about a new client."

"A big one?"

"Potentially *very* big."

"How'd you hear about it? You were gone all weekend."

She wasn't sure confiding in Charlotte was the way to go. Jack wouldn't like that she'd seen the information on his phone, and she didn't want to put Charlotte in the middle. "Let's just say the information practically popped up in front of me."

"Well, that's good. I'm happy for you," Charlotte said. "But you'll let me know if you need any help?"

"I will," Allie promised. "Thank you."

CHAPTER THIRTEEN

THE NEXT MORNING, Allie and Harvey arrived at her office early. She'd discovered through a phone call to the strip mall management office that a CPA had taken over the location where the lawyer who'd handled her adoption used to be. She could barely wait to call the CPA's office to see if they had any information about where the lawyer was now.

Finally, a little after nine o'clock, she was able to get someone on the phone. A woman, who introduced herself as the receptionist, told her the CPA, Felicia Monroe, was with a client and would call Allie back.

Allie had trouble concentrating on anything as she waited for the call.

When her phone finally rang, she nearly jumped out of her chair. "Allie Miller."

"Hello, Ms. Miller. This is Felicia Monroe. What can I do for you?" The woman sounded at least as old as Allie's mother, possibly close to retirement age.

"Thank you for getting back to me so quickly," Allie began. Her nerves were jangling. "I'm trying to find a lawyer who used to be located in the office you now occupy."

"You're talking about Gerry Stone?"

"Yes. Can you tell me if there's a way I can reach him?"

"I'm sorry to say that he passed away, oh—" She paused as if thinking about it. "Probably five years ago. I took over this office almost eight years ago when he retired."

"Do you by any chance know what might have happened to his files? Did he have a partner or anything?"

"Not that I know of. You might check with his wife to see if she knows where his files are."

"I did some checking on the internet yesterday, and according to what I found, his wife died last year." Allie was confident now that the obit she'd read yesterday was the right one for the lawyer.

"I'm sorry to hear that," Felicia said. "What about his kids? I seem to remember he had two or three. I didn't know him very well. My husband knew him better, since we used to have an accounting firm in another office in the same shopping center. But he's gone now, too."

"I'm sorry."

"Don't be."

"Excuse me?"

"He was a lying, cheating son of a bitch."

"Oh." Allie didn't know what else to say. "Well, thank you for the information."

"It wasn't much."

"Every little bit helps. If you think of anything else, please let me know."

"It's none of my business, but may I ask why you're trying to find Gerry?"

"He's the lawyer who handled my adoption. I'm trying to locate my biological parents."

"Well, good luck with that, honey." Felicia's words were thick with sarcasm. "His law license was suspended at least twice for his less-than-ethical adoption practices."

Not a surprise to Allie. "As in, charging a boat-load of money on top of legal and medical expenses?"

"That's just the tip of the iceberg." Before Allie could ask her what she meant, Felicia continued, "I have another call. Good luck to you." She disconnected.

Allie called Charlotte to fill her in but got her voice mail. "Call me when you get this. I have news."

Allie set aside her personal matters to focus on work, but it wasn't easy. She pushed ahead and did extensive research on the beach town of Fairleigh before contacting several people in town who might have the inside scoop on what they were looking to accomplish with a new ad campaign.

What she discovered was that no one knew what she was talking about. She finally worked her way up to the mayor's office. As soon as the words were out of her mouth, she was put on hold.

After several minutes, the woman she'd been speaking to came back on the line. "I'm going to transfer you to Charles Wittmer, the deputy mayor."

"Charles Wittmer," he greeted Allie a few seconds later.

She introduced herself, but he cut her off before she could state her purpose.

"I understand you're under the impression that we're accepting proposals for a new advertising campaign?"

"That's correct."

"I'm afraid your information is incorrect. May I ask how you heard this?"

What could she say—"I peeked at someone's text message"? "That's not important," she said and forged on quickly. "So you're telling me you *don't* want to launch a campaign to bring back tourists after your town was devastated by Hurricane Lorraine two years ago?"

"Well…"

"I understand a lot of construction work has been completed since then." She recited what she'd learned online. "A new boardwalk, reopened businesses, a new Ferris wheel. Even a center to showcase the many talented artists in your town and the surrounding area."

"That's all true, but we're not looking for a PR firm or advertising agency, or whatever you claim to be." He was clearly hesitant about admitting to the promotion.

She pushed on, undaunted. "Even when statistics show that almost forty percent of the rental properties in your town haven't been rented for more than sixty percent of this summer? Isn't that a problem for your vacation homeowners?"

"We do still have a lot of construction going on, so that's part of the problem."

"But the study I read didn't include rental properties that were being repaired and unable to be occupied."

The deputy mayor was silent for a while. Allie almost thought they had been disconnected until he said, "We already know what firm we want." He was decidedly unhappy about revealing the information. "So I'm afraid all the research you've done is for naught."

She had to think fast before he hung up. "Wouldn't you like a second opinion? Another option?"

"This isn't a medical problem where a second opinion is a good idea. We've already contacted a competent firm."

"They might be competent, but do they know as much about your town as I do?" An idea popped into her head. "Are they related to a self-sustaining artist who would have insight into what would bring more artists to your community?"

"Who would this artist be?" His skepticism was building.

"Charlotte Harrington is my…cousin." She wasn't sure she was related to Charlotte, but she definitely had access to her and her ideas.

"Charlotte Harrington?" he inquired, a touch

of interest in his tone. "The same artist who had shows in New York and Boston over the last year?"

"You know her work?"

If he recognized Charlotte's name, he was probably the impetus behind the artists' workhouse in Fairleigh that she'd read about. This was hopeful.

"Oh, yes. She's very good. Her pastels are extraordinary." He paused. "I'll tell you what. If you could bring Ms. Harrington into the campaign, we'd take a look at what you come up with."

"Absolutely!" Charlotte wouldn't have a problem with that. It would mean promotion for both the town and Charlotte. How could she not go along with it?

And Allie bet Jack hadn't even thought about using Charlotte in the campaign.

The deputy mayor gave her more specifics on what they wanted, as well as the fact that they needed the campaign rolled out before the Fourth of July.

"That's only a couple weeks from now." She'd expected they'd want a fall or winter campaign.

"Exactly. We know we're late on this, but we're hoping to boost not only our summer tourist population but the fall, as well."

She asked him some questions about what went on in the fall and winter in Fairleigh, getting creative ideas that she needed to start working on right away. They disconnected a few minutes later.

Satisfied with the outcome, she added a few

things to the notes she'd taken. She had a fairly good idea of what Jack and his firm could do from seeing his presentation last week. She had stiff competition. Her only advantage was that he didn't know he had a competitor.

What would he say if he knew what she'd done after seeing the partial text message on his phone? She couldn't dwell on it. That was the only way to survive in this business—seize every opportunity. Hadn't she learned talent only went so far? You needed to have an edge because there were always people out there who would go even farther to land accounts. Some even broke the law.

She knew that for a fact. She'd witnessed it not once but several times.

She wished she could be as upstanding as Jack wanted her to be, but she didn't have a large company to lean on anymore. She had to do whatever it took to survive.

CHARLOTTE HAD GOTTEN an early start in her art studio Monday morning and was surprised to get a call from Allie so early in the day. "That's a step forward," Charlotte said when Allie told her about talking to the CPA who took over the adoption lawyer's office. "Maybe one of the lawyer's kids will contact you soon."

"I hope so." Allie switched subjects. "Hey, how would you like to go on a road trip with me?"

"I'm pretty busy—"

"This would be work related."

Charlotte was skeptical. "Really? Explain."

Allie told her about talking to the deputy mayor of Fairleigh and how impressed he was that Allie knew Charlotte. "I told him we were cousins. I hope you don't mind."

Charlotte laughed. "Not at all. Since people think we're twins, we must be related somehow. I do wish you'd checked with me before you volunteered my services, though. I have a lot going on right now, especially with my art show coming up."

"You're right. I'm sorry. I thought you might enjoy the town and getting away for a day or two."

"I'm sure I will. Sounds like fun. I guess I can take some pictures and do some sketching."

"Perfect! I knew you'd be okay with it."

Not exactly, but Charlotte was willing to help Allie out, especially since she'd just lost the animal-food account.

"Oh! I almost forgot. The DNA test should arrive today or tomorrow," Charlotte said. "Maybe we can swab our cheeks and get the test mailed off before heading to Fairleigh."

"Sounds like a plan," Allie said. "Let me figure out the best time to go. It should be about two hours from your place. Do you have a preference as to what day?"

"As long as we can take care of the DNA test beforehand, so we can get that out of the way, it doesn't matter to me." Then she added, "But I'd like to have enough time there to get a few pictures and do a little sketching. Fairleigh has some great stone structures—hopefully they weren't all destroyed by the hurricane."

"Good idea. I can work on the campaign while you do your thing."

They ended their call. Charlotte had barely set the phone down when it rang again. Thinking Allie had something to add to their conversation, she was surprised to see a number on caller ID she didn't recognize. "Hello?"

"Is this Charlotte Harrington?" The woman on the other end sounded frail, not like a typical telemarketer.

"Yes, it is." Maybe it was a charity looking for money?

"This is Marie Hanover. You left me a message to call you?"

"Oh, yes!" Charlotte hadn't recognized the voice. Marie sounded so fragile since the last time she'd spoken to her mother's friend. "How are you?"

"Not so good, I'm afraid. I've been having dizzy spells. The doctors aren't sure why."

"I'm sorry to hear that," Charlotte told her.

Charlotte recalled Marie was about ten years older than her mother, which meant Marie must be in her early eighties.

"How are you doing, Charlotte?" Marie asked. "Still painting your pictures?"

Charlotte smiled. Over the years, so many people had belittled her artwork as just a hobby. She'd stopped worrying about it a long time ago, once she was able to support herself with her "little hobby."

"Yes, I have a show in a few weeks."

"How nice for you!"

Charlotte had to get to the reason she called Marie. "I need some information. I was wondering if you could tell me anything about my mother's finances back around the time she was adopting me."

"Her finances? What do you want to know?"

Charlotte sucked in a breath and related the story. "I was going through her old bank statements and discovered she suddenly had a large deposit. A *very* large deposit. Thirty thousand dollars. Then a few days later, she wrote a check to Cash for the same amount. I can't read the signature on the back of the check, so I don't know who cashed it. And this all took place right around the time of my birth."

Marie was quiet for quite a while. "That was a very long time ago. Maybe you should leave it in the past."

"I can't let it go. I need to find out about my adoption. That's where this all started." She told Marie about meeting Allie and how they were born on the same day, but in different states. "She's digging on her end, and I'm doing the same on mine. We already know her parents paid thirty thousand dollars to a lawyer for her, so it seems like my mother paid the same amount for me. Maybe even to the same lawyer. We need answers."

"But what will you gain by digging up the past? I doubt this money has anything to do with your adoption. A coincidence, I'm sure."

"Then what did she use it for? Did she buy something expensive?"

"Maybe she took out a loan and then lent it to someone," Marie suggested. "Who knows?"

Charlotte would bet her art supplies that Marie knew more than she was letting on. "Does the name Gerard Stone sound familiar? He was a lawyer that might have been involved in my adoption."

"Oh, dear." Marie's voice lowered to a near whisper. "I'm afraid I need to go lie down. I'm feeling a dizzy spell coming."

How convenient.

"If you think of anything else, please let me know."

But Marie had already disconnected.

Why was Charlotte getting the distinct impression that Marie knew more than she was telling?

JACK HAD LEFT early from work on Monday to visit his grandfather in the rehab center. Granddad still wasn't pleased about not being home, but at least he'd stopped blaming everyone around him.

He was happy to hear Empire won the animal-food account, though. He wasn't familiar with Allie's company, but he said of the third competitor, "DP is a second-rate organization." He went on to spout off about the fiasco concerning Allie's ex-boyfriend. "They actually thought using extortion to get accounts would work. Can you believe that?"

"I don't think anyone still at DP was involved in any of that," Jack said with authority, now that Allie had been forced to confide in him.

"Doesn't matter. They hired criminals in the first place. Should've known better."

Allie had sworn she didn't know a thing about her ex's extortion plan, but she had no trouble pushing the envelope when it came to business. Was there more she hadn't told him about her dealings with her ex?

Fortunately, Granddad calmed down as soon as Jack told him about the Fairleigh job, and Jack was able to leave while his grandfather was in a better mood.

Jack had brought casual clothes with him to work that morning, so he left the rehab center and went to his grandfather's house to change before picking Allie up for dinner. He no sooner unlocked the door when he got her text.

Harvey gone.

That might be the saddest text in the fewest amount of words that Jack had ever received. He answered her right away.

I'll be there in fifteen. Dress comfortably.

He quickly changed into plaid shorts, a collared sport shirt and boat shoes. He would suggest they go to a sports pub, figuring the energetic atmosphere was more what she needed, rather than a quiet restaurant where she might dwell on losing Harvey.

"Hey," he said when she answered her door a little while later. She didn't say anything in return, merely turned away, leaving the door open for him to enter. She was obviously in pain, and he would be hurting in a different way if he didn't stop focusing on how well her jeans fit over her firm butt. He nearly groaned aloud, reminding himself about his higher purpose for being here.

Why did he have to be so attracted to a woman who had vowed to avoid anything more than friendship with men? *Damn* all the men who came before him who'd caused her to be so afraid.

He entered her apartment and shut the door behind him. Harvey's empty crate sat where he and Allie had placed it last week, like a beacon to remind Allie the dog was gone. Possibly for good.

"I thought we could go to Kit's Pub over on Chestnut," he said. "Unless you'd like somewhere quieter. Kit's will be busy, what with the Red Sox game tonight."

"Kit's is fine." She'd gone into her bedroom. He could barely make out her words. "I'll be right there."

"No hurry." That was a lie, since Jack was having a difficult time holding himself back. He desperately wanted to take her mind off Harvey as well as fulfill their basic desires. He wanted to walk directly into her bedroom, throw her down on her bed and kiss her senseless until she realized her vow was ridiculous and she wanted him as much as he wanted her.

He held himself in check only because he knew he couldn't be the settling-down kind of man she needed him to be.

On the short drive to dinner, Jack tried his best to keep the conversation away from Harvey. Since work was off-limits and the weather was too general a subject, he asked, "Did you find the adoption lawyer yet?"

Allie nodded. "There's a CPA in his old office now, but she knew him. She verified the lawyer was the same as the one I found the obit for." She told him what she'd discovered last night. "She knew him because she and her husband used to rent another office in that shopping center at the same time the lawyer was there."

She told him about the lawyer's kids she'd found on Facebook, sounding stronger and more like herself as she went on. "The oldest daughter sent me a message today."

He glanced at her before backing into a parallel parking space on the street about a block from Kit's. "That's great. What did she say?"

"Unfortunately, she doesn't have her dad's files. When he died, his practice was sold to another lawyer. She gave me his name, but she didn't know if he still had files going back that far."

"What happens if he doesn't have your file? Is there somewhere else to look?"

"I don't know. The daughter, Caroline, did say there's a chance her brother might have her dad's personal files. They have a storage unit somewhere nearby, and there are things in it they haven't been through yet. I guess they're all busy with work and family." She shrugged and got out of the car. "You know how it is."

He got out, too. "We could offer to go through the storage unit if it comes to that."

They walked side-by-side on the uneven cement pavement. "I hope we won't have to go that far," she said.

They reached the front of Kit's Pub, and the noise level went up as soon as Jack opened the oversize wooden door. They were shown to a counter-height table in the corner, making it slightly easier to talk over the noise in the place. High on the walls were flat-screen TVs in different sizes. Below them hung sports paraphernalia and pictures of local teams of all ages that the pub supported.

As soon as they placed drink orders and their server departed, Allie leaned in and said, "Thank you."

"For what?"

"For this." She spread her arms. "For dinner, for taking my mind off Harvey. For all of it." She stopped, her lip quivering slightly. "This might not work out, you know."

"Dinner? Why wouldn't it work out?"

"No, not dinner. I'm talking about Harvey. The people checking him out tonight might decide he's not the dog for them."

"That's true," he said. "But you *do* know he'll be adopted by someone eventually, right?"

She shrugged, her focus on her fingernails.

"I mean it, Allie. It's going to happen. You need to be prepared."

"Okay."

"Hey." He reached across the small table and lifted her chin with his index finger until her eyes met his. "What is it?"

"I don't know," she said almost too quietly to hear. "I guess I didn't expect to get so attached to him."

"Kind of backfired on you, didn't it?" He was being flippant on purpose.

She traced her finger along a ridge in the table. "I've never had any living thing be so dependent on me before, and at first it was frightening."

"And then?"

She lifted her gaze to look at him. "And then I realized how easy it was to take in a living thing that's been abandoned and love it unconditionally. It made me realize how much my parents really do love me. It's not like I didn't know that before, but after having Harvey—" She stopped suddenly and looked down. As if she couldn't get out the words.

"You finally believe you're worth loving?"

She gave a slight nod. "I know that sounds crazy. I guess a part of me took their love for granted, not really believing they could truly love me because I wasn't their biological child."

He reached out for her hand. "I'm glad Harvey showed you differently."

"Me, too." She smiled at him, and he smiled back.

"What are you getting to eat?" He opened her menu and set it in front of her. "My favorites are their jalapeño burger and the Buffalo chicken sandwich."

"I think I'll just have a garden salad." She lacked any enthusiasm even after her epiphany.

He needed to figure out some way to liven her up, because after tonight, he'd be spending a lot of overtime working on the Fairleigh project.

ALLIE TRULY WASN'T HUNGRY. She'd become attached to a dog in a mere week. A dog, for heaven's sake.

A dog who'd chewed her shoes when they first met.

A dog who also worshipped her with his big, brown eyes when she was least expecting it.

He didn't care if she was successful with her advertising agency. He didn't expect her to find a husband and make a family. As long as she fed him on time, he was happy.

Just like Allie, he'd been given away at birth. They'd both been lucky to be loved by caring people.

She didn't want to give Harvey to anyone else, but she didn't know how to stop the process.

She swallowed the lump in her throat and peered across the table at Jack, who was trying his best to make her feel better. He really was a sweet guy.

"Maybe I'll have the chicken Caesar wrap instead of a salad." She didn't know if she could force it down, but seeing his eyes light up at her words was worth it. She couldn't help but feel good about his concern.

They enjoyed a pleasant dinner, keeping track of the Red Sox game and commenting on it as they ate. Allie had relaxed enough to force down a few bites, and before she knew it, her wrap was nearly gone.

"I guess I was hungrier than I thought." She pulled out her wallet.

"Put that away," he instructed her. "I asked you to dinner, and I'll pay the check."

"But you only did it to cheer me up." She pulled out a charge card that was close to being maxed out. Letting him pay would be the smart thing to do.

"That's not the only reason." He was looking at her, his meaning clear.

"I—"

"Don't get the wrong idea. I'm not a 'pay for dinner and expect sex' kind of guy." He waggled his eyebrows. "Although…"

She grinned. "I know—you wouldn't turn it down."

He winked at her. "So you *have* thought about it."

More than she would ever let on to him. "Maybe."

Her face heated as he leaned closer across the table and lowered his voice. "Want to share those thoughts?"

She balled a paper napkin and tossed it at him. He laughed and so did she. "Come on, I need to get home." She rose from her seat and slung her purse over one shoulder.

"At your service," he said as he rose, too.

She began walking toward the exit and heard him say, "The sooner we get to your place, the sooner you can tell me about those thoughts of yours."

She turned her head in his direction and stuck out her tongue.

He chuckled and said, "That's a good start."

CHARLOTTE HAD LONG lost the light in her studio, so she'd stopped working on the Newport doorway she'd sketched and taken a box of her mother's files downstairs to spread out on the kitchen table.

The box contained tax returns and every pay stub her mother had ever received.

"Wow. Mom never threw out *anything*."

Charlotte went directly to the envelope with *1986*

on it in her mother's handwriting, hoping to discover that she'd been given a bonus of thirty thousand dollars that year.

No luck. Every pay stub was exactly the same, at least until she came to October, when it appeared her mother had been given a salary increase of about fifty dollars in take-home pay each pay period. At that point, she still wasn't even making thirty thousand dollars a year.

Where the heck did that money come from?

Before searching another box, Charlotte looked at the pay stubs from the year before, in case her mother had received the money then and put it in a savings account to draw interest before moving it into her checking account.

Again, no indication that her mother ever received a bonus of any kind.

Charlotte returned all the records to the box and hauled it upstairs. She had several other boxes from the attic that she'd put in her studio. The first one held the rest of her mother's tax returns. Charlotte didn't think they'd be any help, so she moved the box aside.

The next one had savings account information. "Voilà!" She didn't bother taking it downstairs, merely searched the folders until she came to the one marked "1986."

She pulled it out and went month by month, perusing savings account statements. Her mother had regularly deposited one hundred dollars in the account every month during that year. The beginning balance on January 1 was a little over eleven thousand dollars. The ending balance on December 31 was less than twelve and a half thousand with accrued interest.

Charlotte checked the year before, and every month of that year her mother had deposited ninety dollars. All of the earlier years' statements showed that as her salary went up, so did her regular deposits into her account.

But there was nothing that indicated she ever had anything close to thirty thousand dollars in the bank.

Charlotte dug through the entire box, hoping to find another savings account or some other clue to the money.

There was nothing.

She sat on the floor of her studio, her legs crossed. She was at a loss. The money had obviously arrived in a lump sum, either as a gift or a loan. Maybe she'd sold something.

Charlotte still couldn't believe it, even though Allie had practically confirmed it. Had her mother really paid cold hard cash to that lawyer in order to adopt Charlotte?

CHAPTER FOURTEEN

JACK AND ALLIE pulled up to her apartment building just as her phone rang.

She dug it out of her purse. "Hello?"

He watched as Allie listened to the person on the other end and her face softened into a smile that grew into a huge grin. "Thanks, Joan, I'll be there to pick him up in a few minutes." She disconnected and, still grinning, turned to Jack. "I need to pick up Harvey. Turns out the couple's dog and Harvey didn't get along, so they're not taking him. Isn't that great?"

"Absolutely." He smiled and shared an idea that had been nagging at him. "Have you thought about adopting him yourself?" He didn't want to see her heartbroken when someone else came along to adopt Harvey, which inevitably would happen.

"Oh, I would love to, but I couldn't. My lifestyle and a dog wouldn't mix."

He hesitated to point out that she and Harvey had been doing quite well for the past week.

She reached for the door handle. "I need to get going. Joan asked if I could pick him up at the Rescue League, otherwise he's there for the night."

"Hold on." He grabbed her arm. "I'll drive you over there."

"But we don't have his crate. He'll be all over your car."

"For a few miles across town, you can hold him."

She appeared to think about it and then said, "If you're sure."

"Positive." He pulled out into the street, and she gave him directions to the Rescue League.

A short while later, they were again parked in front of Allie's apartment building. This time, Harvey was on her lap, full of energy. As much as he really wanted to at least kiss her good-night, Jack doubted Harvey would settle down long enough for that to happen.

He couldn't have been more surprised when Allie said, "Want to come up and celebrate Harvey's homecoming?"

His eyes widened. She had to know what she was doing, didn't she? Or maybe she really did just want to celebrate Harvey's return.

Even though his common sense said, "Go home," his body said, "Why not?"—and that's what came out of his mouth.

Allie was practically bouncing as much as Harvey as she and the dog got on the elevator in front of him. She was as excited as he'd ever seen her, and Jack couldn't help but enjoy the two of them.

When they entered Allie's dark apartment and she turned on lights, she asked, "What would you like to drink? I don't think I have champagne, but we can toast Harvey's return anyway." She named the drink choices while closing her bedroom door and moving barriers so Harvey could be out of his crate, though not out of sight, causing trouble. But he must have been tired after his evening of socializing because he immediately went into his crate on his own, curled up on his blanket and closed his eyes.

"What kind of beer do you have?" Jack asked.

She named a local microbrewery.

"Sounds good." When she asked if he wanted a glass, he said, "Bottle's fine. What are you having?"

In reply, she returned from the kitchen with two beers in hand, giving him one. They clinked bottles and grinned at each other. "To Harvey," she said.

"To Harvey," he repeated. They both took long drinks of the flavorful brew, their gazes never wavering.

Then Allie put her bottle down on the coffee table and reached out to take his. She set it down next to hers and held out her hand.

Not knowing exactly where she was going with this, he took her hand and allowed her to lead him to the couch. She put both hands on his shoulders and gave him a nudge. "Sit."

He did as instructed. Then she removed her shoes, and the next thing he knew, she was straddling his lap, facing him. Their mouths met in a rush. Their passion ignited instantaneously from spark to wildfire.

ALLIE COULDN'T GET enough of Jack. She'd held herself back from giving over to her overwhelming attraction to him for way too long. But after he was
so sweet to her tonight, she knew it was the right
thing to do. She could trust this man. This man
who knew how she was hurting at the possible loss
of Harvey. This man who had been kind to her
parents, was a good friend to Charlotte. This man
wouldn't hurt her. She was sure of it.

So sure that she was prepared to give herself to
him, body and soul.

His mouth was sexy, tasting like the beer they'd
just drunk, and oh, so very hot.

She adjusted her pelvis to feel his hard erection
against her most sensitive spot. He groaned, grabbing her hips when she moved against him.

"Are you sure you know what you're doing?"
His words came between kisses in a gasp. "You're
treading on dangerous ground."

She chuckled, deep in her throat. "Trust me. I'm
completely aware of my actions." She moved her
hips again to punctuate her statement.

She was as clearheaded as ever. She'd already
been emotional about Harvey's departure, and was
glad now that she'd stayed away from alcohol at
dinner so she could be sure this was a rational decision.

Her hands roamed his upper body, loving the
play of his muscles in his arms and chest. His
amazing abdominal muscles twitched when her

hand lightly fluttered over them. She flattened her hand on his stomach, reaching beneath his waistband with her thumb to touch and tease the skin there.

He groaned and grabbed at her mischievous hand, holding it hostage behind her back. Meanwhile, his other hand traveled her body, stopping to concentrate on certain areas—the nape of her neck, the inside of her elbow, the bare skin above her breasts she'd never known was so sensitive—as if memorizing them.

She wore a deep blue tank top under a sheer blue top, and she sucked in a breath when his hand slipped under and untucked her tank top from her jeans. She nearly cried out in ecstasy when he touched her bare back with his hands—hands so hot they nearly burned her.

Jack released her hand so he could use both of his to caress her entire back from waist to shoulders. He moaned. "No bra?"

She giggled. "Built into the tank top."

He moaned louder, and she wiggled her pelvis, loving the feeling of power as well as the heat he intensified in her core.

Allie raised her hands over her head as Jack stripped off her sheer top, leaving her in the tank. He tossed the blouse aside and lowered one strap of the tank, lightly nipping at her shoulder.

She giggled.

Then he focused on her breasts, using his thumb

and forefinger to tease her nipples through the light support of the tank top's cups.

Their gazes met and held.

"Are you absolutely sure about this?" His words came out raspy, about as sexy as a voice could get. "You know I can't make you promises beyond tonight."

This was her chance to stop things before they went too far. He was giving her an out.

Which made her want him even more.

In answer, she crossed her arms and stripped her tank top over her head, tossing it in the same direction as her blouse.

Taking that as the yes it was intended to be, Jack immediately grasped her breasts in both hands. His thumbs teased her nipples, and her core went from hot to molten. She nearly burst into flames when his mouth replaced his hands on her breasts.

Before she realized it, he had her on her back on the couch, and he was on top of her. The weight of his body on hers was a heady sensation she'd only dreamed about, both asleep and awake. She wrapped her legs around his waist, anxious to feel his erection again.

She ran her hands over his back. More than anything, she wanted to be skin to skin. She tugged at his shirt and he cooperated by removing it. Her hands roamed his bare chest, sliding down his abdomen to his belt.

He unbuckled it with less-than-steady hands and

stripped it off quickly. That gave her access to the top button of his plaid shorts as well as his zipper and the pleasure beyond that she could only imagine.

Before opening his pants, she teased him with her thumb, running it slowly up and down the length of his solid shaft until she could see in his face that he couldn't take much more.

He moved out of her reach and took off her jeans, leaving her in scanty blue underpants. She watched in wonder as his gaze took in all of her while his hands caressed. His fingers inched up her inner thigh, teasing her as he slowly moved the thin cloth to the side to access her most intimate and sensitive region, which pulsated as if screaming for release.

All thought left her as his mouth joined his fingers in giving her the pleasure she craved.

Then, with her legs wrapped around his waist, he lifted her from the couch. On the way to her bedroom, she heard him shut and latch Harvey's crate door.

JACK WAS STARTLED awake by a whimper coming from Harvey. The dog probably needed to go out, but Jack didn't want to move. He was too comfortable in Allie's bed, her naked body curled into his.

He smiled at the memory of how she'd responded to his every touch, every movement. He ignored the guilt that nagged at him, knowing he couldn't give Allie more than a pleasurable night here and there.

Harvey whimpered again, and Allie moved.

"Stay here," he whispered close to her ear. "I'll take care of him."

"Mmm."

He was tempted to wake her and go for round three, but Harvey was insistent.

The bedside clock said almost three-thirty. He pulled on his underwear and shorts, thinking he should probably leave after taking Harvey out. Tomorrow was a workday, and he didn't want to overstay his welcome. Besides, sleeping together was one thing. Spending the entire night and waking up to face each other the next morning was quite another.

The last thing he needed was to have Allie misinterpret him spending the night to mean he wanted a committed relationship.

He donned the rest of his clothes and shoes in the living room. "Come on, boy," he said quietly while he fastened Harvey's leash. They hurried down to the street in the elevator and were back in Allie's apartment in minutes. He got Harvey settled in his crate and made sure the latch was secure.

Jack should have walked out of Allie's apartment and gone home, but he couldn't help himself. He went back into her bedroom. He'd intended merely to watch her sleep for a minute, but he couldn't resist leaning down to kiss her lightly on the forehead. He straightened and turned to leave.

"Jack?"

He spun around.

Allie hadn't moved. "Are you leaving?" Her voice was low, sexy from sleep.

"I thought it was for the best." He scrambled for an excuse. "We both have work tomorrow."

"Right."

He returned to the bed and sat down. She curled into his body and rubbed his back. He automatically put a hand on her hip, which was only covered by the sheet.

"You don't have to go," she said. "Unless you really need to."

He was sorely tempted to stay, especially when the sheet slipped to reveal her breasts. His fingers itched to stroke her flesh, now that he'd begun to learn what would make her scream and what would make her beg for more.

"I'd need to get up very early if I stayed," he said. "I don't have clothes for work, so I'd drive all the way to Newport and back."

Unexpectedly her hand touched his knee, and he flinched. Her fingers inched their way up his inner thigh.

"Whatever." Her words were nonchalant, teasing, daring him to go without experiencing her passion one more time. "Leave now. Leave later. Doesn't matter to me."

He stood, already missing her touch. In record time, he stripped off first his clothes and then the sheet that barely covered a beautifully naked Allie.

He was on top of her and inside her before he could remember why it *wasn't* a good idea for him to spend the night.

CHARLOTTE WAS UP early the next morning. She'd already showered and eaten breakfast and was on her last sip of coffee by the time Jack pulled up in front of his house.

"Hey, there." She waved from her porch as he was getting out of his car. "You were out early this morning."

His face turned bright red.

Charlotte's jaw literally dropped when understanding dawned. She quickly covered her open mouth with her hand. "Never mind!" She had clearly embarrassed him by catching him doing the walk of shame.

He laughed it off and walked across the street to her porch.

"I'm so sorry! I wasn't prying. I was making conversation." She hoped he'd been with Allie, but she wouldn't ask him—she'd carefully pry it out of Allie. Unless he'd been with someone else? Charlotte really should stay out of it just in case.

"Don't worry about it," Jack said. He checked his watch and looked up at Charlotte. "Have any more of that coffee?"

"Absolutely. Come on in."

Jack followed Charlotte straight to her kitchen.

She poured him a cup, and he asked, "What're you doing up so early? Couldn't sleep?"

"No, I'm stressed," she told him. "Between my art show in three weeks that I'm not prepared for and the mystery of my mother's money, the appearance of my exact double and so many questions about my adoption—" She took a breath. "You can understand why I'm not sleeping well."

"Allie mentioned you sent for a DNA test. Has it arrived?"

"I was hoping for yesterday, but it will probably come today."

"How long will it take to get the results?"

She shrugged. "I don't know for sure. The lab said it depends on how busy they are." She filled him in on her conversation with Marie. "I've got the distinct feeling there's more that she's not telling me."

"I agree. Does she have any kids or someone else who might know what she's hiding?"

"That's a thought. I think she has a daughter several years older than I am. But I don't know how to contact her. I haven't seen her in at least a decade. She wasn't at my mother's funeral, which is the last time I saw Marie."

They talked for a few more minutes before Jack pointed to her laptop on the kitchen counter. "Mind if I check my email quickly? My laptop's in my car, and I need to see if I've gotten an update on an account."

"Sure. I'll be right back. I need to run upstairs for the pictures I'm having framed. If I don't take them today, I might end up having to do it myself. And I don't have time for that."

"Good luck with that! And thanks for the coffee." He drained the last of it and set the cup in the sink. "I'll let myself out if you're not back before I finish."

"Sounds good. Talk to you later."

JACK'S JAW DROPPED when he opened Charlotte's laptop.

Was it a simple, but weird, coincidence that the website for Fairleigh, Connecticut, was open and glaring at him? The same town that wanted to hire Empire to help boost their tourism?

He didn't bother checking his email and instead closed the computer.

Did Allie somehow know about the town's needs, too? Was that why she'd closed her laptop so quickly when he came to pick her up last night? Had she been looking at the town's website?

He'd never talked about the town or the account with Allie, unless he'd said something in his sleep, which he seriously doubted. What other connection could there be to explain why Charlotte was checking out that specific town?

He left Charlotte's and grabbed his things from his car. He unlocked his front door, entered and dropped everything right inside. Then he pulled out his cell phone and called his office.

"Stan, it's Jack." He paced the length of his living room. "Who else knows about this Fairleigh deal?"

"No one that I know of." Stan sounded bewildered at the question. "You're the only one I've told. No one else in the office even knows yet, unless you said something."

"I haven't discussed it with anyone." Except his grandfather. But Granddad wouldn't have talked about it.

"Okay, thanks, Stan. I might just be paranoid, but let me know if you find out that the news actually did leak. I'm working from home this morning. Call my cell if you hear anything."

They disconnected, and Jack headed upstairs for a shower.

A little while later, he was eating breakfast and finally reading his email when he decided to check out the Fairleigh website himself. Might someone in the mayor's office have posted something there about wanting a new advertising campaign? According to Stan's info, they didn't want to waste the time it would take to open it up for competition. That's why it was so hush-hush. The town council had only just voted on moving forward with the plan at their meeting Friday evening.

The first thing he saw on the town's website was an ad for an annual art show. Maybe that was why

Charlotte had been looking at the website. Had he gone ballistic for no reason?

He exhaled and his blood pressure returned to normal. What a relief.

When had he become so suspicious? Was it because he knew how Allie chose to conduct business?

Deciding to head into the office now that the mystery was solved, he ran into Charlotte packing up her own car. "Need any help with those?" he asked.

"I'm good." She struggled to hold on to several tubes that he assumed held her work.

He crossed the street to talk to her. "Hey, I couldn't help noticing when I opened your laptop that you had a website open for Fairleigh, Connecticut. Do you have anything to do with the art stuff that goes on there?"

"Funny you should ask. I've never been there, but I'm going to check it out. Probably one day this week."

"Why the sudden interest? Don't you have a show to prepare for?"

"That's what I said to Allie when she asked me to go with her. But she convinced me that I could get some work in while we're there."

Jack chose his words carefully. "Allie told you about the advertising campaign Fairleigh's looking at doing?"

"Oh, so you know about it?" Charlotte obviously hadn't been told not to say anything.

"I do."

Did Allie already know he was working on the campaign, too? He'd been under the impression from Stan that there was no competition for this account. When had that changed?

"I should get to work," he said abruptly. He had to figure out what was going on if he wanted to get his grandfather's firm back on its financial feet. The Naturally Healthy Animal Food income would last only so long.

ALLIE AWOKE TO the sound of her phone alarm going off. She hit the snooze button and glanced around the room. She was alone.

The last thing she remembered, although vaguely, was Jack kissing her goodbye. He'd done such a good job of satisfying her after she'd lured him back to bed that she'd passed out immediately afterward.

She stretched out in the bed, her pleasantly strained muscles reminding her of the night's activities. The smile on her face felt permanent.

When the alarm sounded again a few minutes later, she turned it off and dragged herself out of bed and into the shower.

She fed and walked Harvey before they headed to her office, her smile still in place as she passed the receptionist's desk.

"Good morning," she said pleasantly to Penny,

who gave her a surprised look. She understood Penny's confusion—Allie wasn't usually a morning person.

Allie couldn't help that she was in such a good mood.

She and Harvey went into her office, and she shut the door. She checked her schedule to see what day would be best for a trip to Fairleigh. Allie still couldn't believe the lucky happenstance that Fairleigh was home to an artists' community and Allie knew a pretty famous artist.

"Hey, it's me," Allie said when Charlotte answered her phone. "How does Thursday sound for Fairleigh?"

"Works for me." Charlotte hesitated a few seconds, then asked in a singsong tone, "So how was your evening?"

"Fine…" She drew out the word, wondering what Charlotte was hinting at. Could Jack have told her about spending the night together? He didn't seem like a kiss-and-tell kind of guy.

"Just fine?" Charlotte prompted.

She filled Charlotte in on dinner with Jack and getting Harvey back.

Charlotte's response was, "Oh."

"Oh, what?"

"Well, I happened to see Jack early this morning—"

"You got me!" In all honesty, Allie was bursting to tell someone. "He spent the night. Are you happy now?"

Charlotte chuckled. "Extremely. And Jack looked pretty happy, too."

Allie grinned. "Really?"

Charlotte laughed. "Yeah, really."

After a few more minutes of chatting, they set a time for Thursday and made a plan for what they wanted to accomplish before disconnecting.

Not ten minutes later, her cell phone rang. She didn't recognize the number. "Hello?"

"It's Jack." His tone was businesslike.

"Hey, how are you?"

"I need to talk to you. Can we meet somewhere? My office, your office?"

"You sound serious. Is everything okay?"

"Not really. Why don't I come to your office? I can be there in ten. Is that okay?"

"Sure." Allie's good mood deflated, and she felt her smile fade. "I'll see you then."

She didn't know what to think. Everything had been fine when he left early this morning. How could things have gone so wrong so quickly? Was he having second thoughts about her?

It wasn't like she had asked him for a commitment. They'd had sex, for goodness' sake. He hadn't given her a chance to be clingy, even if she happened to be that kind of woman.

Which she wasn't.

She touched up her lipstick and put away anything that had to do with Fairleigh.

Her phone rang. Penny was calling to say she had a visitor.

"Send him back." Allie rubbed her sweaty hands together and chastised herself for being worried about nothing. She met him halfway down the hall and saw the stern look on his face.

She gestured to her office, her arm shaking. "Come in." She pulled a straight-backed chair closer to her desk chair, and they both sat. "What's going on?"

He didn't speak right away. His chest moved as he breathed in and out several times. Then he stood up and paced the length of her office, which wasn't very big.

"Would you spit it out already?" she pleaded.

He stopped pacing and faced her. "I know we made a pact about not letting business get in the way, but I need you to drop any work you're doing for the town of Fairleigh."

"I can't do that," she said. How had he found out that she knew about it? "I need that account."

"So do I."

"And you think your company should be saved while mine goes bankrupt?"

"Allie."

She couldn't look at him. How could he ask her to do such a thing?

He sat down, his voice gentler. "How did you

find out about it, Allie? Empire was asked exclusively to put together a marketing plan."

She faced him. "I was very persuasive, and they're willing to listen to my ideas."

"But how did you find out about it in the first place?" he repeated.

Allie didn't want to admit what she'd done. "Why does it matter? I found out and seized the opportunity. I did what was necessary to be given a chance at the account."

"So that's how it is with you."

"What do you mean?"

"You don't care who gets hurt as long as you win."

Allie stared at him. "That's not true."

"What about Harvey? You didn't care if he was shuffled around. You just used him for your own gain." He paused. "Is that what you did with me? Used me to get the Fairleigh information?"

"If I hadn't fostered Harvey, then someone else would have. And I didn't purposely use you to get information."

"Purposely? So you admit you used me?"

"No!" Her raised voice could probably be heard throughout the floor of the office building.

"I don't get it," he said tightly. "No one but Stan and I knew about Fairleigh outside of the town's council. Stan's text message said—" He glared at Allie. "That's it. You saw his text message, didn't you?"

She stared back at him, not giving him any more ammunition.

"You did. That's how you knew. And you never even mentioned it on the ride home from your parents'. What did you do, figure out my password?" He pulled his cell phone from his pocket and held it out to her. "Here. Is there anything else you'd like to know? Feel free to check all my text messages and emails."

Allie swallowed, hating that he was so angry at her, but she was just as angry. Business was business. She did what she had to in order to survive. "I didn't break into your phone, and I don't care what your password is."

He looked at her as if he was trying to put all the pieces together. "Oh, I get it. You just saw the beginning of the message and took it from there?"

"Ding, ding, ding! See, I did nothing wrong."

"How can you say that?" He ran both hands through his hair. "You read a private message."

"If it was so private, then you shouldn't have left your phone sitting on the kitchen counter."

"So it's my fault that you stole the information?"

"I didn't steal anything. It was in plain sight."

"What about your ex's extortion plan? Are you sure you didn't know about that? Maybe you even suggested it?"

Allie gritted her teeth. "Are you calling me a liar? Of course I didn't know about it. Just because

I'm not all by the book like you, doesn't mean I'd do something intentionally illegal."

Her anger boiled over. Not only at him, but at herself. She knew she shouldn't have trusted him. She opened her office door, hoping he'd take the hint to leave.

He did.

CHAPTER FIFTEEN

ALLIE STARED AT her closed office door, unable to move. Jack had a lot of nerve.

She mumbled to her empty office, "How dare he think he can waltz in here and call me a liar?"

She went back to her desk, pulling open her bottom drawer to retrieve her file on Fairleigh. She slammed it on top of her desk, even more determined to create an ad campaign that would make Jack's look like a second grader's attempt.

Allie opened the file and made an instantaneous decision when she saw the deputy mayor's name. She quickly dialed Charlotte's number.

When Charlotte answered, Allie said, "I changed my mind. Are you free to go to Fairleigh today instead of Thursday?"

"Today? Let me think a minute. I'm just leaving the framing studio." The sound of cars and people could be heard. "I think today is good. Are we spending the night since we'll be getting a later start?"

Allie hadn't thought of that. It would be well after lunchtime when they arrived. She needed this account, and being in the town would give her an edge over Jack.

"We could play it by ear," Allie said. "Pack

an overnight bag, and if we decide to stay, we'll be prepared."

"Okay. What time will you get here?"

Allie looked at the clock on her computer. "I can probably be at your place by eleven-thirty, and we can be in Fairleigh a little after two. I'd like to eat lunch when we get there. Check out a local place and maybe talk to some people to find out what they like about the town." Pursuing clients had been so much easier when she had a team of dedicated employees to take on different tasks—now she had to do everything herself.

"Sounds good," Charlotte said. "I'll be ready."

They disconnected and Allie packed up her things. "Now what're we gonna do with you?" she asked Harvey. The trip might get complicated if she had him along. Restaurants weren't keen on dogs in their establishments unless they were service animals. Same went with a lot of motels if she and Charlotte decided to spend the night.

She went down the hallway to Penny's desk. "I know it's last minute, but do you know of a kennel who would keep Harvey overnight? I need to go out of town on business."

Penny perked up. "Well, actually I'd love to take him. He's the sweetest thing."

That had been way too easy. "Are you sure?"

"Yes, I really want to do it. We've always had dogs, and I'm sure my Jazz will get along with Harvey. She's never met another dog she doesn't like."

"If you're positive it's not an imposition." What was she doing, trying to talk Penny out of it? "Can I leave him here and stop by with his food and toys on my way out of town?"

"Perfect."

Allie collected her purse and brief case, all the while assuring Harvey that Penny would take good care of him. Then she drove to her apartment, packed for the night and drove back to her office to drop off Harvey's things for Penny.

She made it to Charlotte's a few minutes earlier than predicted, glad to see Jack's car wasn't at his house. The last thing she needed was to run into him again. Especially so soon.

For a mere second, she felt the pain of his distrust. She'd convinced herself that he was different from the other men she'd known. How wrong she'd been yet again. She shoved the thoughts away, refusing to dwell on Jack, whether the scenario involved business or anything more personal and intimate.

"Hey!" Charlotte waved from her porch when Allie pulled up in front of her house. "Come on in." She stopped and looked at Allie carefully. "Are you okay?"

Allie shrugged. "I'll be fine."

They were barely inside Charlotte's house when she asked, "Want to talk about it?"

Allie didn't, but she found herself saying, "Jack."

Charlotte frowned. "Lover's spat?"

"More than that. He thinks I'm a liar."

"A liar? It's not about that Fairleigh thing, is it? He saw the website open on my laptop this morning. He asked me about it, and I thought he already knew that you were after it, too. He did seem a little odd, though."

"That explains why he came to my office."

"He did?"

"He wanted to know how I found out about the account, and then he went on to tell me I'm deceitful and a liar."

"Those are strong words," Charlotte said. "But why would he say such things? Did you tell him how you knew about the account?"

Allie shook her head. "I couldn't tell him I saw a text message on his phone, but he eventually guessed it anyway."

"You looked at his phone?" Charlotte's eyebrows shot up. "But isn't that like cheating? Getting the information that way?"

Allie shook her head. "No way. I've told you this business can be like that. You do what needs to be done to get the job, and then you get the job done well."

"I still don't see how that's ethical, reading someone else's text message."

"It's no big deal. He left it out at my parents'. It was right there on the counter. He got a text message and I thought it might be about the animal-food account, so I looked at it. There was only a partial message, but it mentioned Fairleigh. I didn't break into his phone to read it or anything. Maybe he should've been more careful about leaving his phone unattended."

"I'm not sure I agree with your logic, Allie. Why can't you rely on your talent instead of being deceitful?"

"You sound like Jack."

"I'm just trying to point out that you're very talented—you don't need to play these games to get ahead, and you might even get farther by being more honest."

"You can say that because you have real talent. But I need to use my other skills to survive. Anyway, can we not talk about this anymore? I don't want to get into an argument. One a day is enough." She pointed to Charlotte's overnight bag. "Are you ready to go?"

"I am. Oh, I got the DNA test in the mail right after you called."

Exactly what Allie needed to put her in a better mood.

"I already wrote a check and filled out the form that goes with it," Charlotte said as if she were ready to burst. They swabbed their cheeks and followed the instructions carefully.

"Where's the nearest post office?" Allie asked as they loaded into her car.

Charlotte directed her, and Allie pulled to the

curb in front. She waited in the car while Charlotte jumped out to mail off their tests.

"All done. I'm so excited," Charlotte said breathlessly.

"Me, too," Allie agreed, and they hit the road.

A few minutes later, Charlotte broke their silence. "So how did you manage to get the people in Fairleigh to give you a chance to woo them with your brilliance?"

Allie smiled. "With a lot of research *and* using your name like a secret password."

From the corner of her eye, Allie saw the pleased smile on Charlotte's face. She had every right to be happy that she was so well-known for her talent.

They drove in silence for a while until Charlotte said, "I'm really disappointed. I can't find anything about my adoption in my mother's files. She saved every single thing, but nothing about that." She turned her body slightly toward Allie. "It's so great that your mother gave you the information she had about your adoption."

"I know," Allie said. "Having the lawyer's name was a good start, but having Felicia Monroe confirm that the obit I found was his helped me find his family members. I just wish his kids knew for sure where his old files were."

"Felicia Monroe?" Charlotte cocked her head. "That name is so familiar. That's the CPA who's in the lawyer's office now?"

"Yes."

Charlotte suddenly straightened in her seat. "That's it! Monroe and Monroe. I've seen the names on my mother's pay stubs from around when I was born. Henry and Felicia Monroe. But shortly after my birth, she went to work for another firm."

Allie's heart rate doubled. "So you're saying she was working in the same shopping center as my adoption lawyer at the time of our births?"

"How could that be right? Didn't you say this Felicia Monroe was now in the same office as the lawyer? Then how could they both have been in the same office at the same time?"

"Because Felicia told me that she and her late husband used to have their business in a different office in the shopping center."

"That means they definitely could have all been there at the same time. This is great! Felicia would probably remember my mother from when she worked for them."

"You should give her a call," Allie suggested. "I'll find the number for you when we get to Fairleigh."

"I'm shaking with excitement." Charlotte held out her hand as proof. "Maybe she can fill in some of the missing pieces of our puzzle."

JACK CALLED HIS ASSISTANT, Emma, from home to tell her what needed to be done in his absence. Then he added, "Get me a reservation for a hotel in Fairleigh, Connecticut, for tonight. You can text me the details."

He'd arranged a face-to-face meeting with the deputy mayor, who seemed to be in charge of this campaign. He hoped Allie didn't beat him to it. "I'm heading down there now and won't be back in the office until at least Thursday morning," he told Emma. "You can reach me on my cell."

Jack packed an overnight bag and locked up his house. He was in his car, ready to go, when Emma called him back.

"I didn't text because I'm having trouble finding you a room in Fairleigh."

"Really?" How could they not have rooms? The whole reason for the ad campaign was to increase tourism. "There's *nothing* available?"

"Actually, there's one room available," she said. "It's in a bed-and-breakfast. I wasn't sure you wanted me to book a room that wasn't in a hotel."

"That's all you could find?"

"I started looking on the internet, but when everything was sold out, I started calling every hotel and bed-and-breakfast in town. Seems there's a big craft show there this week. There's a room available only because someone canceled."

"Book it. Do it quick before we lose it," Jack told her. He really wanted to stay in Fairleigh, not a few towns away. "Thanks for finding it."

By one-thirty, he was driving past the sign proclaiming Welcome to the Historic Town of Fairleigh, Connecticut. Below it, the slogan read Something for Everyone.

And the creative juices were already flowing.

Right away, he could see that wasn't specific enough. "Something" could mean anything from checkers tournaments to marathons to pie-eating contests. His job was to find out what those some-things were and play them up.

He went directly to the address of the B and B where Emma had him booked. Even though it was before check-in time, he thought he'd see if he could get in anyway.

"Your room is ready for you," the innkeeper told him. She was a woman in her thirties with her hair in a bun and a no-nonsense attitude. "Do you need more than one key?"

"One will be fine." Unlike last night, he would definitely be alone tonight.

She showed him to his room on the second floor and left him alone. He tossed his overnight bag to the side and put his laptop case next to the antique oak desk. The room was on the front corner of the Victorian-style house, and it had large windows looking out in two directions. He opened a window and smelled the ocean immediately as the water was about two blocks away.

He'd driven past a brand-new pier on his way, obviously built since the hurricane. There had been quaint shops and lots of people walking around, maybe because of the craft show Emma had told him about. A few blocks down to the right, he noticed the road had been barricaded for two blocks, and tents were set up. The craft show was obviously a big deal.

He went back downstairs and found the innkeeper. "Can you give me a recommendation for lunch?"

He listened to several choices and decided the diner in the center of town would give him the most contact with people, so he ran back upstairs, washed up and got dressed like a tourist. In khaki shorts and a T-shirt, he headed to the diner.

As soon as he opened the diner's door, he saw her. His heart pounded in his chest. He should have known Allie would come here as soon as possible. He hadn't counted on her beating him here, though.

She faced away from him in the booth where she and Charlotte were sitting. Before he could back out the door undetected, Charlotte saw him and waved. Her welcoming smile told him Allie hadn't confided in her about what had happened that morning. Either that or she didn't care.

"Look, it's Jack!" she said to Allie, loud enough for him to hear since it wasn't a very big restaurant and they were in the second booth from the door.

Allie didn't turn around.

He waved to Charlotte, hoping the hostess would come forward quickly to seat him far away from the women.

"Come join us," Charlotte said, to which Allie said, "Shh!"

He took the few steps to their table. "I don't want to intrude."

Allie didn't look at him.

"You're not intruding, is he, Allie?"

Allie didn't reply, but then he could clearly read the answer on her face.

Charlotte looked from Allie to Jack to Allie again. She slid over in her seat to make room for Jack. "Sit down," she ordered, which was very unlike Charlotte. "I know you're both after the same client, but you need to work out your other issues. I want to be friends with both of you, but I can't play referee."

He sat down, unwilling to make a scene in the restaurant.

Charlotte folded her hands on the table and demanded, "Who's going to talk first?"

ALLIE HAD NEVER wanted to force Charlotte to take sides.

"I'm waiting," Charlotte said through a clenched jaw.

Not wanting to upset Charlotte even more, Allie spoke up. "Jack doesn't like how I found out about Fairleigh." She looked directly at Charlotte as if Jack wasn't even there.

"I can understand that," Charlotte said. "But why can't you apologize and move forward?"

"I have nothing to apologize for," Allie said.

Jack spoke up before Allie could continue. "She doesn't think she's done anything wrong."

"Is that what you want? An apology?" Allie finally looked at him, her eyes narrowed. "Fine. I'm sorry. Now are you happy? I'm sorry that you left your phone out where I could read your text message."

Jack's eyes widened. "You call that an apology?"

"Move over." Charlotte nudged Jack. "I need to get out."

He stood and then so did she. After he sat down again at her urging, Charlotte stood at the end of the table and said very distinctly, "I'm going to the ladies' room. When I get back, I expect you'll have worked things out. If not, then pretend you did, because I care a lot about both of you, and I won't stand by and have you mad at each other." She spun on her heel and walked away, leaving Allie stunned by her vehement outburst.

"She's pretty upset," Jack said.

"No kidding." Allie couldn't contain her sarcasm.

"Maybe for Charlotte's sake, we could be civil. At least when she's around."

She stared at him. He had a good point. "I could do that. For Charlotte's sake."

"I probably should be more careful about where I leave my phone."

"And I should keep my eyes to myself."

His mouth turned up ever so slightly. "I know you're having a hard time keeping your business afloat. I can appreciate how desperate you must be."

"Desperate? How do you know about my finances?"

He hesitated. "Your dad mentioned it."

"My dad?" She lowered her voice when she realized she'd practically shouted. "My dad? What did he say?"

"Just that he knew you were struggling financially after losing your job."

That was putting it mildly. More like bobbing in the ocean and trying to stay afloat long enough to suck in oxygen before being dragged under the water again.

She looked at her hands and then up at him. "Does he also know that I was blacklisted by every advertising agency in New England? Empire wouldn't even give me an entry-level job." Jack's eyes widened and she added, "You and I agreed to not discuss business, so I never brought it up."

"I didn't know that," he said. "I'm not involved in the hiring process, although I do know we haven't been able to hire anyone new for at least two years. The only new hires have been as replacements for employees who left the firm."

He stretched his hand out to her, palm up. "I'm sorry for what I said earlier. I don't believe you knew about your ex's illegal activities."

She hesitated long enough that he had to know she felt pressured, then placed her hand in his. "Thank you."

Charlotte was suddenly standing at the end of the table. "Good. I'm happy to see we're getting along again. It's about time. I've been standing near the door watching you." She nudged Jack, and he made room for her on the bench seat. "The waitress over there says this place is known for their lobster roll, so that's what I'm having. What about you two?"

AFTER THEIR FOOD CAME—all three ordered lobster rolls—none of them spoke as they ate. Jack had to agree that this was a great choice for lunch.

"Where are you two staying?" he asked. "I'm assuming you're spending the night?"

"We don't have a room yet," Charlotte said.

Jack raised his eyebrows. "You're gonna have trouble if you don't already have a reservation. My assistant could only get me a room at a local bed-and-breakfast. According to her, it was the last place in town."

"Oh, no. Maybe we should find ourselves a room before we do anything else," Charlotte suggested to Allie, who hadn't said anything for a while.

"I'm staying at Fairleigh Manor," Jack told them and mentioned a few other places for them to try.

"If we can't find something," Allie finally said, "then we can drive home late tonight."

For some odd reason, Jack didn't want her to

leave. Now that they'd forged a peace agreement, however temporary, he wanted to continue where they'd left off when he had departed from her bed early that morning.

Had it only been half a day ago that he hadn't wanted to leave her?

So much had happened since then.

He watched as the two women discussed the pros and cons of leaving late tonight. They were so similar, yet so different. It was easy to see how he could have been confused at Emily's wedding, but now that he knew both women, he would never confuse them again.

He picked up the bill the server dropped off. "I'd better get going. I'll pay this on the way out." He pulled out a credit card and started to get up. "Listen, let me know if you don't find a room. Mine's pretty big, and we could probably scrounge up a rollaway bed. You two could take the king bed." He was looking at Allie as he spoke. "I'm sure we could make it work." He gave them a little wave and stepped to the cash register, his back to the two women.

All he could think about was how good Allie would look and feel if she were in that king-size bed with him tonight.

"I'M GLAD HE'S finally gone," Allie said when Jack left the restaurant.

"No, you're not," Charlotte said.

She was right. Allie's mouth had begun to water when he was talking about his king-size bed. Her body tingled in all the places he'd touched over and over again during the night.

How had everything gone so wrong?

"Allie, did you hear me?" Charlotte said.

"What did you say?" Allie blinked a few times to clear her head.

"I asked if you were ready to go. If Jack's right, getting a room will be difficult."

"I don't understand why they need an advertising campaign to bring in tourists if they don't have enough hotel rooms for the ones they're already attracting." Allie wiped her mouth and took a last sip of her soda. "Let's go to the coffee shop around the corner. They advertised free Wi-Fi. I can pull up a list of hotels on my laptop and we'll make some calls."

With that decided, they headed to the coffee shop, giving Allie an opportunity to see another small business in town.

Soon they were already halfway through their list with no luck. "I don't think we're going to find a room," Charlotte said. "Why don't we take Jack up on his offer?"

Allie wasn't about to commit to staying with Jack unless absolutely necessary. "Let's go meet the deputy mayor and then decide. We might not need to spend the night if we can see enough of the town before dark."

Charlotte seemed reluctant to agree, but they headed to the town hall anyway.

They went through a lax security check and were directed to a reception desk. "We'd like to speak to Deputy Mayor Wittmer, please."

"I'm sorry," the young woman at the desk told her. "The Deputy Mayor is in a meeting. Do you have an appointment?"

"No, but I'm sure he'll want to speak to us." Allie gave their names. She knew she should have called ahead, and she would have in any other situation. She'd blame that slip-up on Jack for being such a distraction.

"You can wait over there if you'd like." The woman pointed to a small seating area with a few vinyl-covered chairs. "Although I can't guarantee he'll see you."

Charlotte and Allie sat down. "Why don't we continue to go down the list of hotels?" Allie suggested.

"I don't think we're going to find anything," Charlotte said, but she opened her phone and dialed the next number on their hand-written list.

Allie was about to dial the last hotel on the list when she got an incoming call. She didn't recognize the number, but it was from Rhode Island.

She stood up. "I'll take this outside," she whispered to Charlotte, who nodded while listening on her own phone.

"Hello?" Allie said as soon as she was outside on the sidewalk.

"Is this Allie Miller?" At Allie's confirmation, the male caller said, "This is Peter Stone. I'm Gerard Stone's son."

"Yes, Peter, thank you for calling."

"My sister filled me in. She says you're looking for your adoption file."

"That's right. I believe your father handled my adoption. Do you have any idea where the file might be?"

"Look, I know my father did bad things in his life, and he made mistakes. But if you need this file because you're looking to sue his estate, then you're out of luck. He died deep in debt. There's no money to be had."

Allie was so taken aback by his assumption that she was speechless for a moment. "Oh, no," she said when she got her voice back. "This is a personal matter. I don't care what your father did or didn't do. I'm just trying to find my birth parents." She went on to explain about meeting Charlotte. "We believe your father may have been the lawyer who also brokered her adoption."

"If that's the case, then I think I can help."

"Oh! That would be wonderful." Allie's heart leaped at the news. They made arrangements for Allie and Charlotte to meet him at his family's storage locker the next night.

She disconnected and hurried back inside to tell Charlotte the good news.

Before she could open her mouth, Jack and a man she could only assume was the deputy mayor came walking down the hall to the reception area.

"Thanks for your time, Chuck," Jack said as he shook the man's hand. "I'll be in touch."

Jack nodded as he walked past Charlotte and Allie. The man was so damn cocky. If he thought he already had the account, he didn't know who he was up against.

CHAPTER SIXTEEN

ALLIE TURNED AWAY from Jack and his obvious satisfaction at having spoken with the deputy mayor first. Did she have time to tell Charlotte about her phone call from Peter Stone?

She whispered to Charlotte, "Let's go over to the receptionist's desk so the deputy mayor can't walk by us." Allie took Charlotte's elbow and guided her. "That was Gerard Stone's son, Peter, on the phone," she said quietly.

Charlotte's head swiveled in Allie's direction, her eyes wide. "What did he say?"

"He wants to meet us at the storage place tomorrow night to go through his dad's files."

Charlotte pursed her lips. "That doesn't sound like the safest place to meet a stranger."

Allie waved away her doubt. "He's *not* a stranger. He's the son of the man who probably has a lot of the answers we've been searching for." She put a finger to her lips when the deputy mayor began walking past them toward his office.

"Mr. Deputy Mayor." Allie greeted him with an outstretched arm, hoping she'd used the correct title to address him.

He slowly put his hand out to shake hers, looking to the receptionist for answers.

"These women were hoping to speak to you," the receptionist told him.

Allie didn't wait for her to continue. "I'm Allie Miller and this is Charlotte Harrington. We spoke over the phone."

As soon as Allie mentioned Charlotte's name, Deputy Mayor Charles Wittmer—or Chuck as she'd heard Jack call him—gave Charlotte his immediate attention.

"Ms. Harrington," he gushed as he put out a hand and held hers in both of his for an awkward amount of time. "What a privilege to meet you."

Charlotte withdrew her hand and said, "Thank you, Mr. Deputy Mayor."

"Please, call me Chuck. We're very informal around here." He addressed Allie. "I must say, you told me you were cousins, but you look like twins."

Charlotte smiled and the man nearly melted.

Thinking quickly, and hoping it would help their cause, Allie said, "Yes, we are twins. It's a long, complicated story."

She was afraid to look at Charlotte after telling the lie, but Allie had to use every trick in her arsenal to get the Fairleigh account.

Then Charlotte took the lead. "Would it be possible for us to speak somewhere private? Like your office?"

"Oh, come right this way, Ms. Harrington." He gestured down the short hall, and they followed him.

"Please, call me Charlotte," she told him when

they were seated in his office. "I believe you and Allie spoke on the phone about increasing tourism." She looked to Allie. "I'll let the two of you speak about that since it's not my area of expertise."

Allie couldn't have coached Charlotte any better when it came to this meeting, even if Chuck did look a little disappointed about his lack of interaction with Charlotte. "Thank you so much for your time, Chuck," Allie began. "I'm sure you and Charlotte will have plenty of time to talk about Charlotte's art and what Fairleigh has planned for local artists."

Chuck looked decidedly more relaxed when he heard that. Now that she had his attention, she brought up the lack of hotel rooms. "I imagine that's because of the craft show?" At his nod, she asked, "What else do you have scheduled over the next three months?"

He opened the calendar on his desktop computer, and Allie was surprised to see there was very little scheduled until September.

Chuck named several summer celebrations and small conventions that previously met in town but had found other locations after Fairleigh was devastated by the hurricane.

They discussed several options that could be managed quickly. "My feeling is that if you get the year-round residents excited about tourism and their town, then they'll invite friends and relatives to visit, and that will be the beginning of a new wave of tourism. Word of mouth is a great place to start."

"I like how you think, Allie."

"Then you'd like us to proceed with an advertising campaign?"

Chuck squinted. "Well, I can't go that far, but I do like where you're headed. We have another company we asked to help us."

"Yes, we know. And I'm not afraid to say that we can definitely do a better job for you."

"And why is that?"

Allie spit out the first thing she could think of. "Well, first of all, we have Charlotte here to entice artists and art lovers like yourself. She'll convince them Fairleigh is a town they need to check out."

Chuck beamed when she spoke about him being an art lover. "That does give you a one-up, but they are a bigger firm and have more assets to draw from."

"More assets aren't always a good thing," she countered.

"Why's that?"

"Because the more people you have involved in something, the more ideas need to come together. In my case, I'm the only person who needs to agree and, if I say so myself, I'm pretty agreeable." She gave him her biggest grin, and he blushed as she expected him to.

Before he could speak, she added, "I also know his company recently took on a large client, so their time will be divided. Whereas my time would be completely yours." Using the fact that Jack had won the animal-food account was something she would have used no matter who he was. At least that's what she told herself.

Chuck scratched his chin. "You do bring up some good points. But I have to say, Mr. Fletcher made some excellent suggestions, too."

"I'm sure he did," Allie said as sweetly as she could. "Charlotte and I are well acquainted with him. He's very good at his job." And excellent at things not at all related to his job. She put her hands to her cheeks when she felt them heat.

"Are you feeling okay?" Chuck asked solicitously.

"What? Oh, I'm fine. Just a little warm." Allie took a few deep breaths and changed the subject back to what she could offer the town. "Maybe we should visit the artists' workplace?"

Chuck looked at the clock. "Oh, dear. I'm afraid they're closed for the day. You will be staying the night, won't you?"

"There's not a room to be had in town," Allie told him. "I don't suppose you know of a town close by that we could try?"

"I'm sure the neighboring towns are full, too. This has always been our biggest week for tourism. Folks from across the country come just for the artisans we have. It's a juried show, so we don't take any and all craftspeople who apply. We're quite choosy."

"Good for you," Allie acknowledged, but that didn't get them a room for the night. She'd be damned if she'd accept Jack's offer, but right now she wasn't seeing an alternative. Going home, even if they both stayed at Charlotte's, would be several hours taken away from making any points with Chuck or even seeing the rest of the town. "We'll figure something out as far as spending the night, but we'd love to take you to dinner and hear more about the town."

"Unfortunately, I've already made plans for dinner."

"With Mr. Fletcher?" Allie knew the answer before the red-faced Chuck nodded. "Then we can all go to dinner together. Jack won't mind—he's actually Charlotte's neighbor." She spoke quickly, rising from her chair as if he'd already agreed. "That will give you and Charlotte time to talk."

"Well—" He looked at Charlotte. "I would like to spend more time talking about your artwork."

"It's all settled, then," Allie said. "I'm sure Mr. Fletcher can make a reservation for four instead of two. I'll call you later to find out the restaurant." She put out her hand to Chuck, hoping to make their exit before he realized he was being manipulated. Charlotte stood, picking up on the hint that they were leaving.

"Before you go," Chuck said quietly, sounding a little embarrassed, "I have something to show you."

Allie almost sighed with relief that he wasn't canceling dinner.

"Come this way." Chuck led them into the hallway and took a left, leading them away from the reception area.

"Oh!" Charlotte stopped suddenly and put both hands over her mouth.

Both Chuck and Charlotte were looking at a gorgeous scene of a deserted beach with the sun coming up over the horizon. The colors—pastels would be Allie's guess—were both vibrant and subtle. She almost felt like part of the scene.

"That's beautiful," Allie said before she noticed the signature. C Harrington.

Charlotte quickly wiped tears from her cheeks, obviously emotional. In a shaky voice she said, "Thank you for showing me this."

"Oh, Ms. Harrington, it's definitely my pleasure to have your work displayed here," Chuck gushed, which he seemed to do on a regular basis. "I actually bought it for my office last year, but everyone loved it so much that I decided to move it out here."

Charlotte touched the man's arm. "I'm glad people are enjoying it."

Allie quickly ended the encounter by reminding them that they needed to arrange accommodations for the night. Charlotte was obviously having trouble keeping herself together.

"We'll see you at dinner." They both waved and hurried outside to the pavement. "Are you okay,

Charlotte?" Allie asked when she pulled her to a bench to sit down.

Charlotte shook her head and covered her face with her hands. Her whole body shook, and Allie couldn't think of anything to do but lightly rub Charlotte's back until she was ready to speak.

Finally Charlotte straightened, staring ahead at the cars driving down the main street. Allie had to strain to hear Charlotte's words. "That was the last scene I completed before my mother's pancreatic cancer diagnosis."

Allie had no words of comfort and pulled a sobbing Charlotte into her arms.

WHEN ALLIE AND CHARLOTTE showed up for dinner, Jack was even more surprised than when the deputy mayor called him to add two to the reservation. He'd expected two of Chuck's coworkers—maybe the mayor himself—not this pair.

How had Allie manipulated Chuck to get invited to dinner?

Chuck walked in with them and took the seat in the booth across from Jack. Charlotte quickly sat next to Chuck, leaving Allie to sit beside Jack.

He purposely didn't give her much room, for which he was rewarded with a look of contempt. "You look nice tonight," he told her, knowing it would only set her farther off course.

The restaurant was a typical touristy place with sea creatures such as starfish and shells on the walls, and paper covering the tables. The menu selection was exactly what Jack expected, with every type of East Coast seafood available, including quahogs, Rhode Island's type of clams.

Jack had wanted a more refined restaurant for dinner, but just as rooms were unavailable, so were restaurant reservations. If not for dropping the deputy mayor's name, as well as Chuck's suggestion to try this restaurant, the four of them might very well have been going through a fast-food drive-through.

"This looks delicious," Allie said to Chuck as she glanced around at the food on the other tables. "Do you eat here often?"

"This is one of my favorite places," he admitted. "And it's not only because my cousin is the owner and chef."

"How nice!" Allie went back to reading the menu. "What do you suggest?"

They talked about the menu for a few more minutes before their server took their drink orders. Jack couldn't help noticing Charlotte was more quiet and subdued than usual. He didn't want to embarrass her in front of Chuck, so he didn't mention it.

At one point, Allie moved in her seat and whispered under her breath from behind her menu, "Can you move over a little? I'm going to fall off."

He smiled sweetly and moved about a quarter of an inch. She responded by shoving her whole body into him, not that she was strong enough to move him.

"Jerk," she whispered, kicking the side of his shin with her shoe.

"Nice talk from such a lovely mouth."

Her cheeks turned pink, just as he'd expected.

"Stop it," she sputtered.

"Is everything okay?" Chuck asked.

Jack had been so caught up in his little battle with Allie that he'd forgotten why he was at dinner in the first place. Their legs were still touching, and he made no move to avoid contact, loving the heat they made together.

"Everything's fine," he told Chuck as he discreetly took Allie's hand beneath the table and entwined their fingers tightly enough that she couldn't pull away. She squeezed her hand to show her displeasure, and he squeezed lightly back. "We were discussing which way we liked our seafood cooked. What's your preference, Chuck? Fried or sautéed?" He settled their hands on his thigh, probably a mistake since his body began acting inappropriately at the proximity of her hand to certain body parts.

Remembering once again that this was a business meeting, he turned his mind back to the menu. After ordering their entrées, Allie and Jack asked Chuck a lot of questions about the town, both intent on producing an excellent advertising campaign and selling Chuck on their own expertise.

"I hope you've found a room for the night?" Chuck directed his question to Charlotte.

"Well—"

Jack spoke up before either of the women could stop him. "Actually, they're staying at the same B and B as I am. I talked to the innkeeper, and she has a very small room for you."

"Really?" Charlotte asked. "That's wonderful. How nice of you." She asked Allie, "Wasn't that nice of him?"

"Just trying to help out." He was rewarded with another kick in the shin from Allie, while she merely smiled at Chuck. Jack released her hand to rub his leg.

Later, when the bill came, Allie was quick to pick up the check.

"We could split it," he suggested, aware of her financial situation.

Allie wouldn't give in. "You bought lunch, so I'll pick up dinner."

They were getting up to leave when Allie asked, "What time should we meet you at the artists' workhouse, Chuck?"

This was news to Jack. No wonder Charlotte had come along. "That sounds like something I'd like to see, too," he said, which got him a jab in the ribs from Allie.

"It opens at ten o'clock tomorrow," Chuck said. "Shall we all meet at the workhouse then?"

They agreed and Chuck departed for his car, leaving Jack and the two women standing in front of the restaurant.

"If you don't want the room at Fairleigh Manor," Jack said, "I can cancel."

"We'll take it," Charlotte said quickly.

"I had them reserve the room on my credit card," he said.

"I'll make sure the charge goes on mine," Allie told him.

"You can pay me back later if you need to keep it on my card," he offered.

"I'll be fine."

Jack wasn't so sure about that.

CHARLOTTE LISTENED TO Allie complain about Jack the entire ride from the restaurant to the hotel.

"That man drives me crazy in less time than it takes to shoo a fly."

Even so, Charlotte couldn't help but enjoy the way Jack and Allie were together.

Their attraction was obvious. If only they didn't allow business to get in the middle of it, they might be on their way to a pretty darn great relationship.

"Good thing you're off men," Charlotte reminded Allie. She pretended to look out the passenger-side window so Allie wouldn't see the smile she couldn't hide.

"I admit I had a little bump in my plan last night," Allie said. "But it's not like we have a relationship or anything."

"Especially since Jack isn't into relationships either."

Allie didn't reply, simply driving the few more blocks to Fairleigh Manor, a Victorian home with a much grander name than the building with its peeling paint and missing cedar roof shingles.

"I didn't realize how late it was getting," Charlotte said when the car was parked.

"Me, either," Allie agreed on a yawn. "I just want to go to sleep and get up in time to grab breakfast and check out the town before we meet with Chuck."

Jack was already in his room when the two women arrived. He came out into the hall as the innkeeper was showing them to their room next to his.

"There's not much room in here," Allie noted when the innkeeper left.

She wasn't kidding. The room had a double bed with only about two feet on either side of it. There was even less space at the end of the bed.

"There's not even a place to put our things," Charlotte said. "I guess we can pile everything here." She put her small suitcase on the bench at the foot of the bed.

Allie had rolled her overnight bag into the room, and she put it next to Charlotte's on the bench. She opened it, grabbing a cosmetic case and what appeared to be a nightshirt. "Where's the bathroom?" she asked Jack and Charlotte.

"We share one," Jack said. "It's across the hall."

"Great."

"There's no one else on this floor, so we're the only ones using it."

"And that's supposed to make things better?" Allie left the room with her things.

"I'll see you in the morning," Jack told Charlotte.

"Good night and thanks." Charlotte waited for Allie to finish, wondering what she could do to get Jack and Allie to realize they should be together. She tried to think like Allie did, looking for any advantage. While brushing her teeth, a plan came to mind. She smiled at herself in the mirror. Someday they'd thank her. Maybe not tonight or tomorrow. But someday.

ALLIE HAD NEVER been more uncomfortable in a bed. Not that the mattress was that bad, but it was Charlotte.

She kicked and squirmed and flailed her arms. Just as Allie would drift off, Charlotte would start her tossing and turning. Allie clung to the edge of the bed that couldn't possibly be as big as a standard double.

She'd never get a wink of sleep at this rate.

She couldn't help visualizing Jack's bed. She knew he was easy to sleep next to, but how could she do that without giving him the wrong idea?

Very, very bad idea.

Charlotte moaned and flung her arm in Allie's direction, hitting her in the back of the head.

Allie finally got out of the torture bed as quietly

as possible, thinking she'd have to find another surface to sleep on. But there was no other furniture in the room to sleep on, and barely enough floor space to walk around the bed. Allie almost reconsidered her decision to sleep somewhere else when Charlotte seemed to have fallen into a deeper, calmer sleep.

But then she began flailing again—Allie had no choice.

She tiptoed to the bedroom door, taking her pillow and the extra blanket from the end of the bed with her. Maybe the hallway would be a better choice. She opened the door quietly and carefully and closed it behind her.

"What's up?"

Jack was coming out of the bathroom. He was shirtless with only his khaki shorts on. Allie's fingers tingled at the memory of his bare skin.

She cleared her head. Not a time for thoughts like that.

"Charlotte's all over the bed. I came out here to sleep in the hallway."

"You don't have to do that." He took her pillow and blanket. "Come with me."

She followed him into his room, knowing full well that it was a bad idea. "This is a bad idea."

"It'll be fine." He began moving pillows around on the bed, using her pillow and the blanket to make a barrier down the middle of the bed. He pointed to his work. "There. The walls of Jericho."

"Huh?" This was a terrible idea.

"It's an old movie. *It Happened One Night.* We should watch it together sometime." He stripped down to his underwear and crawled into one side. "Come on. You need some sleep." He rolled over, his back to her, while she stood and watched.

Sleeping in the bed with him couldn't possibly be as bad as sleeping with dear Charlotte—Charlotte of the Newport Ballet and Karate Company.

She shut off the light on her side and climbed into bed. Turning on her side, her back to Jack, she tried not to think about how close he was to her. His soft, even breathing told her he was probably asleep already.

Damn. Why had business gotten between them? Her pulse pounded so loudly she thought he might hear it.

She reviewed her plan for tomorrow, wondering what Jack had in mind. He'd already horned in on their visit to the artists' workhouse, although the more time they spent together, the more she'd know about his plans for the town. She was determined to win this account after losing the last one to him.

She'd set her cell phone alarm so she'd be up bright and early to go for a walk before breakfast, but she'd forgotten her phone in her room. Charlotte had mentioned she wanted to go out to sketch in the morning, so they would be splitting up until they met at the workhouse. Ideally, Allie would wake up on her own in time to do what she needed to do.

She was nearly drifting off when she felt movement. Jack had turned over. Was he going to make a move toward her? Could she be strong and tell him no?

Her heart raced until she heard him breathe softly and regularly again. She relaxed and eventually fell sleep.

She wasn't sure how much later it was that she suddenly woke to movement on the other side of the bed. The pillows between them were being tossed aside, and Jack's strong arm came around her middle to pull her to him. As they spooned, his hand slid under her nightshirt to comfortably cup her breast.

As if that's how they slept every night.

"Jack, you're naked!" Now that her nightshirt had ridden up because of his fondling, she couldn't ignore what was now pressing against her own bare skin.

"Oh, yeah. I didn't want to seem too eager earlier." His words whispered in her ear were deep and gravelly from sleep. He couldn't have sounded sexier if he'd tried.

She wiggled to move away from him, even if it was reluctantly. "And now?"

He kissed her neck just below her ear, and she didn't care anymore. Her nightshirt landed on the floor, and she begged him to make love to her.

CHAPTER SEVENTEEN

JACK WOKE TO the sun peeking through the drapes. He sat straight up, the sheet covering his chest falling forward, when he realized how late it must be. The bedside clock said nearly eight o'clock. He got out of bed and noticed the pillows at his feet, and the memories of the night he'd had with Allie came back in a whoosh.

Jack grinned. He hadn't dreamt it.

He leaned over the bed to pick up the pillow she'd slept on. Yep, definitely smelled like her citrus shampoo. Also cold to the touch. She must have gotten up a while ago.

He opened the door slightly and saw no one was using the bathroom. He hopped into the shower, noticing one bath towel had been used already.

Once in the shower, he remembered more clearly how he and Allie had spent the night. He smiled, remembering the time she'd spent touching and kissing every inch of him.

After showering he got out the door in no time, so he explored the streets of Fairleigh. He noticed several boarded-up businesses. They'd obviously not been able to survive the hurricane devastation.

"Excuse me," he said to a middle-aged couple

walking in his direction. "May I ask you a few questions about this town?"

"Of course," the woman answered immediately.

"I work for an advertising firm that's been tasked with bringing tourism back to Fairleigh. Are you tourists or do you live here?"

"We're locals," the man said. "Twenty years ago, we left Kansas and opened a flower shop here in town. We wanted to be near the water."

"And you've done okay since the hurricane?"

"Not exactly, but luckily we have insurance. Not all the businesses in town were covered. And either help from FEMA came too late, or it wasn't enough and some people couldn't reopen."

"I see." Jack wasn't surprised by their answer. "How do you see the town now? Are you still glad to be here despite tourism being down?"

"I'm sure it will come back," the woman told him confidently.

"Why's that?"

"Because the people here love this town, and they're willing to do what's necessary to revive it. Just because a few people didn't reopen their businesses doesn't mean the town will fall apart. I see it as opportunities for others to start businesses here and be successful."

"I appreciate your opinion on the matter." Jack gave her his business card. "If you think of anything else that might be useful, please don't hesitate to contact me."

They all went on their way, and Jack stopped to speak to several more people on the street as well as some shop owners as the stores began to open.

He finally came to a restaurant that served only breakfast. Figuring that was a good place to get some coffee and food, and meet a few more locals, he opened the door and stepped inside.

There was nothing special about the place except for a homey atmosphere that Jack couldn't put his finger on. The furniture was metal, lots of small tables and chairs with the ability to be moved around, and it had obviously been used hard over the years. The walls were freshly painted, and an old-fashioned case held muffins, scones and all sorts of baked goods with a sign proclaiming they were freshly made on the premises.

"Hey, Jack!" Chuck was seated at a small table for two. An older man occupied the other chair.

Jack went over to greet Chuck.

"This is my uncle, Maurice Weber," Chuck said by way of introduction.

Jack shook hands with both men.

"Would you like to join us?" Chuck offered.

Before Jack could answer, they'd borrowed an empty chair from another table and placed it at theirs.

Jack sat while Chuck caught their waitress's attention. He gave Jack a questioning look as he said to their waitress, "Coffee?" to which Jack nodded gratefully. "The menu's on the chalkboard up there," Chuck told him.

"Jack is part of that advertising firm I was telling you about that we contacted about tourism," Chuck explained to his uncle.

"Great to meet you, Jack. You've got a big job to do if you're gonna get this town hopping again." Maurice took a sip of his coffee before the waitress brought Jack a fresh cup and refilled the other men's cups.

"I'll have the egg sandwich with bacon," Jack told their waitress.

"Good choice," Chuck said.

Jack took advantage of having Chuck's uncle available, questioning him as he had other locals.

"I think if we can get something going with the artists' workhouse, that will bring in tourists," Maurice said. "People want that dose of culture along with the relaxation Fairleigh provides."

"Maybe something like a wine-and-cheese open house with featured artists?" Jack suggested.

Both men straightened, their eyes wide with excitement. "That would be a great idea," Chuck said. "Especially if we had artists who are known to people." He turned to his uncle. "Charlotte Harrington is in town with her twin sister, Allie Miller. They're competing for the advertising account against Jack here." He sipped his coffee and reminded his uncle that Charlotte had done the beach scene hanging outside his office in the town hall.

Meanwhile, Jack couldn't get past the twin sister remark. Was that what Allie had told him, knowing Chuck was a fan of Charlotte's? Had she used Charlotte?

How underhanded and devious was that?

ALLIE HEADED STRAIGHT to the water after showering and dressing in casual wear. Charlotte had already left their room, and Allie wanted to be long gone before Jack woke up.

She needed to talk to someone about what had happened between Jack and her. And making the assumption that Charlotte had headed to the ocean, she walked in that direction, too.

Allie needed reassurance that she wasn't being stupid by sleeping with Jack. She could no longer deny that there was something between them. She felt it even when they weren't together. Something kept her coming back to him, and not only for sex.

Regardless, should she have pushed him away last night? Told him she wasn't interested? Talk about being of two minds. Her body kept saying yes, and even though her head should have told her mouth to say no, her head seemed to know better than to ruin an explosive night of pleasure.

She spotted Charlotte on a far-off dock, her back to the water as she sat cross-legged on the structure, obviously concentrating on the buildings close to the water.

Allie walked slowly toward Charlotte, not wanting to interrupt her concentration. Finally she stopped at the dock not too far from Charlotte and walked to the end of it. Several boats were tied to what appeared to be newly built structures. Judging by the pictures she'd seen, Hurricane Lorraine had taken a toll on this town, from wiping out docks and sinking boats to flooding businesses and homes with up to several feet of water.

It was surprising that this town was even operational after all that destruction.

"Hey, Allie!" Charlotte called out to her and waved.

Allie made her way to where Charlotte was working and sat down beside her.

"You were gone when I got out of the shower this morning," Allie said.

"I wanted to catch the sunrise over the water." She pulled up the pictures she'd taken on her camera.

"Those are gorgeous!"

Charlotte smiled. "Thanks." She put the camera into its case. "Sleep okay?" She had her head turned away from Allie.

"Sure," Allie said. "You?"

Then she saw Charlotte's smile. "So you know I slept in Jack's bed."

"Uh-huh." Charlotte's grin grew bigger. "You're welcome."

Allie was confused.

"I never kick and thrash in my sleep," Charlotte

explained. "Didn't you notice that I only flailed around when you'd finally get comfortable?"

Allie's eyes widened. "You were faking? Why would you do that?"

"Because you two belong together. You should see your face when you're near him. It's obvious to everyone around that there's something special going on between you."

"And you thought you needed to push us together?" Allie wasn't sure if she was happy or angry about Charlotte's deception.

"Neither of you was doing anything to fix things on your own. I figured if you at least had sex, then you could figure out the rest after."

"Except I left his room before he woke up this morning," Allie admitted.

Charlotte appeared crestfallen. "You two haven't worked things out?"

"Beyond physical, no."

"Then you need to go find him."

"I can't," Allie said. "I don't know how we can be together. He has no respect for me."

"I think you took the wrong meaning from his words. I think he has great respect for your talent. Maybe you should concentrate on that and not worry about trying to bad-mouth him to the client."

"Bad-mouth? When did I do that?"

"When you told Chuck that Jack's company just got a big new contract and wouldn't have enough time for Fairleigh."

"It's true."

"But you didn't have to mention it."

Allie thought about it. "I guess I could tone it down a little."

She needed some time alone to get her head straight before meeting Chuck at ten. "I've gotta go," she told Charlotte. "I'll meet you at the artists' workhouse at ten? Checkout's at eleven, so we should pack the car before we go to the workhouse. If I miss you, leave your stuff with the innkeeper."

Charlotte nodded. "I'm sorry if I made things more complicated for you."

"It's not your fault." Allie took full responsibility for her actions. "Though I wouldn't have expected you to be so devious. You were pretty believable with your thrashing."

Charlotte gave her a guilty grin. "It really was completely out of character for me."

Allie said goodbye and went on her way, pondering Charlotte's advice. A few minutes later she saw Jack in the distance coming in her direction. Was she up to having a conversation right now? She had a lot of other things on her mind.

When they were within a few feet of each other, they both stopped. Neither spoke right away. Finally Jack, with a distinctly annoyed look, said, "Are you really going around telling lies about my company to get this account?"

That was the last thing she'd expected him to say.

"Well, good morning to you, too!" She started to walk past him, but he caught her arm.

"I mean it, Allie. Is that what you're doing?"

She met his glare and realized how angry he was. "What are you talking about?"

He stared at her, and she switched her weight from one foot to the other as if he were a teacher about to dole out detention. "Chuck just told me that you said my company didn't have the time to handle his account."

"It's the truth."

"No, it's not. We have plenty of employees who will work hard for him, and you know it. I thought we had a deal about being honest with each other."

"Look, it just came out. And, besides, I told Chuck that before we made our deal. You want me to go talk to him?"

Without hesitation, Jack said, "Yes. That's exactly what I want. I won't have you ruining my reputation."

She knew what it was like to have her reputation ruined. "I'll speak to him." Maybe Charlotte had been right about Allie relying more on her talent instead of trying to mislead people. Maybe she needed to make some changes.

CHARLOTTE SAW ALLIE and Jack in the distance. Already guilty over setting them up last night, she felt even worse when she could see from their body language that their conversation wasn't going well.

She gathered her things—she wanted to have a shower before meeting everyone at the artists' workhouse. Taking sides would be a bad decision on Charlotte's part. Jack and Allie were adults, able to work out their own problems.

About an hour later, Charlotte reached the artists' workhouse a few minutes early. Since the main door was unlocked, she went inside to take a look around.

She was very impressed by the use of the building, which didn't look like much on the outside. Peeking through the windows of the locked doors as she went down the hallway, she found there were separate rooms where artists could set up a studio to work on anything from pottery to oil painting to textiles. Several of the studios looked vacant.

How wonderful would it be if there was a facility like this closer to Newport? Not that she needed a space herself, but she'd love to be able to interact with other artists. Sometimes her work was too solitary. She'd needed that solitude since her mother passed away, but lately she felt herself coming out of it and craving more human interaction.

Between having Jack as her neighbor, as well as her friend, and meeting Allie, with whom she'd bonded nearly immediately, Charlotte found herself awakening for the first time in many months.

"There you are," Chuck said when Charlotte came back outside. Both Allie and Jack were with him, each appearing dour, their body language even worse.

"I'm sorry. I was looking around. The door was unlocked, so I checked out the studios. I'm very impressed with the setup."

Chuck beamed and went on to explain that the artists were carefully chosen and they paid a rental fee for their space.

After several more questions as they toured the building, mostly from Charlotte, Chuck said, "If we're done here, I'd like to have you all come back to town hall. I need to discuss the direction we'd like to go advertising-wise with Mayor Silvia as well as the city planner."

"But we haven't presented anything to you," Allie said.

"I believe I've gotten a good sense from both companies about the direction you'd like to go with the campaign," Chuck said. "We need to get this up and running as soon as possible. Can we meet at noon, if that works for the three of you?"

"Are you sure you need me there?" Charlotte didn't want to be in the way.

"Of course, Ms. Harrington...Charlotte. You play a very important role here."

Charlotte couldn't help but notice the satisfied look on Allie's face at Chuck's remark. It would be wonderful if Allie got the job, but she knew Jack also needed the account to keep his grandfather's company stable.

Chuck walked to his car, backed out of his space and pulled into the street, leaving Charlotte standing in the middle of Jack and Allie. A very uncomfortable position to say the least.

Allie's phone went off. "It's Peter Stone," she told Charlotte and answered the call. She walked a distance from Charlotte and Jack.

"He's the son of the lawyer who handled her adoption," Charlotte explained to Jack. "We're meeting him tonight to go through his father's files."

"Where are you meeting?" Jack asked.

"At a storage company in Cranston," Charlotte answered.

"I don't like it," Jack said. "What if this guy isn't who he says he is? Could be dangerous."

Charlotte had considered it, but Allie had been so sure about Peter being aboveboard.

"There are two of us and one of him," Charlotte reminded him. "We'll be fine."

"Not if he doesn't show up alone."

Allie returned, speaking directly to Charlotte as if Jack weren't there. "Peter was just confirming for tonight."

"I don't like that you two are going alone," Jack told her. "You don't know who this guy is."

Allie stared at him a second. "What do you care? You've made it clear how you feel about me and my actions. We'll be fine."

"Don't you watch movies?" Jack asked, lowering his voice. *"The Silence of the Lambs?"*

"That's ridiculous," Allie said. "Now you're trying to scare us."

"Darn right I am," Jack told her. "I can be there as a backup—"

"No way." Allie practically yelled the words. "I'm not having you scare the guy off. If you come anywhere near that storage area tonight, I'll have no problem calling the police and telling them you're stalking me." She paused. "You know how deceitful I can be." She turned on her heel and got into her car, obviously expecting Charlotte to follow.

"I guess we'll see you at town hall in a little while," Charlotte said quietly to Jack, who nodded and walked to his own car.

ALLIE AND CHARLOTTE arrived at town hall right before Jack. They were shown into a small conference room, where Chuck and the others were already seated. The group rose as the women entered, and Chuck made the introductions when Jack appeared close behind them.

"This is Mayor Silvia and our city planner, Bob Connelly, who's also a local architect," Chuck explained. "Our town is so small that most of our administrative positions, excluding police chief, mayor, deputy mayor, and our support staff, are volunteer positions. That's why meeting over lunch works best for Bob." He gestured to the platter of sandwiches. "Please help yourself."

Allie was too nervous to eat, but she helped herself to a bottle of water.

"Let's get started," Mayor Silvia suggested. "Since Chuck here said you both have some great ideas to get tourism going again, here's what we propose—both companies work together on the campaign."

"I'm sorry, Mr. Mayor," Allie said quickly. "I'm afraid that's impossible." What the heck were these guys thinking? She couldn't work with Jack. And he didn't trust her enough to work with her.

The mayor looked at her a moment, his deep-set dark eyes penetrating. "Then I'm the one who's sorry, Ms. Miller. If we have to choose, then the job will have to go to Empire."

"But why?" Allie hoped it hadn't come out like a whine.

"They're a larger company with more employees and expertise who can get the job done more efficiently. We need a quick turnaround, as this needs to be done before the Fourth of July. Though we'd prefer if you work together, as you have Ms. Harrington, the artist, as your expert."

Allie needed this job. She needed the money. She looked at Jack, who was having a side conversation with the city planner. Jack must be pleased. *Could* she work with him for the next two weeks? Once it was over, they could go their own ways.

Both Jack and Charlotte had told her to depend on her talent, but she hadn't been able to convince these clients. She only had Charlotte keeping her in the mix.

Against her better judgment, she had no other choice, especially after losing the animal-food account. "On second thought, I would very much appreciate the opportunity to work on this project with Empire." She half stood to lean over the table to shake hands with the mayor as well as the other two gentlemen. She never even glanced at Jack.

After almost an hour of discussion on particulars, the meeting adjourned, and Allie and Charlotte were on their way out of town.

Allie's phone rang a little while into their drive. Since she was at the wheel, she didn't answer. "It's Jack," she told Charlotte. "I'll call him back later." Much later. If she felt like it.

Charlotte's phone rang. "Hello? Oh, hi, Jack."

Did she have to sound so perky and pleased to speak to the guy?

"Okay, I'll talk to Allie and get back to you."

They disconnected, and Charlotte said, "He told me we left so quickly that we didn't get a chance to set up a meeting to start working on the campaign."

"I'll check my schedule." Allie's response came out more sarcastic than she'd intended. "Sorry, I don't mean to take it out on you. I'm ticked off that I'll have to work with Jack."

"It'll only be two weeks, since they want the plan rolled out before the Fourth of July. It'll go quickly."

"I know." She also knew Charlotte was probably hoping Allie and Jack would work things out during their time together.

That was a lost cause.

CHAPTER EIGHTEEN

Since Jack found fewer than half a dozen storage places with the actual address of Cranston when he did an internet search, it wasn't difficult to locate the one where Allie and Charlotte were meeting this guy Peter. He wasn't about to let them go off alone, but he also wouldn't let them know he was there.

At the third one, he saw Allie's car parked next to Charlotte's, so he parked nearby and went into the small office to speak to someone. He was hoping they had cameras set up so he could watch the scene from afar. He had his doubts that they'd be that sophisticated.

"Hi," he said to the young man with stringy hair behind the counter. The clerk didn't bother glancing up from his phone. "I was wondering if you have cameras set up in your facility."

"Yeah, we do," he said, looking up briefly before going back to concentrating on his phone. "The entire facility's under constant surveillance."

That sounded more like an advertising pitch than the truth.

"Would it be possible to watch? I'm concerned about two women who are meeting a stranger here."

"Sorry, man, we can't do that. We can look at the footage only after the fact."

"Oh, okay, thanks." He was ready to leave to search the halls for the Allie and Charlotte when he thought of something. "I'm not sure where they are. Can you look up a name and tell me where the unit is?"

"We're not allowed to do that, either." He went back to tapping on his phone.

Jack pulled a twenty from his wallet. "What if I say I can't remember which unit is mine?"

"You didn't say you had a unit, too." The guy was either high or not very bright.

Now Jack just needed to remember the guy's name. He knew the lawyer was Gerard Stone, but couldn't remember the son's first name.

"Can you look me up? The last name is Stone."

The guy set his phone down and punched in some information on the outdated computer behind the counter.

"Peter Stone?" The guy never looked up.

"Right."

"Unit three sixty-five."

"That's it. Thanks. Can you remind me how to get there? It's been a while since I've been here." Jack took a chance the guy wasn't going to figure out he'd given the information out to the wrong person. He hadn't even asked for ID.

"Go around the corner and through entrance C,

up the stairs to the third floor." The guy went back to his phone, laughing at something on his screen.

"Thanks so much." Jack pocketed the money.

Jack followed the guy's directions, and as soon as he opened the fire door on the third level, he heard a loud discussion.

Allie and a man were arguing.

"There's no way we're paying for information that's rightfully ours." Allie was adamant, and if the guy knew her even a little, he'd realize she wouldn't back down.

"Look," the guy said, "if you want the file, you'll have to pay. My family needs the money. Thanks to my dad's legal debt, my mom had to move in with her sister."

"That's not our fault," Allie told him. "Now let us see our files or I'll make a call to my lawyer."

"Get out!" The man suddenly became angry and shoved Charlotte into the hallway.

That was all Jack could take. He was about to step forward when Allie yelled, "Stay away from her!" She grabbed something that looked like a pipe and held it up as if ready to strike, placing herself between the two of them.

The guy put his hands up. "Hey, no need for violence." He was probably five-seven or -eight and two hundred pounds, all in his gut.

"You're not getting a cent from us," Allie reminded him. "Now give us our files."

"Okay, okay. I had to give it a shot." He appeared

to consider his options before reluctantly asking, "What year was it again?"

"1986. April." Charlotte spoke up.

The guy moved some boxes around while the women watched. He huffed and puffed as he worked. Finally he pulled out a box and dropped it in front of Allie. "Here it is."

The two women pounced on the box, opening it to rifle through the folders inside. "Here's the Miller file, Eleanor and Bart," Allie said as she pulled it from the box. "And here's the Harrington file." She looked at Charlotte. "Your mom's first name was Grace?" At Charlotte's nod, Allie handed her the folder.

The women sat side by side on the cement floor, their backs against the cement. Each had their own folders in hand, just staring at them.

"If that's all," Peter said, "I've gotta get going."

Neither of the women even took notice of Peter as he rolled the door closed, locked the storage unit and left.

ALLIE'S STOMACH WAS about to revolt.

"We actually have these in our hands." Charlotte wiped a tear from her cheek. "Are you ready to open the files?"

Allie only nodded. Words were impossible for her right now.

They opened the files, and both went for their original birth certificates.

"This is a Rhode Island birth certificate. Not a New York one," Charlotte noted. "How can that be?"

"We can figure out that part later," Allie said. "Read what yours says."

"Baby Girl born on April 16, 1986," Charlotte read and went on to name the hospital in Cranston.

"Same here," Allie said quietly. She swallowed, unable to even imagine what they would discover about themselves.

Charlotte's next word gave Allie chills. "Mother—"

"Barbara Sherwood." Both women said the name at the same time, and they immediately knew what that meant. "We're really twins," Allie said on a sob.

They dropped their files and hugged for a long time. Allie had a biological sister. Not just a sister, but a twin sister. She never wanted to let her go. She'd found something she hadn't known she'd been looking for.

"What else does it say?" Allie asked when they finally disconnected. She pulled tissues from her purse, handed one to Charlotte and wiped her own tears, as well.

"The Father space is blank."

"Mine, too," Allie said. "She must not have known who he was, or maybe he was married and she didn't want to name him." Allie didn't really care. Her birth mother had split them up, probably for the money, never giving them another thought.

"This says our mother was twenty when she gave birth," Charlotte said. "That's pretty young. Especially to have twins."

"If our parents paid thirty thousand each," Allie reminded her, "I'm sure she had a big payday."

They searched through their respective files to see what other information was there.

"Here's a page of notes that seem to have been made by the lawyer," Charlotte said. She squinted to read the handwritten page. "This says something about our mother being an inmate at the Cranston Women's Correctional Institute." She turned to Allie. "Does that mean she was in jail when she was pregnant with us?"

Allie looked at the page of nearly identical notes in her own file. "Sounds like it."

"I wonder where she is now." Charlotte sounded wistful, while Allie had no interest in finding out or ever meeting their biological mother. Eleanor Miller would always be her mother.

"We can do an internet search for her later," Allie said to placate Charlotte, who merely nodded.

They looked at each other. "We're actually sisters. Twins," Charlotte said. "It seems unreal."

"I know," Allie agreed. "I wish we'd known each other our entire lives." Her voice broke as she spoke. Damn. She never cried.

They hugged again, and when they broke apart,

Allie realized that Jack had been a silent witness to the entire thing. He stood with his back against the wall, obviously not wanting to interrupt.

"Where did you come from? I thought I told you to stay away." Allie smiled at him through her tears, though, and she realized his eyes were red. She stood and went over to hug him, their earlier disagreement be damned.

"I was hoping to see you take on that guy with, what, a pipe?"

She nodded. "Sometimes you gotta do what you gotta do."

He put his arms around her and squeezed. No hug had felt better except the one from her twin sister, who decided to join the embrace.

Allie whispered in Jack's ear, "I guess telling people that Charlotte and I are twins wasn't a lie, after all."

"WE NEED TO CELEBRATE," Charlotte said a few minutes later with no ideas in mind.

"I bought a bottle of champagne this afternoon, and it's chilling in my fridge," Allie said. "I was hoping we'd have something to celebrate." She looked at Jack. "You're welcome to join us."

"Of course he is," Charlotte said, wishing the two of them would make up already. "If not for him, we might never have met."

"That's true." Allie said.

They all had their own cars after getting back

into town earlier that day, so Charlotte had a few minutes alone to ponder what she thought she knew and what she'd learned tonight.

Things didn't add up. Why was her corrected birth certificate from the state of New York and not Rhode Island like her original? She'd used it her entire life. How could her adoptive mother have picked her up in New York if she was born in Rhode Island?

Allie's information seemed so clear, whereas Charlotte's made her question everything except her relationship to Allie.

All three of them arrived at Allie's apartment at the same time. Harvey barked in greeting from his crate, and Allie immediately let him out. She'd picked him up that afternoon from Penny.

"I'll take him out," Jack offered and hooked the leash to Harvey's collar. They headed out the door.

While Jack was gone, Allie got the champagne from the fridge as well as three glasses. "You're pretty quiet," she said to Charlotte.

"I guess I've got more questions than answers right now," Charlotte admitted.

Allie removed the foil, untwisted the metal cage and held a kitchen towel over the top of the bottle. With little effort, she twisted the bottle, uncorking the champagne successfully.

"At least we have the big question answered," Allie said.

"But why did my mother tell me I was born in

New York? And how on earth did she manage to get me a birth certificate from that state? I'm wondering if it's a forgery."

"That's possible, I guess," Allie agreed as she poured the bubbly into the glasses.

"My hands are still shaking," Charlotte confided to Allie. "I have an actual sister."

Allie's smile was genuine. "And a twin sister, no less. Should we start dressing alike since we missed doing that as kids?"

The women laughed, coming up with several things they'd missed out on, like taking each other's place or playing pranks on strangers.

With all three glasses half full, they heard Jack coming back with Harvey, who was so glad to be home that he ran around the apartment several times before settling down.

"I'm really happy for both of you," Jack said as he lifted a glass. "I hope you each get what you've been looking for from this wonderful news."

"To being twins!" Both women spoke at once, and they laughed. Then they all clinked glasses and took sips of their champagne.

"I've got to take off," Jack said a few minutes later, "but let's meet tomorrow to get the Fairleigh project off the ground." He put his empty glass on the counter and said to Allie, "My office at nine?"

"You don't need me, do you?" Charlotte asked. "I really don't know anything about what you guys do."

"I think we can handle it," Allie told her. "We'll save you for face-to-face meetings."

With that settled, Jack took off, leaving the two women alone to digest their incredible news.

THE NEXT DAY, Jack went early to the rehab center to visit his grandfather. He hadn't been there in several days and discovered Granddad had improved considerably.

"You seem bothered by something," Granddad said as Jack pulled a chair closer to where his grandfather was seated.

Jack shrugged. Even Granddad could see he was torn. Should he end things with Allie once they finish with the Fairleigh project? "I've got a lot on my mind. You know, business stuff."

"Looks like there's more to it than that." Granddad was obviously doing better to be so observant.

They discussed the animal-food account as well as the Fairleigh account.

"Good job, Jack," his grandfather said with a big smile. "I'm proud of you. Now tell me about this woman you have to work with."

"She's one to watch out for." Jack began explaining her maneuvers, and his grandfather's demeanor changed abruptly.

"You've got to cut yourself loose from her," Granddad ordered gruffly. "She's a devil in disguise, and you can't trust that she won't hurt Empire with her tactics."

"I wouldn't go that far," Jack said, unable to stop himself from defending her. "For example, she's actually fallen for the dog she's been fostering."

"So what? She still wiggled her way into the Fairleigh account."

Jack was no longer so upset about how Allie had found out about the account, so he hadn't shared that tidbit with his grandfather. "In the long run, we'll do a better job for Fairleigh *with* Allie's help."

"Even though she was deceptive about being related to this artist?"

"True," Jack admitted. "But it turns out they *are* related. They're twins, adopted to different families as infants." He took a different strategy, feeling as if he needed to present both sides to Granddad. "I'm pretty sure you've met Allie before. She came in to interview for a job a few months ago."

After finding out that Allie had interviewed with Empire, Jack had requested her file from HR and discovered that his grandfather had given the go-ahead to hire her, but he'd been overruled by several others who thought she would be a bad influence after her run-in with law enforcement.

"Tell me more about her." Granddad waited patiently.

Jack told him about her background, including both her time at DP and the accounts she had now in her own business.

"If I wanted to hire her, she must have a spark. I never hire anyone without it. Maybe she *will* be good for the Fairleigh campaign. If she works out, maybe we try to hire her."

Jack wasn't so sure that was a good idea, but he'd handle it when and if the time came.

He left the rehab center a little while later, wondering why he'd defended Allie to his grandfather. He headed to his office, where he was to meet her, and he found Allie standing at his office door.

"Your receptionist told me to come back."

She wore high heels with black pants and a white silky blouse that was ruffled at the bottom. The first few top buttons were open, and she wore a large necklace with stones the same color as her eyes.

Those eyes. Damn those eyes.

He reluctantly looked away and said, "Let's go into the conference room." He gathered his laptop and his file on Fairleigh and led the way.

She carried a large burgundy tote bag over her shoulder, more like a feminine brief case than a purse. She pulled out a laptop and several pages of handwritten notes on a legal pad.

She hadn't said a word since explaining her arrival at his office door.

"Before we begin," Jack said, "I want to get something straight."

She stared at him until he continued.

"If this business relationship is going to work, then you need to promise that you'll be honest. No deception."

She glanced away and then back at him. "Deal."

He wasn't sure if he could trust her. "We've made that deal before."

"I know." Her tone was serious. "I'm trying hard to be more like both you and Charlotte want me to be."

"We're not trying to change you."

She nodded. "I know. But I also know that you both think I have talent that I should be relying on more, and I'm beginning to think you're right. Though I wish I'd been able to showcase that before the Fairleigh account was awarded."

"What's brought about this change of heart?"

She shrugged. "I'm not sure. I think it has something to do with Charlotte being my sister. It's as if she fills a hole in my life, and when I look at her and her life, I can see how mine could be if I allowed it."

"Wow. That's great."

Neither spoke for a few minutes, and then she said, "We should get to work." They hadn't discussed their future, but they had two weeks for that.

"Where would you like to start?" He wanted to give her the opportunity to voice her ideas before he threw his own at her.

"I know the town's budget isn't very large," Allie began formally, as if speaking to a stranger, "so I thought we might be able to get Chuck or someone interviewed on the local news about how the town is coming back after the devastation of Hurricane Lorraine."

That was actually brilliant. He'd hoped to get them a radio ad because it would be less expensive than a TV ad, but Allie's suggestion was free.

"I like it," he admitted. "I'm not sure Chuck is the right person to do it, but we can revisit that later." He typed on his laptop, wondering if she had any more impressive ideas.

"There's also a free newspaper in Fairleigh," she said. "I haven't checked it out yet, but getting ads in that and papers for surrounding towns might be worthwhile if the price isn't too high."

Another good idea.

Jack had known Allie was intelligent, but he hadn't realized she was so creative.

"I was also thinking they need a website and a Twitter account, as well as a Facebook account." Allie checked her notes. "We can come up with a hashtag like #FairleighIsBack and get people to tweet upcoming events and post them on Facebook."

Jack's excitement about the campaign escalated. Allie was really good at her job.

"The artists probably have their own accounts," Jack added. "I'm sure they would tweet something about Fairleigh if we ask."

"I like that," Allie said. "Maybe come up with a widget they can download for their personal websites."

Jack sat up a little straighter after getting her approval. "Fairleigh also needs a new motto on the sign coming into town."

"That was my impression, too," Allie said, "but when I mentioned it to Chuck, he said the motto can't be changed. Something about it being there from the time of the town's inception. They've tried out different things, but there's a group in town who complain too loudly to ignore."

"Really? That's too bad." He hadn't known about not being able to change it, but Allie had done her homework thoroughly. Jack could definitely see how she must have impressed his grandfather.

They spent the next hour deciding who would do what and when they should meet again.

Jack didn't want Allie to go. He thought about inviting her to lunch, wanted to hear more about how she was doing after finding out about her twin sister, but thought better of it.

He didn't want her to get the wrong idea.

Even if he had begun to have second thoughts about discontinuing their relationship.

Relationship.

That was a word he never used when it came to the women he dated.

But he was definitely using the word now when it came to Allie.

ALLIE LEFT JACK'S OFFICE feeling good about how the meeting had gone. They certainly had been businesslike, hardly a personal word between them after their opening discussion.

Business, strictly business. That's what she needed to remember, even if she had a difficult time concentrating when he was wearing that perfectly fit suit and she was well aware of the sexy body beneath his clothes.

She picked up a sandwich on the way to her office. She'd barely taken her first bite when she decided to call her mom. It had been too late to call her last night to tell her the news about Charlotte, and this morning she'd been busy working on ideas for her meeting with Jack.

"Hi, Mom," Allie greeted her when she answered. "Do you have a minute?"

"For you, always." Her mom really was the best. How would Allie's life have been if she'd been raised by a twenty-year-old ex-con?

"You sound like you're in a good mood, Allison, what's going on?"

"Well—" Allie suddenly got choked up. She swallowed and started again. "Charlotte and I found out last night that we're twins. We haven't gotten back the DNA test yet, but that's a technicality. I have a biological sister."

"Oh, Allison, I'm so happy for you both." Her mother was crying, but Allie knew they were tears of joy. "How wonderful to find each other. I want to hear all the details."

Allie explained everything they knew, from

having the same mother on the same date in the same hospital to the fact that her biological mother was very young and a prison inmate when she gave birth.

"She was in prison?" Mom exclaimed. "Oh, my. And so young. Poor thing." Allie's adoptive mother—or her real mother, as she would always think of her—was a mom through and through. She was even concerned about the woman who gave up her babies for money, seemingly without a care whether or not they were separated.

"She sold us," Allie insisted. "And split us up. She didn't care about us, just the money."

"Maybe she didn't know you went to different families," her mother pointed out. "You don't know what the lawyer was up to. Didn't you tell me he was disciplined several times during his career?"

"True," Allie said. "But she could have taken the time to find out what happened to us."

"I'm sure there's a good reason, sweetheart. You need to forgive and forget."

Allie wasn't as forgiving as her mother. Maybe time would soften Allie's attitude about the woman who gave birth to her.

"Besides," her mother continued, "if not for her, we wouldn't have been so blessed to have you in our lives."

That was exactly what Allie needed to hear, even if she hadn't realized it until her mother spoke the words. "Thank you, Mom. Thank you for raising me. I love you." This was one time she wished she were standing in front of her mom so she could give her a big hug.

Mom sounded surprised. "I love you, too, sweetheart. More than you'll ever know." She paused and then added, "We need to have a party."

"A party?" Allie smiled and blinked the moisture from her eyes.

"Yes, we need to welcome Charlotte into the family."

"Wait a minute," Allie said. "Don't be in such a rush. She's still pretty raw since losing her adoptive mother. And she has more questions than ever about her adoption." She explained about Charlotte's birth certificate from New York.

"I understand," Mom said. "I promise we won't pressure her. Let's make it an 'Allison found her sister' party instead."

Allie laughed, appreciating her mom and realizing she could never tell her fully how much she meant to her.

"I really do love you, Mom." She choked up as she said it. What was with her? She never got this emotional.

"I love you, too," her mom responded. "So can we have the party?"

Allie laughed and wiped at the tear that escaped down her cheek. "Yes, we can have the party. As long as we do it after I finish this account. Which will be by the Fourth of July."

"Then let's do a big party for the Fourth."

"Let me check with Charlotte. I'm pretty sure her art show is the weekend before, but I'll double-check."

"I'd love to go see her work," Mom exclaimed. "Do you think that would be okay? I don't want to overwhelm her."

"How about I talk with her and see how she's feeling?"

"Yes, you talk to her. And if she's not comfort-able with me coming or if she wants to hold off on a party, then you let me know. The last thing I want is to alienate your sister." She laughed. "How funny is it that I'm not talking about Rachael when I say 'your sister'?"

Allie smiled. "Very weird, Mom. Very, very weird."

"Listen, we'll set the date soon, if Charlotte is okay with it, and you *will* be bringing Jack with you, right? He's the reason the two of you met in the first place."

"Mom—"

"Uh-oh. What?"

"I don't think Jack will want to come."

"Why not? Did we do something wrong when he was here?"

"No, no, it's me. I've disappointed him, and I don't think he wants to have anything to do with me once this campaign ends."

"Then apologize to him, Allison. Don't you want him at least as a friend?"

"I'm sorry to disappoint you," Allie said, leaving off the "again." "I just don't see how Jack and I will recover."

"You never disappoint me," her mother said. "I'm always proud of you. I'm disappointed that you and Jack aren't together."

"I'm sure someone else will come along," she tried to assure her mother.

"But not someone like Jack. Watching the two of you—the sparks between you—reminds me of your father and me when we were falling in love."

CHAPTER NINETEEN

CHARLOTTE WAS IN her home studio when the phone rang. "Good afternoon, my dear sister!" she answered when she saw that it was Allie's number.

Allie laughed as expected. "I still can't quite get over all this."

"Neither can I," Charlotte agreed. "In one second we found out we were twins. Our lives *should* have changed, but life's still going on as usual."

"Good way to put it," Allie said. "Hey, I talked to my mom earlier to tell her our news, and she's very excited for us."

"I'm glad she's taking it well," Charlotte said, wondering how her own mother would have responded to Charlotte finding her long lost sister.

"Me, too," Allie said. "But my mom's a mom, and I guess she wants all her kiddos happy. She can see how happy this has made me, so that's all that matters to her."

"How lucky that you have her," Charlotte said wistfully.

"I know—she's great. And actually she'd like to have a party to celebrate our news. If that's okay with you. I told her not to push you into accepting my whole family all at once."

"That sounds wonderful," Charlotte said. "When was she thinking?"

The two women discussed what Allie's mother had in mind, and then Allie said, "My mom would love to speak to you, to welcome you and invite you personally."

"I'd like that. I'm anxious to meet her."

"I'll text you her phone number, and then you can call her whenever you're ready."

"Sounds good. I need to finish up some things for my art show next week, but I'll call her later today."

They ended their call, and Charlotte felt a warmth envelop her. She had been given the gift of the large family she'd always wanted.

Several hours later, Charlotte finished packing up some of her things that she had to transport to the show. She looked at the phone.

She wanted to talk to Allie's mother, but she had another call to make first—to Felicia Monroe.

"Hello, Ms. Monroe," Charlotte said when Felicia's answering machine message was over. "This is Charlotte Harrington. I believe you knew my mother, Grace Harrington. I have a few questions about my mom I'm hoping you can answer." She left her phone number and disconnected.

Next she called Allie's mother. "Hello, Mrs. Miller. This is Charlotte Harrington," she greeted her.

"Oh, my dear, it's so good to hear from you." Mrs. Miller couldn't have been more excited. "And please, call me Eleanor. There's no need to be formal. You're my daughter's twin sister. That makes you family."

Before Charlotte could say anything, Eleanor continued. "I'm so sorry. Allie warned me not to be too pushy."

"That's okay," Charlotte assured her. "I'm as thrilled about the news as you are."

"Allie told me about your mother. I'm very sorry for your loss, dear."

"Thank you. It was devastating to lose her, especially when I had no other family."

"Well, you do now," Eleanor told her. "You can have as little or as much family as you want."

Tears came to Charlotte's eyes. Last night when she and Allie had read their birth certificates together, Charlotte hadn't realized what a huge gift the information would bring.

"Thank you, Eleanor. You have no idea how much that means to me."

They talked a few minutes, and then Eleanor brought up the subject of Allie and Jack. "She tells me they have no interest in being a couple."

"Well—"

"So there *is* something going on. I knew it. The spark between them is so obvious."

"I agree," Charlotte said. "If only they'd keep business out of it, they might have a chance."

"So what shall we do?"

Charlotte laughed. "What are you thinking?"

They spent the next few minutes discussing the best way to handle the situation. They both had the same goal, and when they disconnected, Charlotte felt really good about her new relationship with Eleanor. And about Jack and Allie's future.

BY THE THIRD DAY of their new working arrangement, Allie was surprised to discover that she was actually looking forward to video chatting with Jack. They'd decided that meeting face-to-face every day in one of their offices was unnecessary and took too much extra time.

Jack had several employees working as a team on the Fairleigh project, and Allie was impressed with their range of talent. One was a web designer, one a graphics expert and the third had an impressive number of media contacts.

"I've arranged for Bob, the city planner, to appear on the local six and eleven o'clock news shows," Allie told Jack, trying to concentrate on work and the notes in front of her instead of remembering how his mouth felt. "Not only can he talk knowledgeably about the rebuilding process, but I also think he's the most personable of the town employees and will make a great impression on the public."

"Good call," Jack said without looking up. He wrote something on a legal pad and requested that one of his employees report on their progress.

Allie half listened, trying to take notes, but knowing the only reason she was even part of this team was because of Charlotte. That fact still nagged at her.

"I talked to Charlotte last night when I got home from work," Jack told her. "She said she was available for the date we'd talked about to be the guest artist at the workhouse." He shuffled some papers. "August something."

"August eighth." Allie was surprised by the twinge in her gut when Jack mentioned talking to Charlotte. How would it be, living across the street from him and seeing him every day? Allie felt a touch of jealousy.

"Sounds right." Jack wrote a note of the date. "A local winery is also setting up a tent, and we've already begun advertising it."

He said more, but Allie didn't catch everything—she was too preoccupied thinking about Jack on a level that wasn't business. Though she didn't know why she tortured herself. He'd made it clear that he didn't want a personal relationship with her, and he didn't agree with the way she conducted business.

How else could she survive? She'd been taught by the best when she started at DP Advertising. If not for Jimmy taking it too far, she'd still be at DP, business as usual.

At DP she would have been praised for getting the scoop on Fairleigh, for using Charlotte as a lure, for fostering Harvey to win the animal-food account.

"Allie?" Jack was speaking to her.

She blinked. "Yes?"

"I asked if you had anything else to add."

"Um, no, that's it for today." But she didn't want him to disconnect. She wanted to talk to him. Really talk to him.

She couldn't explain her reaction to him. She should move ahead and not look back.

"Same time tomorrow, then," Jack said, and they disconnected.

Probably for the best.

When she compared Jack to the other men she'd dated, he was almost the exact opposite.

Maybe Jack was simply too good for her. He wasn't a Jimmy, who landed in jail, or a Tony, who never mentioned his wife and three kids, or even a Steve, who sold fake designer purses as a sideline to his bartending gig.

She needed to tamp down her feelings for him— they were beginning to consume her.

Besides, Jack had always made it clear he wasn't into relationships. He'd warned her that sex with him was up to her, but it had to be with no strings attached.

Problem was, now she wanted those strings.

Not that it would ever work out. They were too different. As hard as she tried, she wasn't sure she'd ever be able to live up to his expectations.

A WEEK LATER, the Fairleigh project was nearly done, and Jack had a different matter on his mind.

It was now clear that his grandfather could no

longer live by himself. But Jack was shocked when his grandfather agreed to move to an assisted living facility in a small town not too far from Jack's house. He hadn't even argued.

Jack had arranged for movers to come and pack up his grandfather's house, so by the time Granddad moved, his things would be in place.

When the day came, Jack drove Granddad to his new home in a lovely establishment that provided all kinds of services, including the security of knowing someone was watching out for him 24/7.

Jack's first idea had been to move Granddad into his own house in Newport. That would have required outside help since Jack would be at work all day, but Granddad wasn't about to "impose," as he phrased it.

"You know you can still change your mind and move into my house with me," Jack said as he parked at the assisted living facility. "I have plenty of room."

"That's for you and your family," Granddad said as he slowly got out of the car.

"You're my family."

"You should have a family of your own. It's about time. What are you, thirtysomething now?"

"Thirty-two," Jack answered. "Since when have you pushed for me or anyone to have a family? You certainly avoided that."

"And I'm paying for it now." Granddad's tone

was serious, full of regret. They walked slowly on
the path to the main entrance.

"How do you figure?"

Granddad had never talked like this before.

"If I'd married your grandmother when she came
to me and said she was pregnant with your mother,
then maybe we would have had more children and
more grandchildren. Then you wouldn't have the
sole burden of my care now."

"It's not a burden," Jack said and meant it. "You
raised me when my mother died and my father
deserted me. I owe you so much."

They reached the main entrance, checked in and
headed down the hallway where his grandfather's
apartment was located. The facility was clean, the
staff friendly. Jack had done his homework when
it came to finding the right place for Granddad. In
addition, there were several other residents whom
his grandfather knew quite well.

"She married someone else," Granddad said suddenly.

"Who did?"

"Your grandmother. I did my duty, paid child
support and took your mother for several weeks
over the summer and the occasional holiday. But I
should've married her mother."

Jack had no words.

"She got tired of waiting for me, so she married someone else." Granddad paused, and his eyes

were bright with tears. "I never should have let her go."

Jack swallowed. Granddad had never spoken about this before. He'd never thought his grandfather had regretted any of his decisions.

Would Jack someday regret letting Allie go, too? The thought of her with another man made his gut churn.

He got his grandfather settled and was ready to leave when Granddad said, "Don't do what I did, son. You need a family. Don't think you can do it all alone and never settle down. Your father made a lot of mistakes with women, and I know you're afraid to turn out just like him. But don't be like me, either, avoiding anyone who would tie you down or push you to look at life differently. In the end, you'll be sorry."

A little while later, as he drove to his office, he couldn't help thinking about Allie. He was attracted to her, loved the sex, the playful banter. Working with her had been great, much better than he'd expected. One of them would express an idea, and the other would add to it. He'd looked forward to speaking with her every day, even if it had been only by video chat.

The emptiness in his chest when he wasn't around her was something he'd never felt before.

Did he have feelings for her?

Honestly? Yes.

Was this what love felt like? He'd never been in love before.

Now what?

AT LAST THE DAY of the party for Allie and Charlotte arrived. Allie had wanted Charlotte to drive
to Allie's parents' with her, but Charlotte had insisted she had things to finish up Friday night and
would be there early the next morning.

Allie went Friday night, knowing her mother
could use her help, which also gave her some time
alone with her mom.

They had stayed up late, talking while working
in the kitchen together. Mom baked and iced a cake
while Allie made dozens of meatballs according to
her mother's recipe.

"You really don't think you and Jack can work
things out?" her mom asked the next morning while
they were having coffee and planning what needed
to be done next.

"Wow, talk about switching subjects," Allie said.
"Where'd that come from?"

"Oh, I just really like Jack and had hoped the
two of you could make a go of it."

"Well, stop hoping, Mom. We're not compatible."
Allie's heart squeezed as she said the words. As if
she had proclaimed their relationship—or whatever
it was that they had—dead. No bringing it back to
life with a defibrillator, no mouth-to-mouth resus-
citation. Dead.

"Shouldn't Charlotte be here soon?" Mom asked.

The kitchen clock said close to noon. "She
thought she'd be here early this morning, but I don't
think she realized how long the trip would be."

Mom must have been anxious about meeting Charlotte, because she kept looking at the clock. Very unlike her mother to be so time conscious and edgy.

The doorbell rang just after noon, and even though she'd been overly excited to meet Charlotte, Mom asked, "Why don't you get that? My hands are sticky."

Which was an outright lie, because she'd just rinsed and dried them on the kitchen towel that hung from the oven handle.

Allie narrowed her eyes, wondering what her mother was up to, but went to answer the door anyway.

Charlotte nearly bowled her over when she came through the doorway and hugged her.

And there, over Charlotte's shoulder, stood Jack.

Allie was speechless, although she should have guessed something was up from her mother's behavior.

"I hope you don't mind that I brought Jack," Charlotte said without meeting Allie's eyes. "Your mom said it would be okay, and I kind of owed him." She sounded out of breath. "If not for him taking me to your brother's wedding, we never would have met."

Allie finally found her tongue. "True." She stepped aside and led them toward the kitchen to meet her mother, but she was already coming into the living room.

"I'm so glad you're here, Jack. Oh, Charlotte!" Mom put her arms out. "I'd recognize you anywhere. You and Allie really *are* identical."

Charlotte hugged Mom, and Allie couldn't quite catch what she whispered to Charlotte, but she definitely heard the name *Jack*.

"Let me show you around," Mom said to Charlotte. They disappeared, leaving Allie alone with Jack.

"I guess you should make yourself comfortable," Allie said without looking at him.

"I wasn't sure about coming, but Charlotte insisted," he said. "You haven't answered my calls or texts."

She shrugged. "I've been busy. With the Fairleigh job over, I needed to keep hustling for new clients. You know how it is." She gestured to the kitchen. "Anyway, I think those two had something to do with you being here."

"You think they plotted?" He appeared to consider the idea. "You might be right, now that I recall the conversation with Charlotte."

"Have a seat. Can I get you a drink?" She decided to treat him like any other guest, even though her heart was crumbling at the sight of him. She'd missed him and hadn't realized how much until right this minute.

"Would you at least look at me, Allie?" Jack's request was nearly a plea. "I've been wanting to speak to you."

She finally met his gaze—he looked very serious. "What is there to say? Our business relation-ship is over."

"But what about our personal one?"

Her eyes widened. "You think we can go back to having fun in the sack, no strings, no talk of busi-ness?" She shook her head. "No way." She couldn't accept a fraction of him. She was in love with *all* of him. The shock of the revelation nearly knocked her over.

"I agree. We can't go back to that," he said. "But I want to have something with you that I've never even considered before. I want a relationship."

"I don't believe you. That's not your style. Be-sides, even though I've realized some of my past mistakes and am working on not repeating them, you don't agree with my business practices. So how could anything between us work out?"

"I've thought about it a lot over the last few days. I think I've avoided relationships before now be-cause, except for my grandfather, everyone else has left me." He paused as if weighing his words. "I think I was also subconsciously comparing you to my father. He lied and cheated to get his way. I know you're trying hard to change, but maybe I was wrong, too. Maybe I was too adamant about doing business my way."

"Maybe?"

His lips twitched. "Okay, I was wrong. Some-times it takes some 'creativity' to stay in business.

I'm not saying I like everything you did, but I'll admit there are other ways to operate than mine."

"I guess that's something."

He put a hand out. "Will you give us a chance?"

"I can't."

His hand dropped to his side. "Why not?"

"Because, as hard as I try, I'll never be the person you want me to be. I'll just disappoint you."

"We'll never agree on everything, but I know you'll never disappoint me."

"Why now? Why are you being so reasonable?" Allie was confused.

His chest rose and fell. "Because I'm in love with you."

She had to consciously keep her jaw from dropping. "You are?"

He held his hand out again. This time she grabbed on, and he pulled her close. "I'm no expert, but I'm pretty sure this is love I'm feeling."

She grinned at him.

"I think I'm feeling the same thing," she said and went on tiptoes to kiss him. "I love you."

"I love you, too," he said between kisses.

A few minutes later, Allie said, "I guess this means we're a couple?"

He grinned. "Yep. Should we tell them?" He nodded to the kitchen.

"I hear quiet clapping and giggling. I'm guessing they already know."

EPILOGUE

Several weeks later

THE AUGUST EVENING was cooling off quickly as the sun went down. Charlotte was unloading her car into her studio, with Allie and Jack's help. It had been a successful weekend. Her Boston art show had gone much better than expected. Charlotte couldn't help beaming.

"I want to hear all about it," Allie said. "I wish Jack and I could have gotten away."

"I have other shows scheduled. It's not every day you get a nephew. So how are Rachael and their new addition doing?" Charlotte asked. Rachael had gone into labor Friday afternoon, so Charlotte had talked Allie and Jack into going to Albany instead of Boston. It was the right place for them to be.

"They're both doing great. He's an adorable baby, and Jack even held him."

"They told me he wasn't as breakable as he appeared, so I gave it a try," Jack joked.

"And they were right?" Charlotte grinned at him.

Jack shrugged. "He was kind of cuddly. He even grabbed on to my finger."

Charlotte quickly went through the mail from the weekend and she let out a gasp.

"What is it?" Allie asked.

"The DNA test!" Charlotte ripped open the envelope.

"Don't tear it before we can read it," Allie joked.

"You know this test is just a formality, right?" Jack probably couldn't help being the practical one of the three. "You already know you're twins."

The women ignored him and read the paper at the same time. They soon grabbed onto each other and tears were flowing.

Jack got them tissues and joined in the hug.

"Now we're official," Charlotte said once they calmed down. "I think there's only one more trip left and my car will be empty. Then we can properly celebrate."

"Last time I provided champagne," Allie said.

"I've got beer in the fridge," Charlotte offered.

They were about to make another trip outside to the car when Charlotte's phone rang. "Someone's calling my cell." She pulled it from her purse and recognized the number immediately. "It's Felicia Monroe. I've got to take this. I've called her several times over the past few weeks and left messages." Charlotte pushed a button on the phone's screen. "Hello?"

"Is this Charlotte Harrington?" The woman on the other end was anything but pleasant.

"Yes, it is."

"This is Felicia Monroe."

"Thank you for calling me back. It's so good to talk to you."

"I can't say the same," Felicia said gruffly. "What the hell do you want?"

Charlotte was taken aback by Felicia's tone. They'd never met, so why did the woman seem to dislike her so much? Because she'd left her several messages?

"I wanted to talk to you about when my mother worked at your CPA office."

"I have nothing to say about that tramp."

"Tramp?" Charlotte repeated. Allie's and Jack's heads swiveled in Charlotte's direction.

A few minutes later, Charlotte ended the phone call without saying another word. She put her phone down and sat in the closest chair.

Allie went to Charlotte, bending down in front of her. "What is it? What did she say?"

Charlotte hesitated then stumbled over her words. "She said to leave her alone. That my mother was a tramp who ruined Felicia's marriage, and as her daughter, I'm probably just like her."

"Who is she to speak like that about you?" Allie's voice rose. "I should call her back and tell her so. Did she say anything else?"

"Isn't that enough?" Charlotte covered her face with her hands. "How can she say that about my mother?"

"Did she have proof about your mother and her husband?" Jack spoke up for the first time.

Charlotte shook her head. "She said my mother

and her husband would meet in a movie theater and then go to a hotel room once a week. This all happened before I was born, but she's obviously not gotten over it."

"Do you think it's even true?" Allie asked.

Charlotte stood suddenly. "The memory box. The one under my bed." She got up from the chair and went up the stairs to the second floor. Her mother would probably have saved things from that time period.

Charlotte returned carrying the ornate oak box. She set it on the dining room table and opened it. "I haven't gone through this because I didn't think I was strong enough. But maybe there's something in here that will prove whether Felicia is telling the truth."

"Or lying," Allie added.

Charlotte opened the box slowly and moved things around. She pulled out ticket stubs and newspaper articles. "Here's Henry Monroe's obituary from the newspaper." She held up a yellowed strip of paper. "That was Felicia's husband."

"That could be because she used to work for the guy," Jack pointed out.

Allie nodded, but Charlotte knew by the pit in her stomach that it meant more than that. "Maybe this affair is what my mother's friend, Marie, didn't want to tell me."

"Oh!" Charlotte put a hand to her mouth. Buried at the bottom of the box was an envelope with her name on it. She pulled it out to show Allie and Jack. "This is my mother's handwriting."

"It doesn't look very old," Allie commented.

"No, it doesn't," Charlotte said. "In fact, I remember buying this stationery for her after she got sick. She wanted to write letters to friends she hadn't seen in a while."

The envelope was sealed, and Charlotte held it in her hand, wondering what the letter said. Wondering if it held any answers to her many questions.

"Maybe we should leave you alone to read it," Jack suggested.

"That's a good idea." Allie hugged Charlotte from behind. "You know where we are if you need us."

"WHAT DO YOU think the letter says?" Allie asked Jack when they walked into his house and were greeted by Harvey. How had she lived her life so long without the joy a dog brought? Jack had surprised her by adopting him the week after the party for her and Charlotte. If she hadn't completely accepted that he loved her before that, she was a total believer afterward.

"Maybe her mother wanted to tell her how much she loved her. She could have been worried that she wouldn't be able to tell her at the end."

"True," Allie agreed. "I guess I'm a little suspicious after that weird conversation with Felicia."

"That *was* strange. Especially after all these years, to hold a grudge against not only Charlotte's mother, but Charlotte, too."

Allie went to the fridge, pulled out a beer and

held it up. At Jack's nod, she pulled a second one out and opened them both.

"Porch?" he asked, and she nodded and followed him outside.

They'd gotten into the habit of staying at Jack's house on weekends and spending weeknights at Allie's apartment because it was closer to work. Allie had come to love Jack's house, and Harvey had made himself at home here, too.

She glanced at Jack as he took a swig of beer.

"What?" he asked.

She smiled. "Nothing."

He took her hand in his and squeezed. "I love you, too."

She squeezed back.

Her life had made a complete turnaround. She couldn't imagine being any happier than she was at that moment.

Maybe she should give her mother more credit about her idea that people were meant to live in pairs. Not only had Allie been born as part of a pair, but now she was paired with a great guy who she adored, even when they were business rivals.

She leaned her head back and looked at the dark sky with all the sparkling stars, wondering how she'd been so lucky to find both Charlotte and Jack in such a large universe.

* * * * *

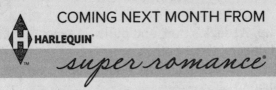
#1988 ABOUT THAT NIGHT
by Beth Andrews

Texas millionaire C.J. Bartasavich is used to being in control. But when he discovers he's going to be a father after a one-night stand with cocktail waitress Ivy Rutherford, suddenly he feels powerless. If he wants a place in his child's life, he'll have to prove to Ivy that he's honorable, kind and worthy of her and her baby's hearts.

#1989 A FAMILY COME TRUE
by Kris Fletcher

Ian North has always helped Darcy Maguire with her baby daughter, because that's what best friends do. But when an unexpected visit means Ian and Darcy have to pretend to be a couple, suddenly everything is *complicated*. The attraction is definitely there...but can they really be a family?

#1990 HER COP PROTECTOR
by Sharon Hartley

Detective Dean Hammer can't get June Latham out of his mind. The veterinary assistant is beautiful, sexy...and frustrating. Dean is certain she knows more than she's letting on about the murders he's investigating. And when she comes under fire herself, he knows he must protect her. But can he get her to trust him with her heart?

#1991 THE GOOD FATHER
Where Secrets are Safe
by Tara Taylor Quinn

For Brett Ackerman, Ella Chandler is the one who got away. Now she's back, asking for his help with a family crisis. But time together leads to a night of passion—and an unexpected pregnancy! Brett never planned to be a father, but maybe this is his chance to be the man Ella needs.